I0699789

# FUNDAMENTALS OF BIOLOGY

## PART 2: REPRODUCTION

PENNY REID

WWW.PENNYREID.NINJA/NEWSLETTER/

# COPYRIGHT

[ 1 ]

# ENDOCRINOLOGY, BRAIN, AND PITUITARY GLAND

***Samantha***

Sunlight. Actual, golden, warm-on-my-face sunlight. My first coherent thought of the day was, *So, this is what it's like to sleep soundly through the night and wake up after sunrise.* The next was, *I feel fucking awesome.*

For the first time in two years, I was well rested and not fighting a caffeine-withdrawal headache.

Maybe I'd died and this was the afterlife, a high-thread-count sheet, a cocoon of perfect warmth, and a brain empty of intrusive thoughts but full of serotonin, the type only made possible by an appropriate length and number of REM cycles. I allowed myself the decadence of drifting there, savoring the delicate pressure of a memory-foam pillow against my temple, the gentle weight of a duvet across my hips, and the luxurious sense of not having a single place I needed to be.

I let myself enjoy this blissful state for exactly eight seconds before my limbs, traitorous as ever, craved movement. So, I began to stretch, arching my toes. But before I could fully commence a morning starfish, I froze. Because my left hand was palming the undeniable reality of another human being.

There's a microsecond between "that's a person" and "which person"

1

that, for most people, might be raw panic. For me, however, it was pure professionalism. I had a procedure for this.

Step one: Assess level of nudity. My left hand, still frozen mid-stretch, confirmed bare skin, but not below-the-waist bare. Chest, maybe? Arm, maybe? Stomach, *definitely*. And a muscly one.

Step two: Identify the person. Keeping my eyes closed, I mentally replayed the previous twelve hours. Had I gone out? No. Had I let anyone into the building? Also no. Had I, at any point, consumed more than the recommended daily allowance of alcohol? Negative.

So, no hookups. No midnight social calls. No one should be in my bed.

Yet, this warm body next to mine definitely existed. And this wasn't a dream, I wasn't asleep. Someone warm and solid and occupying a scandalous percentage of my mattress.

Step three: Confirm position. With the meticulousness of a bomb technician, I moved my fingertips. Male, for sure. Hairless chest, ridged with muscle. Not moving, which meant asleep or possibly dead. Breath? Yes, regular, slow, and deep. So, not dead. I could feel his chest rise and fall beneath the new position of my left hand.

Step four: Open eyes, assess the scene, and—*oh my God!*

This wasn't the afterlife. This was a penthouse apartment in the Lower East Side of Manhattan.

And I was spooning Andreas Kristiansen.

Not just spooning, but aggressively spooning. I was *ladling* him, as though sometime in the night I'd turned into an octopus and decided his body was my favorite rock to cling to. My left leg hooked over both of his, my left arm splayed across his chest and under his shirt, and my face nestled in the crook of his neck like a needy baby possum.

My stomach folded itself into an origami crane. *How did this happen?*

Meanwhile, Andreas, for his part, either didn't mind or hadn't yet noticed. He lay mostly on his back, turned slightly toward me, the soft sound of his breathing barely audible. Shifting backward and reversing out of his neck, I tilted my head and readjusted my temple on the pillow. His face was less than six inches from mine, so close I could see the individual eyelashes resting on his cheek, the faintest pink flush along his jaw.

Step five: Detach with minimal jostling.

I tried. I really, really tried to execute an elegant, silent disengagement. What happened instead was I pulled my arm back, but in my haste, whacked him square in the solar plexus. Andreas grunted and flinched, which caused me to overcompensate. I attempted to roll away and simultaneously kick off the duvet, but gravity betrayed me. *Damn gravity, always letting me down!*

I tumbled off the edge of the mattress and landed on the carpet with a muffled thud.

For a moment, I just lay there, listening to the pounding of my heart in my ears, contemplating how in the heck we'd ended up in bed together.

Above me, I heard Andreas take a deep breath. A moment later, he peered over the edge of the bed. He blinked, hair sticking up in sleep-wild directions, and regarded me with what felt like cool, clinical detachment. "Are you injured?" he asked, voice husky from sleep.

I scrambled to an upright sitting position, heat flooding my cheeks. "No, I'm fine," I lied, even as I clutched my tailbone, which would absolutely be bruised by lunch.

Andreas's gaze did a quick vertical scan, pausing at my legs, then darting back to my face. "Good," he said stiffly, an unmistakable yet faint blush blooming over his cheeks.

*Is he embarrassed? Good!* Who did he think he was? Climbing into bed with me?

I pushed my hair out of my face, indignance flaring in my chest. "I, uh —why are you in my bed?" I demanded.

Sitting up fully, Andreas righted his shirt in a way that felt oddly modest and careful, and then cleared his throat. "You are mistaken. This is my room."

I looked around. Oh my God!

He was right. The massive window, the bare walls, the sheer size of the bed—I was in the main bedroom. His bedroom.

I pressed my palms to my eyes. "Oh fuck. I sleepwalked again."

"Correct. You came in around three. You did not respond to verbal cues."

Dropping my hands, I refused to feel mortified as I assessed the situation. Yes, I'd sleepwalked into his room and climbed into his bed and ladled him aggressively, but he just stated that he'd been aware of my invasion for several hours, and was cognizant when it happened, and had done . . . what? Anything? He just let me *sleep* with him?

"You tried to wake me up?" I squinted at him.

He nodded, still stiff and serious. "Only at first. Then I remembered your roommate said you were a sleepwalker, and you told me yourself you have insomnia. It can be dangerous to wake a sleepwalker, so I let you sleep."

*Hmm.* There was some logic there. *And yet—*

"So, your solution was to let me"—I gestured, indicating the proximity of our bodies—"occupy your personal space all night?"

The pink on his cheeks burned brighter and he cleared his throat again, saying with a hint of defensiveness, "It seemed to work. You slept well."

I stared at him, noticing, to my utter incredulity, how this expression he currently wore made him look ridiculously adorable. *What is he thinking? What is this expression?*

Not quite embarrassed, but something like it. Not regretful. Definitely not ashamed. More like . . . bashful?

*That's it.*

Huffing a short laugh, I rolled my eyes at myself, even as my lungs burned with confusion. I didn't understand him. Why would he be shy about it? Wasn't he the one who let me sleep in his bed? WHATEVER!

Since I was still on the floor, I checked to ensure my oversized T-shirt covered me to mid-thigh and did my best to ignore my lack of pants. "Well, then"—I forced a calm confidence into my voice I didn't quite feel —"I apologize for sleepwalking into your bedroom last night. I will barricade my door from the inside to keep it from happening again."

"Is that safe?" Andreas stood, tugging on the front of his button-up, long-sleeve pajama shirt. I noted against my will that Andreas wore a dashing matching blue-and-white pin-striped pajama set. You know, the ones with the mother-of-pearl buttons, piping at the wrists, and a pocket at the left breast. Basically, they were the pajama equivalent of an expensive suit.

In that moment, the stark dichotomy between us struck me. Andreas in his suit of fancy pajamas, likely costing more than my entire wardrobe, and me in my oversized, four-dollar cotton T-shirt. The last fifteen years had taken us on completely contrasting paths. We were not the same.

Andreas reached for his phone while I mused over our surface level differences, but also the invisible ones. Our upbringing, education, and life experiences. Suddenly, I felt immensely curious about him, where in the world he'd been, what he'd been doing, who he'd met, who his friends were. Had he gone to college? I had no idea.

I could look it up online, but I didn't want to read about Andreas. I wanted to know about his past from him.

I was so busy with my own thoughts that I didn't notice he'd extended his hand to me until he said, "Do you need help standing?"

"Um—" I didn't need a hand, but his hand was so nice. Therefore I did what any self-respecting hand aficionado would do. I accepted his fingers.

He hauled me up, steady and effortlessly. But instead of releasing me, he held on. "Are you sure you are not hurt?" he asked, voice suddenly softer.

My brain short-circuiting on the gentleness of his tone, I blinked at him dumbly for several seconds. But then I caught my reflection in the mirror behind him and my hair was in a full-blown Einstein-on-MDMA situation. Yeesh.

Extracting myself from his grip, I crossed my arms and backed up a step. "I'm fine. And I think I'm late for work."

His eyes flicked down to my legs, then back up, and he straightened his spine before speaking. "You have to work today?"

"Yes."

Andreas's eyes narrowed. "Today is Sunday."

*Aw crap.*

"That—that's right." I spoke and nodded haltingly while fumbling with improvised bravado. "But for a PhD student who has to fight for lab time, there is no such thing as a weekend. So, I better get to it."

I marched around him, but then spun in the doorway, remembering something I'd meant to ask yesterday. "Oh, so. Andreas. Was the adoption paperwork filed? When will it be final?" For good measure, I tacked on some humor. "Just want to know when to start addressing you as *father dearest.*"

I noticed his jaw tighten at my joke. Pushing his hands into his pajama pockets, he leveled me with his trademark bored stare. "Unlike PhD student labs, courts recognize weekends and are closed until Monday." He sounded calm, but I sensed an undercurrent of odd aggression. Or maybe my vibe-checker was on the fritz this morning. Highly possible given my unconscious brain's choices.

He went on. "I have pulled some strings to get it fast-tracked. Everything should be finalized before Thanksgiving."

"That's good. Thank you." This felt like the first real, official step toward revenge. The engagement was all a show, but this adoption was legally binding. Perhaps my subconscious would avoid his bedroom once everything was final.

On that note. "Oh, again, since I'm apparently sleepwalking, I should barricade my door—"

"Do you think that's safe?" He shuffled a step forward.

"—but you should probably lock your door at night. If I somehow get past the barricade and door, I don't want to impose on you again. I am really sorry about last night."

Andreas openly inspected me. The silence stretched for so long, I thought he might not respond, and I was just about to leave when he finally said, "I will keep that in mind."

Hoping that statement was his way of politely agreeing, I nodded, then darted out, speed walking back to my side of the apartment. Once safely in the sanctuary of the bathroom, I braced my hands against the cool countertop, stared into the mirror, and tried to process the previous five minutes.

My hair was a fright. My shirt was askew. I still felt the ghostly imprint of Andreas's hand on my skin.

One night into living with him, and I'd already been betrayed by my subconscious brain. I had to get a handle on myself. I was an adult. A scientist. A woman with a mission and that mission came first.

And yet, the only thing I could think about, as I stared at my reflection, was how good it had felt to be held by him. Even if he hadn't meant it that way. Even if he was, very soon, going to be my legal father.

I groaned into the sink, then splashed water on my face. "Get it together, Sam," I whispered.

But my skin still tingled where his hand had touched mine, and somewhere in my chest, something soft and dangerous took deeper root.

* * *

If I were being honest, I needed the cold late-autumn air. I needed the sting, because my brain had been running a fever since approximately 8:45 AM, which was when I'd tumbled out of Andreas's bed.

I hadn't even managed to put on my shoes before fleeing the apartment, waving off Andreas's offer of coffee. Instead, I'd clutched them to my chest like a security blanket. Tara, who seemed to have the tact of a Buddhist monk and the judgmental restraint of a golden retriever, merely greeted me when I appeared on the sidewalk.

"I'm teaching a kickboxing class tonight. Want to come?" Tara asked as soon as she pulled into traffic.

"Yes. Please. What time?" Anything to postpone going back to Andreas's apartment.

"Nine."

I thought for a moment. "That works. I'll finish up work around six, grab a bite, then we can head straight there? I'll digest while I check out the gym."

"Sounds good." Tara flipped on her turn signal and the remainder of the drive passed in silence.

I spent it recalling all the boys I'd left before, every strategy for extracting inconvenient feelings or letting them die on the vine. Usually, disentangling myself was as easy as identifying a man's most repugnant opinion and, if necessary, blowing it out of proportion until I couldn't see the good anymore. But Andreas hadn't cooperated last night, sharing none of his repugnant opinions.

My second strategy was typically foolproof and involved asking myself: What was so special about this guy, anyway? What did I actually like about him?

I mean, sure. Andreas was handsome. So were lots of guys. And he was a kisser of rare talent, so that was something special. And he was thoughtful, smart, and strategic. And he seemed to genuinely care about doing the right thing, even if it made his life difficult. And I've known him forever. *And his hands . . .*

DON'T THINK ABOUT HIS HANDS!

Squeezing my eyes shut, I gave my head a quick shake to dispel the image of Andreas's gorgeous hands and decided to talk myself out of liking him later. For the remainder of the car ride, I stayed busy by making a mental task list of all the work waiting for me at the lab.

But the lab was even less successful as a distraction. My hands shook so badly during pipetting that I had to recalibrate the digital reader three times, which is, for anyone keeping score, three more times than I'd ever miscalibrated it during all my years of grad school. By 2:00 PM, I'd gotten so little work done, I abandoned the blessedly empty lab and worked instead on a project Dmitry had emailed to me last week. He'd asked me to read through his methods section. I edited it for him instead, adding new citations and fleshing out a few of his placeholders.

The only thing that kept me grounded was the knowledge that, after work, I'd hopefully get to burn off at least a fraction of my anxious energy doing violence to some heavy bags in Tara's kickboxing class.

That was my new plan: punch things.

When 5:30 PM rolled around I figured enough was enough. I texted Tara, changed in the locker room, and made my way downstairs. Standing just outside the front doors of the biology building, blue scarf wound up to my nose, I searched the curb for the familiar hulk of Tara's Mercedes. The wind had me blinking against the cold.

Movement flickered at the edge of my vision. A man, tall, moving forward purposefully, strode up the far side of the street. His suit was an expensive blue-gray, not the fun blue of a retro car but the cold, almost metallic blue of a winter sky right before it snows. He wore a cashmere overcoat that looked incredibly soft. It reminded me of Andreas's. *Don't think about Andreas!*

Refocusing on the man, I noted his hair was cut close on the sides, styled just enough on top that it seemed to mock lesser men who dared to try the look. *Huh. He sorta looks like Andreas : . .*

Before I could chide myself for thinking about Andreas again, I registered who this man was, and every neuron in my prefrontal cortex fired at once.

Henrik Kristiansen.

Andreas's half brother, the one Andreas had described as "unpredictable and often resorts to physical violence."

Henrik's stare locked on me at exactly that moment. A pulse of adrenaline had me standing straighter.

*Run.*

# [ 2 ]

# THE FEMALE REPRODUCTIVE SYSTEM

***Samantha***

Henrik's eyes were glacial and blue enough to make you believe in recessive gene dominance. His gaze met mine with an energy so openly malevolent it was practically scented with testosterone.

I tried not to look rattled. My hand went for my campus badge a full second before my brain gave it the order. Henrik's stride lengthened. He cut across the sidewalk without once glancing for traffic, because obviously the cars would stop for him. They did.

"Samantha!" he called, voice friendly and entirely at odds with the felony violence in his gaze. He lifted a hand, palm up, as if inviting me to a sociable game of Russian roulette.

I took a step back toward the biology building, thumbed the badge, and held it at the ready. "Henrik," I called back, forcing calm into my voice. "Didn't realize you were allowed outside of a cage without a leash."

He grinned, flashing teeth. My fear made them look both whiter and sharper than possible. "Rumors of my incarceration have been greatly overexaggerated."

As he approached, I did my best to hide my movements and intentions. The moment he got within ten strides, I scanned in, pulled the door open,

9

and slipped through, letting it close with hydraulic slowness between us as he ran to grab the handle.

Too late. It clicked shut with me on the inside and him on the outside. Thank God.

Henrik's features twisted with anger and he pounded on the glass door. Internally, I gave myself a high five for not flinching. Outwardly, I slowly crossed my arms and pasted on an unperturbed smile. Apparently resigned to the impenetrable partition between us, Henrik huffed a laugh and placed one palm flat against the glass. The look he gave me belonged on a National Geographic special.

"What, not even a handshake?"

"I don't like being touched by violent offenders." I shrugged.

He huffed another laugh and pushed away from the building, his eyes scanning me openly. I took the opportunity to calm my racing heart and inspect him as well.

Up close, Henrik looked older than Tobias. Less pretty boy, more "CEO of Fight Club." His nose had clearly been broken more than once, but rather than diminish his beauty, it only enhanced the suggestion that he was dangerous. His hair was much lighter than Andreas's, but not quite the golden white of his older brother's.

His smile widened as it settled on mine again. "You're a coward, Samantha. Just like your father."

If he wanted to anger me, he succeeded. I'd always suspected Tobias and Henrik had something to do with what happened to my father. I decided to take his current statement as proof.

I smiled back, showing all my teeth. "Oh? Most people just tell me I have his eyes."

Henrik leaned in again, forehead nearly touching the glass, his blue eyes boring into me. "You're not as clever as you think. Or as safe. I'd have caught you, if I wanted to."

I pretended to check my phone, though my hands shook so much I almost dropped it. "Then why didn't you? Worried I'd get blood on your expensive coat?"

Henrik chuckled. It was a deep, rolling sound that might have been pleasant in another context, like, say, a commercial for luxury vodka, or an ad for a private island. "You know, listening to Andreas is a mistake. He makes promises he can't keep, and he doesn't know anything about taking care of a woman." Henrik gave me a quick, lascivious once-over, licking his lips as he added, "Maybe you and I could reach an agreement instead. Unlike my little brother who has no experience, I know what I'm doing."

I cringed at the thought, an honest expression, and shook my head. "No, thank you. I prefer my men to walk upright." I gave him a look, then turned my back on him for two seconds, just to see what he'd do.

What he did was pound once, hard, on the glass with the side of his fist. It made me flinch and triggered a wave of heat down my spine.

I spun, holding my phone like it was a can of mace. "Leave. Or I'm calling the police."

He pressed his hands together, prayerlike, then splayed them wide in a performance of mockery. "You don't even want to know why I'm here?"

"No."

He looked over both shoulders, scanning the sidewalk. "It's good you're cautious. It means you actually understand what's at stake."

That, for some reason, angered me more than anything else he'd said so far. "I know exactly what's at stake." I'd lived through losing every-thing. It was time for this psychopath to know how it felt.

Henrik grinned again, and there was something feral about it. "I know about the addendum." He sing-songed the statement like a taunt. "To the will, right? You plan to have a baby. Are you two already trying?"

For a moment, I literally could not speak. My ears rang with an icy static, and every drop of blood in my body tried to leave at once.

He knew about the will. And about the grandchild clause. Andreas had been right to be paranoid.

Henrik laughed at my silence. "You're not even denying it?" His eyes dropped to my stomach. "Are you knocked up already?"

I managed to get my tongue unstuck. "Henrik, why are you here? You don't need to stalk me to know what's happening. Just text Tobias and get your briefing."

He leaned back, clearly enjoying himself. "Tobias doesn't know how to get things done." Then he lowered his voice to something deeper. "And because I want you to hear it from me that nothing is guaranteed. Nine months is a long time. Anything can happen."

I did not respond. There was nothing to say to that.

His smile faded, replaced by a darker and flatter expression. "I'm not going to let my Genetix be inherited by a fucking fetus. So, if you have a death wish, keep playing house with my little brother. But don't get too comfortable."

Henrik didn't move, not at first. He just let his words hang in the cold air, hands pressed to the glass, mouth twisting in the approximation of a smile. I stayed where I was, just on the other side of the door, thumb still white-knuckled around my phone, wondering why I hadn't called the police yet.

If he wanted to intimidate me, he was succeeding beyond his wildest expectations.

I watched as he pulled a phone from his coat, thumbed a text or maybe took a photo. Then, like he'd grown bored with the whole "terrorize Sam" event, he took a step away from the door, rocked back on his heels, and surveyed the street. For a heartbeat, I thought he'd leave. But instead, he pivoted on one shoe and scanned the sidewalk, head cocked in a way that was at once predatory and weirdly expectant.

I followed his gaze and saw why.

Not too far away, a black Mercedes pulled up, then idled. A moment later, the driver's-side door popped open and out stepped Tara, all five foot, eight inches of her, hair up in the same efficient ponytail as mine. She wore a navy windbreaker, dark leggings, and sneakers, but the way she moved made the clothes look tactical.

Henrik squinted at her. I watched, fascinated, as the gears turned in his head. For a second, I wondered if he would assume Tara was me. As Tara walked toward us with long, unhurried strides, Henrik started forward, his interest likely piqued.

At fifty feet, his shoulders bunched and he glanced back at me with unmistakable confusion. But then he turned back and met Tara halfway up the steps to the building.

"Hey," Tara called out, voice calm.

Henrik stopped, shoulders rolling back, and for a moment I thought he might just bowl her over. Instead, he put on that same flat, professional smile. "You're not Samantha," he said.

"Nope," Tara agreed, shifting her weight, then continuing to walk up the stairs and around him with a casual authority. "Just a friend."

The words hung there as Henrik turned back toward the building, watching her. Eventually, he released a laugh that didn't touch his eyes.

"Well, since Samantha won't come out to play, maybe I could play with you."

"I wouldn't advise that," Tara replied, inspecting me, then mouthing the words, *Are you okay?*

I nodded, but then shifted my focus back to Henrik, not wanting to take my eyes off him for even a second.

She turned her back to me and he looked her over, top to toe, and I saw a flash of something—caution, maybe, or the animal calculation that precedes an attack. "Why? You some sort of ninja or something?"

"Something like that," Tara said, and took one step closer.

There was a stillness then, the kind of hush that comes before an avalanche. Henrik continued openly sizing her up, then darted a glance at me through the glass. I tried not to look like I was cowering, but there was a zero percent chance I was fooling anyone.

"Tell your friend to come out and talk like an adult," Henrik said, voice still soft but edged now.

"Nah."

Henrik's smile dropped. "'Nah?'"

"That's right. Nah."

He laughed again, but this time it was short, almost a bark. "You're serious."

She said something that sounded like "Deadly," but since she faced away from me, I couldn't be sure.

And then, as if they'd been following pre-rehearsed choreography, they both moved.

It was fast. I barely registered the blur of Henrik's hand as he reached for Tara's neck, or the way Tara stepped inside the grab, twisted his wrist, and drove a knee into his gut so hard it lifted him an inch off the cement. He doubled over, more from surprise than pain, but Tara was already behind him, one arm around his throat, the other pinning his wrist. Henrik tried to elbow her but she shifted, swept his feet, and brought him down in a controlled sprawl on the cold concrete.

He thrashed, kicked out, tried to roll. Tara let him, but only enough to humiliate him further, and then—when he growled and went for her ponytail—she caught his arm, bent it backward, and held it at an angle that seemed impossible.

Henrik let out a curse so loud it reverberated through the glass.

"Let. Go," Tara said.

Henrik, to his credit, tried one last time to flip her. She let him get just enough leverage to think he had a shot, then shifted her knee into the small of his back, and he went face-down with a yelp.

"I told you to let go," Tara said, voice steady, not even breathing hard.

Henrik's reply was a string of expletives in what sounded like Swedish, though it might have just been the universal language of defeat. Tara let him go, slow, never giving him her back. To his credit, he didn't even try to stand. She stepped away and kept her eyes on him, posture relaxed but ready.

In that moment, I really, really wanted to go to Tara's kickboxing class.

Tara straightened, brushed her hands together like she'd just finished a particularly annoying round of weeding a garden, and said, "He's not armed. You can come out, Sam."

For a few heartbeats, I just watched Henrik, face-down, still trying to recover his dignity if not his wind. Then I pushed open the door, adrenaline burning through my veins, and hurried down the steps. I gave Henrik as wide a berth as the stairs allowed.

He looked up at me, eyes glassy with rage and, maybe, confusion. "You think you're safe? You're not," he spat.

"Get in the car, Sam," Tara said, never looking away from Henrik still sprawled on the ground.

I did as she instructed, rushing for the door, opening it, and catapulting myself inside. I had never wanted anything more in my life than to be inside a locked Mercedes, surrounded by reinforced steel, and speeding away from this entire encounter.

What felt like seconds later, Tara slid in behind the wheel, yanked her own door shut, and had the car in gear before I'd even managed to get my seat belt buckled. My hands shook so hard I had to use both of them to thread the latch through the buckle.

"Are you really okay? Did he touch you?" she asked, eyes darting between me and the road.

"He didn't touch me, and I am okay," I said, and not believing it. The adrenaline was leaving my system and now I was shaking all over. "Thank you."

Tara gave me a smile, but it looked tight. "May I suggest I take you home now and you skip kickboxing tonight?"

"Uh . . . okay." I nodded, agreeing with her. I would go, just not tonight.

She grinned, the real kind this time. "Come next week, okay?"

I nodded again.

We merged into traffic, leaving Henrik behind. The car was silent except for the muted thump of tires over potholes and the steady thrum of my pulse, which refused to slow down.

I was shaken, and scared, and my hands weren't going to stop trembling for at least a year, but there was something else under the surface—a kind of bright, savage relief. And, deep down, a quiet, vengeful satisfaction. Henrik had fallen for the smoke screen. He thought we were trying for a baby.

The truth would never occur to him, not until it was too late. And by then, Genetix would be mine.

# [ 3 ]

# THE MALE REPRODUCTIVE SYSTEM

***Samantha***

I sensed Tara's gaze move over me every so often in the rearview mirror as I pressed my palms together, knuckles white, and tried to will my heart to slow. She said nothing, bless her, and seemed to be unbothered by the altercation with Henrik. Meanwhile, I was playing it on loop in my brain. She'd thrown a grown man to the ground and made it look easy. And now, she behaved as though roughing Henrik up was the same as assisting an innocuous, little old lady cross the street. Maybe, to her, she had. Maybe I was an innocuous little old lady.

We drove in silence for a block, then two, the hum of the engine and the rhythmic tick of the turn signal the only sounds besides my own ragged breathing. At the next red light, I spoke without planning to.

"Can you drive around for a bit before heading back to the apartment? I just need a few minutes." My voice sounded too thin, almost childlike. I hated that, but didn't have the energy to make it tougher.

Tara nodded, eyes flickering to me in the mirror. "Sure. But I'll have to let Andreas know. I just told him we were on our way and if we're running late, he'll want to know. Is that okay?"

For a second, I bristled at the idea of being surveilled, but the feeling faded just as quickly as it arrived. I had no problem with Andreas keeping tabs on me. Not after today. He was right about his brothers and he was right about Henrik in particular. It wasn't paranoia if it was warranted.

"Yes, of course. That's fine." I exhaled and tried to melt my spine into the seat.

Tara thumbed her phone at the next stoplight, probably sending a perfectly bland update. It dawned on me that this was my life now. Status reports. Driver/bodyguard. The prospect didn't even feel dystopian; it felt reasonable given the stakes.

The Mercedes glided through city blocks where people in expensive yoga pants jogged with their dogs and didn't have to wonder whether some Scandinavian sociopath was plotting to end their nonexistent pregnancy. I envied them, a little. Or maybe a lot. I'd never admit that out loud, even under torture, which I now suspected Henrik would be happy to provide, gratis.

After two turns, Tara spoke again, voice pitched low. "You handled yourself really well. I know you're probably shaken, but you kept your head." She paused. "Most people don't."

I tried to snort, but it sounded more like a hiccup. "I hid behind glass, Tara."

"And you didn't run. You made him work for it. I've seen plenty of people freeze up or faint, or try to punch back and end up with a concussion. You, though—you got out of the situation, kept your wits and your phone, waited for me, stayed focused. Good job."

I didn't know what to say to that, so I just nodded.

By the third left turn, my hands had stopped shaking. The adrenaline ebbed, which meant a wave of exhaustion washed over me, threatening to knock me out cold right there in the back seat. I watched the city scroll by through the tinted window and let my mind go blank for the first time since I recognized Henrik's face.

The thought emerged, *Why had Henrik called my dad a coward?* I didn't know. Either way, the next steps were clear. I had to be smarter, meaner, and better prepared. There was no room for error, not when people like the Kristiansens existed.

I waited until my pulse slowed, until I could speak without feeling like my tongue would tie itself in a hangman's knot, before instructing Tara, "You can take me back to the apartment now."

Tara caught my gaze in the mirror, checked my face, then nodded.

"Got it." She steered us into traffic and in five more minutes we were pulling up outside the apartment building.

By then, I felt almost like myself again. I thanked Tara, even though I knew she didn't need to be thanked, and grabbed my backpack from the floor. I lifted my hand to the door handle when I caught sight of Andreas on the sidewalk.

He stood with his arms folded, eyes on the Mercedes, body angled toward the street like he was preparing to intercept a riot or maybe chase down a rogue food truck. He wore a charcoal sweater that probably cost more than my monthly rent at my old apartment, and for some reason, the sight of him, there, clearly waiting for me in the dwindling daylight and cold, made me want to cry.

Before I could even pull the door handle, Andreas was at the back window, knocking. The knock was polite, but the force behind it suggested he was two seconds from tearing off the whole door.

Tara unlocked the car, and he pulled the back door open, his silhouette momentarily filling the frame. His eyes, usually half-mast and unreadable, were liquid and alive. There was a tightness in his jaw and a wildness in the way he scanned my face, like he was searching for injuries or evidence of trauma that might not be visible to the naked eye.

He did not speak, not right away. The air inside the car seemed to freeze, and then, suddenly, he reached inside, grabbed me by the shoulder, and pulled me out.

I stumbled but he caught me. I was now pressed against him, my chin nearly to his chest, his arm locked around my back, his hand fisting the fabric of my jacket. It was a full-body hug, the kind meant to keep a person from falling apart, or maybe to keep the world from taking them away.

He seemed to be vibrating. Not a lot, just enough for me to notice. His heart was a trip-hammer, beating through his chest so fast it made my own skip a few measures.

He held me, and only after a long moment, did he speak. "He didn't hurt you, did he? Did he touch you?"

I shook my head, unable to find words. My throat was blocked by something big and jagged and stupid. Tears burned behind my eyelids, but I refused to let them fall. I could smell his skin and his cologne and, faintly, the chamomile tea he must have been drinking when he got Tara's text.

He stepped back, but only enough to look me in the eyes. "You're sure?"

I nodded again, trying to manage a reply, but all that came out was, "I'm okay. I'm fine."

His hand tightened on my upper arm and his voice dropped to a whisper. "You have to stay inside the building until your guard arrives from now on. Promise me. God, if something had happened to you, if he had hurt you . . ."

That nearly undid me. He sounded so genuinely upset, so real and so raw, that I had to look away. My vision swam for a second, and I realized my entire body was cold, except for the spots where his hands gripped me. They were warm, unreasonably so.

"It's okay," I managed, but it sounded pathetic, even to me.

He shook his head. "It is not okay. I am sorry. I—" His words jammed together, tangled and sharp. "I will not let it happen again."

My chest hurt with the effort it took to not cry. For a moment, I wondered if this was all for show. But the pulse pounding under his skin, the way he kept glancing at my face and then away, like it was physically painful to see me scared, told me otherwise. He was afraid. For me.

That, more than anything, made me feel oddly safe, safer than I'd felt in a long time. I had someone looking out for me, checking in, waiting for me to come home.

Not allowing myself to think too much about it, I buried my face in his chest and let myself be held. I was so tired, so wrung out, that I didn't care if the whole city watched. The pressure of his embrace was grounding, a force field against the rest of the world.

Tara stepped away, silent and invisible as a shadow, giving us space. For the first time in a long time, I let myself be comforted. I let myself believe that maybe, in this one thing, I wasn't alone.

We stood like that for a long time, not speaking, just breathing each other's air, until my heart slowed and my thoughts grew quiet. When I finally looked up, Andreas's eyes were less wild, but the concern in them hadn't faded.

"You're really okay?" he asked, softer this time.

"Yeah," I said. "I'm okay now."

He nodded, but didn't let go. If anything, his grip tightened for a heartbeat, then loosened just enough for him to tuck a lock of my hair behind my ear, an oddly delicate gesture.

He glanced toward the doorman, who had come out of his booth and now stood a respectful distance away, pretending to be interested in the curb. "Let us go inside," Andreas said, but didn't move.

I stepped away first, feeling steadier, and walked through the lobby. He followed and hovered at my side like a satellite, orbiting, always within arm's reach. I didn't mind. The further we got from the sidewalk, the less I felt the urge to look over my shoulder.

We entered the elevator, and only then did he speak again, voice low and meant for me alone. "Tara texted me that you did everything right. She said you were smart and you kept your head."

I tried to smile, but my lips wouldn't quite obey. "Mostly I just didn't want to be the star of a true crime documentary."

Andreas almost smiled. "I would not let that happen."

The elevator chimed and we walked in silence to the apartment. He opened the door and ushered me inside. For a second, I stood there, taking in the warmth of the space, the faint aroma of coffee and whatever savory dish Andreas was having for dinner.

I dropped my bag in the entryway and turned to look at him. He studied me for a moment, then closed the distance and wrapped me in another hug. This one was less urgent, more careful. It felt like a promise, or maybe an apology.

I let myself relax. I let him hold me up. And there were no cameras here. This wasn't for show.

"Thank you," I whispered, not sure if I was thanking him for the hug, for worrying, or for being exactly who I needed in this moment.

He didn't answer, but he didn't need to. He just held on, and I held back, and for the next minute, that was enough.

* * *

After an indeterminate period of time spent hugging in the hallway, I finally talked myself into pulling away. I'd had a shitty night, and accepting comfort, leaning on Andreas was appropriate given Henrik's threatening antics—but only to a point!

Now it was time for me to pull myself together, even if he was warm and smelled good and his body felt amazing. I needed to rely on myself.

*Andreas won't always be here to comfort me.*

Extracting my body, I gave him a vague smile, then stepped out of his orbit. Kicking off my shoes by the door, I picked them up and placed them in the closet, hung up my jacket, and ditched my backpack. I then drifted to the living room wordlessly, gravitating to the couch not out of conscious thought, but because it was the first surface that promised softness. The cushions were unfamiliar but not unfriendly, and I let myself sink into the plush expanse, arms crossed tightly over my stomach.

I sensed Andreas hover for exactly three seconds, standing behind the couch, before vanishing. I heard him moving in the kitchen. Glass clinking, something ceramic rattling, the faint, deliberate pop of an electric kettle's button.

I focused on the sounds he made while I scanned the interior of his apartment. I hadn't taken the time to really look at this room before. Taking note of the details now felt therapeutic, pulling me out of my head, forcing me into the present. The living room had the kind of curving, expensive lines you see in extremely old houses, and the books on the shelves were battered and dog-eared and grouped in weird little cliques, not for aesthetics but for accessibility.

I also noticed a collection of sheet music, which stood out to me since it was the only sheet music on the shelf. The sheets were lovingly stored between layers of acid-free paper and were within a black linen box. I soon realized why he owned the collection. The composer was his mother, Augustina Loretto, and there were notations and scribbles in the margin of the first page. I assumed these notes were her handwriting. The sheets of music felt precious and private, so I didn't look through them. I put them back safely on the shelf where I'd found them.

On the coffee table, a single remote lay on a glass tray which also contained a pitcher of water, four stacked glasses, four white linen napkins, a blank notepad, and a single fountain pen. The windows swallowed half a city block and spit it back in watercolor versions of itself. It was all so . . . intentional. And elegant. And functional.

*I wonder what that remote controls?* There was no TV in the room, not that I could see.

Andreas returned with a tray holding two mugs and a small plate, each item selected and positioned with so much care that I wondered if he'd spent the better part of the last fifteen minutes searching the internet for "appropriate beverages and snacks for traumatized guests." He set the tray down on the table, keeping it a safe distance from my knees, then sat on the opposite end of the couch, not quite facing me. Three feet of high-grade leather sofa between us.

"Thank you." It came out unsteady, too loud. I picked up the mug—the light golden liquid inside was, I assumed, tea—grateful for the anchor, and stared at the plate of cookies. After a long pause, I leaned closer and inspected them, the gears in my brain moving sluggishly.

"Are these . . . shortbread with jam?" I finally managed.

Andreas nodded, not looking at me. "Yes. I recall, those were your favorite when we were kids."

I squinted at the cookies, then at him. Then, on autopilot, I picked one up and took a bite. The taste yanked me instantly back to the memory of a kitchen in the Hamptons, my mom humming and rolling the dough into balls, little dots of red jam in the center of the thumbprint I made with my own hands.

The flavor was exactly right—lemony, buttery, with the sharp hit of raspberry jam on the roof of my mouth. The nostalgia gut-punched me so hard my eyes stung, but all I did was chew in silence. They tasted *exactly* the same as my mom's. Even the jam, which she'd make every summer over the Fourth of July from raspberry bushes she'd grown at our home in Connecticut. She'd then bring jars to the Hamptons and make shortbread in the Kristiansens' vacation home kitchen.

*How'd he do that?*

"How did you do that?" The question tumbled out of me. "These taste just like my mom's."

His face a composed mask, Andreas fidgeted with his mug, then set it down without drinking. He glanced sideways at me, then away, then back. Tension stretched between us and had become its own entity—less a cloud, more a flock of birds with nowhere to land.

He cleared his throat. "Do you regret it?"

I licked a crumb off my thumb, then stared at him. "Regret what? Eating the cookie? I never regret cookies."

He didn't blink. "No. Agreeing to this plan. To inherit Genetix. Now that you know what Henrik is like."

I studied him, trying to figure out if this was a test, or a trap, or simply raw honesty. "No. If anything, meeting Henrik and seeing for myself first-hand how unhinged he is, makes me even more certain that taking over those Genetix shares is the right thing. I can't imagine someone like him being in charge of my father's company. Tobias is bad enough, but Henrik . . ."

I let the thought trail off, not because I didn't have a million adjectives to tack on, but because I'd already reached the upper limit of my emotional output for the day.

Andreas nodded. "He is very dangerous." He spoke without inflection, as if reading from a file. Or a police report. Or a court record.

I sipped the tea, which was hot and herbal and probably blended for maximum relaxation. My hands had stopped shaking, but my insides still felt wobbly.

"He's been arrested many times," Andreas continued, voice low. "My father's connections and money have kept him out of jail, mostly."

"Has he ever killed someone?" I asked, surprising myself with the bluntness of the question. But I felt like it was an important one.

Andreas went very still, his profile sharp in the light from the huge window. Eventually, he met my gaze. "No. Not quite."

The phrase hung in the air, grim and striking me as both vague and precise. Andreas kept saying Henrik was dangerous. I wanted to quantify it so I could prepare myself.

"What do you mean, 'not quite'?" My stomach twisted again.

"He beat someone so badly, they almost died. But not quite." Andreas sounded clinical, not cold, but like he'd spent years reciting these facts to himself.

"And he was never punished?" I pressed.

Andreas shrugged, though it was more a collapse of the shoulders. "Oskar had the case dropped and buried, paid off the family, and placed Henrik under a type of house arrest for almost two years afterward. But when Oskar's illness progressed, no one was paying attention. Henrik has been more or less unchecked since my father fell into a coma. So, a few months now."

I exhaled and rubbed my forehead, a headache pooling behind my eyes. "If anything, I think maybe I should have more bodyguards."

I sensed Andreas move. When I glanced up at him, he seemed to have perked up and now sat straighter.

"I can make the larger team more visible."

I gave him a sidelong look. "You already have a larger team?"

He blinked once, and then his eyes dropped. "Uh . . . I do."

I squinted. "Please explain."

Andreas's chest rose with a deep inhale, giving me the sense that he'd decided something, or was surrendering to something. "The truth is, you have four bodyguards already, but only Tara is obvious to you. Whenever we have been together, we have a team of six. I have requested that they be discreet, so as to not make you uncomfortable."

Setting down my tea, I laughed. But it was a shaky, bewildered sound. "Even when you walked me home on Thursday?"

"Yes," he said. His tone held an edge of belligerence. Or perhaps it was defensiveness. "And even prior, I placed a team of four on you before we had coffee at the café. As soon as I made first contact through my assistant, Elio. By making contact, I knew I had potentially opened you up to my brothers' scrutiny. I wanted to be certain you were safe."

I simply looked at him, mind whirling through every moment of the past few weeks, searching for any sighting of a security detail. I hadn't noticed a thing, and what did that say about my lack of spidey-senses? Was this a compliment to Andreas's security team, or an indictment of my own observational skills? Or both?

Perhaps I was too tired at present to muster outrage at this news, or perhaps my pragmaticism immediately recognized the logic and prudence of his actions. Whatever it was, I didn't feel irritation. I felt resigned.

"I guess I should thank you." I reached for and took a sip of my tea.

Andreas looked up, uncertainty flickering in his eyes. "Are you angry with me?"

Tilting my head, I thought about it, wanting to be certain before responding. "No. Actually. I'm not even a little angry. Thank you for keeping me safe. And if I haven't thanked you for this yet, then allow me to say, thank you for helping me gain controlling interest in my father's company."

His relief was nearly palpable, though he tried to cover it by taking a careful sip of his own tea.

"Are you open to having a larger visible team?" he asked, his tone striking me as carefully conversational.

"Maybe if I'm in a public place for a long time." I debated the matter. "And I think I should probably warn the building security at my department to keep an eye out. What do you think?"

Andreas nodded immediately. "Yes. I agree. I will make arrangements."

He hesitated, then set his mug down again. "Are you sure you do not regret agreeing to this inheritance scheme?"

I set my mug down too, thinking carefully. "No. As I said, I'm really glad—relieved, even—that I finally agreed to it. Again, if Henrik were to inherit Genetix, I can't imagine how he would treat the employees, or how he'd use the wealth and power gained in his sadistic pursuits."

Andreas nodded, but it was a slow gesture. "Yes. I agree. I felt—I feel —similar. Which is why I pushed you so hard. I apologize if, at the time, I—"

"I get it now," I cut in. "You were right to push. You were right to place a security team on me as soon as you made first contact. And I probably wouldn't have listened to you about Henrik or Tobias until I experienced their maliciousness firsthand. I'm sorry I was so resistant. And I really am glad we've teamed up to take them down."

He still looked like he wanted to say something else, but instead he nodded, apparently accepting my words.

A shiver ran through me, originating somewhere deep. I realized I still felt rattled, still floating a few feet above my own body, watching myself from the ceiling.

Perhaps Andreas noticed because he asked, "May I hug you again?"

I lifted an eyebrow at him, then gave in to the impulse to make a joke. "Do I smell that good? It's just soap. I'll give you the name of the brand."

A faint smile ghosted his mouth, but he shook his head. "It must have been frightening for you. But, truthfully, this is for me. I am also shaken, just thinking about what might have happened."

I stared at him, and the urge to make another joke disappeared. Not letting myself think too much about it, I scooted forward on the couch, and opened my arms.

He didn't hesitate. He closed the distance between us in a single, smooth motion, sliding to me, and pulled me into a tight, two-armed embrace. His body felt rigid at first, as though he might be afraid of breaking me, but then I felt the slow, deliberate loosening of tension, the way he let his chin dip down to rest in the curve of my shoulder, the way his fingers flexed and then stilled on my back.

I let myself be held, but after a moment, I squeezed him back, firmer, the way you'd hug a friend after a funeral. I wanted him to feel comforted, too, not just obligated to protect me or keep me from falling apart. I wanted him to know I saw him, and his fears, and for this moment at least, we were both safe.

Neither of us moved. Like before in the hallway, it could have been two minutes or twenty. The city beyond the windows glowed and shifted, but inside, the only movement was our breathing.

$$[ 4 ]$$

# SEXUAL DIFFERENTIATION

***Samantha***

Sunlight tickled my eyelids, which was strange, because my bedroom didn't face east and—hold on.

I wasn't in my bed.

This pillow felt too solid, too warm, and, if I really paid attention, way too much like human muscle. There was the clean scent of laundry detergent, yes, but also a deeper, spicy note. Rosemary, cologne, and warm skin. My left arm was numb from the angle, and my right leg was slung over something firm and unyielding, with my heel pressed hard against the outside of a knee that was definitely not my own unless I'd suddenly developed superhuman flexibility skilz.

I opened one eye and found an expanse of blue silk immediately in front of my nose. It shimmered in the morning light. I recognized the exact shade, not cornflower, not navy, but the rich, almost iridescent blue reserved for high-end men's pajama suits.

*Of course*. Because the my subconscious could always be trusted to make things maximally weird. *I sleepwalked. Again.*

Shifting incrementally, I confirmed the following: My face was smashed against Andreas Kristiansen's shoulder. My body was three-fourths on top of him, one-fourth on the couch, like I'd lost a wrestling match with both gravity and personal boundaries. My left arm was threaded beneath our rib cages, and his right arm was wrapped all the way around my back, palm splayed flat and proprietarily across my bottom.

He was asleep. Or—as I lifted my head from his chest—he looked asleep. He could have been dead, but the steady rise and fall of his chest, plus the faint sound of him breathing, suggested otherwise. My thighs, like some kind of traitorous heat-seeking missiles, had made themselves very much at home straddling his. For a moment I marveled at the contrast; his legs, thick and hard, compared to my own, which were encased in the jersey cotton sleep pants I'd thrown on last night.

Tilting my head back and staring at the ceiling, I tried to reverse engineer the sequence of events that had deposited me in this arrangement. Last night, after the Henrik incident, I'd sat on the couch with Andreas. We drank tea, ate cookies, talked in a way that was two degrees too honest, and then, at some point, we'd hugged. I distinctly remembered hugging him.

Then I went to my room, changed into pajamas, brushed my teeth, took the time to do my entire skincare regiment—which was unusual for me, I mostly considered the purchasing of cosmetic items aspirational in nature—and then I went into my room, barricaded the door with furniture and the bins full of my stuff, and I went to sleep.

But then I must have left my room and sleepwalked, right on top of Andreas.

And he must have, for whatever reason, decided it was preferable to let a full-grown woman use him as a pillow rather than disturb her. *He's so weird.*

My psychiatrist was going to have a field day. The time had come. I couldn't put it off. I had to schedule an appointment. I would call her first thing when I got to work, insurance be damned.

Closing my eyes, I weighed my options.

Option A: Extract myself from this sexy European cuddle trap without waking him. This would require flexibility, stealth, and possibly a team of riggers from Cirque du Soleil.

Option B: Accept my fate, go back to sleep, and deal with the fallout later. Pros: no immediate effort. Cons: inevitable awkwardness.

Option C: Use the opportunity to analyze Andreas until I spotted a flaw. Did he snore? Was he a sleep-talker? Would he, if I yelled "Fire!"

abandon me for the nearest exit? If I stared at him long enough, would his face reveal a previously unseen defect? Was he, in the immortal words of Cher from *Clueless,* actually a Monet—put together from far away but a total mess up close?

I decided on option A, only because the sun was rising rapidly and I needed to get to work sooner rather than later.

I began the detachment process—disengage left arm, lift head, and pivot right leg off his lap. What I failed to account for was the fact that Andreas's grip on my butt was, even in sleep, tenacious.

As soon as I tried to slide away, his arm cinched tighter, and his other hand came up to grip my upper thigh, pulling me flush against him. I froze. Because, ladies, he had a massive third-leg situation going on. Andreas's unmistakable erection pressed indecently—but so delightfully —against my vagina, and the last tendrils of my sleepiness fled in an instant.

Then, quite suddenly, Andreas awoke. One moment comatose, the next his eyes flying open, expression blank. He blinked several times, then his gaze zeroed in on me, wide and fuzzy, but not surprised.

"Good morning," I said, because what else does one say in this situation? There is no script for waking up on someone's lap, unless you're in an anime, and I lacked the requisite blue hair, DD cup size, and accidental panty flash.

Plus, being totally honest, since last night, when he'd hugged me on the sidewalk, I now felt this low hum of tension, something like electricity, when we were together. A hyperawareness. It made thinking difficult and kept getting in the way of clever word choice.

Andreas blinked at me again, and I watched as his brain caught up with the situation, specifically the time, place, person, limb arrangement, and hand position. His cheeks did that fascinating thing where they turned pink and the color bloomed outward. With a flinching motion, he loosened his grip, his hands flying away, and he took a deep breath.

"Samantha." His voice was so hoarse I wondered if he'd slept at all. "Did you sleep well?"

"I . . . think so?" I scootched backward, away from his mast of morning wood. His hands returned to my body as though to steady me, settling lightly on my waist. "What happened?" I asked, fairly certain I knew, but I wanted to hear his side.

"I was sitting on the couch after you left, reading. Around midnight, you came out of your room, sleepwalking again."

I groaned and covered my face with both hands. "Did I—oh God. Did I say anything? Or do anything weird? I mean, other than sit on your lap."

He considered this, then shook his head. "No. You were walking to my room, I think. I called out your name. You stopped, stood there for a moment. You turned and walked over to me. Then you, uh, you sat on me, as you are now, and went to sleep. Or, I guess, stayed asleep, but in this position." He swallowed, the sound audible and oddly endearing.

"So, you just . . . let me sleep on you. All night." I could feel the flush creeping up my own neck now, both from frustration and a growing sense of something less platonic. And, you know, the aforementioned hyper-awareness.

Andreas nodded, turning his head away to yawn. When he finished, he glanced back at me, and for a split second, his eyes flicked down to my mouth. It was subtle—blink and you'd miss it—but I didn't miss it.

*Oh no! Does my breath stink?*

I covered my mouth as more upsetting possibilities unsexified situation. I must've drooled on him. Or snored. Or, worst of all, ground my teeth. Nothing sexy about teeth grinding.

I needed to say something. Anything. But without letting him smell my morning breath.

"Are your legs okay?" I blurted, still holding my hand in front of my mouth like a female judge on *Iron Chef Japan.* "Can you feel them? Will you ever walk again? Have I paralyzed you?"

He regarded me with a mixture of what looked like amusement and something I couldn't name, glancing at the hand covering my mouth and lifting an eyebrow. "They are a little—uh—stiff," he said, and the way he said it, slow and deliberate, sent a little shiver down my back.

I snorted, then cringed. Nothing sexy about snorting. Or cringing. I mean, name one situation where it's sexy to cringe.

And yet I still sat on his lap, straddling him, and I knew—though I could no longer feel it due to my earlier scootch back—his very hard cock was mere inches from my very open legs.

*Yeeeeeah.* I needed to get off his lap. Like, right now.

"Anyway!" Turning my face to the side to point my morning breath elsewhere, I set my hands on the couch behind him and pushed, forcing my legs to work even as they protested. My hips spasmed, obviously not liking the position my unconscious brain had preferred for last night's sleep.

I felt Andreas's hands on my waist tighten, probably thinking I might face-plant without assistance, but then he let me go. Ungracefully, I dismounted his lap. My inner thighs ached, reminding me of that one time in elementary school when I'd been forced to ride a horse for six hours. *THE WORST!*

Finally separated from the ridiculously sexy man I shared an apartment and revenge destiny with, I pushed my back against the arm of the couch and brought my knees up, wrapping my arms around my legs.

Once I was off, he immediately reached to the side and placed a throw pillow on his lap, clearing his throat. Andreas was in another fancy pajama set. I suspected the top had been perfectly pressed last night before he'd donned it. Perhaps it had also been buttoned up to his collarbones, but the top two buttons were undone now, hinting at the smooth skin beneath and the elegance of his bone structure. And, boy oh boy, did he give good clavicle.

Tearing my eyes away, I made a mental note to one day count how many pajama sets this man owned, because so far I'd seen two, and each looked like it came with a monogrammed handkerchief and a complimentary monocle.

Thank goodness I'd put on a huge long-sleeve T-shirt and baggy sweatpants last night. In all honesty, I'd chosen these clothes just in case I did sleepwalk. I didn't want to wake up pantsless like yesterday.

But . . . *Hmm.*

Maybe I should do the opposite tonight? Perhaps if I felt uncomfortable going to bed I wouldn't sleepwalk. Maybe I should sleep in a negligee, just to see if my subconscious was less likely to parade around the apartment in lace and silk.

I peeked at him and caught him watching me. Andreas's eyes dropped and he straightened his posture, folding his hands on top of the throw pillow. His cheeks, for the record, had still not faded back to their baseline hue. If anything, they'd gone from pink to red.

That hyperawareness buzzed beneath my skin and twisted in my stomach, making me speak before I'd vetted the words. "Sorry again for, uh, invading your personal space. We should put a bell around my neck so you can hear me coming," I joked, and then internally reprimanded myself for the stupid joke.

I hated this. I was second-guessing everything coming out of my mouth. Horseback riding for six hours wasn't the worst, this was *the worst!*

He shook his head. "There is no need to apologize. The last thing I want is for you to feel like you must restrict yourself here. This is your home, too. Please." Andreas hesitated, as though thinking through his words carefully before saying them, then continued. "I know this situation with my brothers is extremely stressful. If this is how your brain chooses to cope, I am glad to be useful."

My eyebrows bounced upward. "Useful?" Goodness. I could think of a few ways to use him, but none of those seemed at all appropriate.

He looked me in the eye, then away, then back. "I want to be useful," he said quietly.

He had no idea where my dirty brain was going, so I asked, "You're telling me you're okay being my personal mattress?" which was the cleanest way I could think of describing my current thoughts. And I made sure to flavor the words with all the incredulity I felt.

There was a beat during which I honestly had no idea what he was thinking and my heart hammered in my chest. He wasn't looking at me anymore. He stared forward, his face in profile.

My whole body tensed because, *Is he thinking what I'm thinking? Is he going to propose a friends-with-benefits situation?* I held my breath, waiting. Waiting. And hoping.

Eventually, Andreas's usual mask of bored indifference slipped over his features.

*So . . . that's a no.*

I was suddenly, viscerally aware of how close we still were on the couch. The entire living room, for all its square footage, shrank to a four-foot radius of us. Silence became uncomfortable—for me—so I scrambled to redirect the conversation.

"Uh, so, on a scale of one to ten, how awful was this for you?" Hopefully he would accept my olive branch of self-deprecation. I didn't want to live in an apartment with someone who felt awkward around me. I didn't want to become Andreas's Dr. James Nieminen.

Andreas glanced at me, apparently considering the question with the seriousness of someone reviewing an offer of employment. "Zero," he finally said. And when my mouth parted and my forehead wrinkled with genuine confusion—because how could that be?—he added, "It is only embarrassing if you are uncomfortable. I am not, was not, uncomfortable."

Staring at him and his serene, dispassionate expression, I realized that he was totally unaffected by what had happened last night and this morning. Maybe women fell asleep on his lap all the time. This was old hat for him. An everyday occurrence.

Okay then.

I will say, his honesty was disarming. It made me want to ask a hundred follow-up questions. Likely, those follow-up questions would reveal too much. Being me, I defaulted to banter instead.

"Well, if you're a zero, then I'm a zero. You're a really good mattress. Like, ten out of ten, would recommend."

Holding my gaze, he said, "Glad to be of service," pitching his voice deeper, quieter than it had been up to now.

*What's this? What's he doing? What's that mean?*

Ugh! This really was the worst. Did liking a person mean I would always be this frazzled and on edge around them? Second-guessing and picking apart their words? I hated this.

Our gazes remained locked for a full five to ten seconds before the tension grew so thick—*again*—it spurred me to stand. Ignoring the renewed protests of my thighs and hips, I made a show of stretching, lifting my arms over my head and faking a theatric and very loud yawn until I felt certain my legs would carry me back to my room. Now I just needed to—

Somewhere down the hallway, the sound of my phone ringing saved me from coming up with a clever post-cuddle exit line.

"Let me get that!" I darted around the couch, nearly kneeing the coffee table in my haste to leave, and jogged toward the bedroom where I should've been sleeping last night. I wouldn't usually rush to answer a call, especially not this early in the morning, but fleeing the scene of my own subconscious crime was a top priority.

When I finally found my phone, it was on the nightstand in the bedroom, still plugged into the charger. I answered with a breathless "Hello?"

"Sam! It's Diya!" Her voice was bright and familiar and a welcome interruption.

"Diya! Hi! HOW ARE YOU?" For the second time that morning, I cringed. This time at the unintentional loudness and breathlessness of my voice.

"Are you—did I interrupt you running a marathon?" She dropped her voice to ask, "Or were you in the middle of something else?" The suggestion in her tone was unmistakable.

"Neither," I said flatly, hating that I felt myself blush. I wasn't a blusher. I never blushed! "Just sprinted across the apartment for the phone. What's up?"

"How are you? How are things? How's engaged life?"

"It's all good. I'm just . . . adjusting." For some reason, Henrik's enraged face from last night picked that moment flash behind my vision. *Psycho.*

"Are you sure you don't want to come back? Pretty sure I heard rats unionizing in the walls yesterday. Sorry you missed it."

I snorted a laugh, which made her laugh. The sound of her laughter grounded me, made the world feel less sharp. In the background, I heard the shouts of hospital workers and the low rumble of what must have been an intercom. She was at the hospital, which meant she'd carved out time for this call in the middle of her insane day. It must've been important.

"Did I leave something behind? Or, why are you calling? Is everything okay?"

"Everything is fine! And, as far as I could tell yesterday, you didn't leave any trace of yourself behind. It's like you were never there. So weird." Her voice trailed off on this last part and I heard her take a deep breath before she continued, "So, the reason I'm calling is because the girls and I want to invite you and Andreas out to dinner Wednesday night. Everyone is still in town. It would just be the four of us. Well, five, including Andreas."

I kicked one of my still-full bins that was parked in the middle of the room. "Dinner Wednesday night with all the ladies? Uh, let me check with Andreas to see if he's free."

From somewhere in the apartment Andreas called out, "I am free Wednesday night for dinner with your friends."

Before I could say anything, Diya said, "Oh! That's great!" Obviously she'd heard him. "We'll eat at Kendra's restaurant. Nakita said that Andreas is vegan?"

I had to clear my throat before I could speak. "Uh, yeah. He is." Kendra worked at a vegan barbecue restaurant not far from Andreas's. "Okay, fine. What time Wednesday?"

After we'd finalized the details (7:00 PM, Smokin Greens BBQ, New York casual) Diya said, "I have to tell you something funny. I was talking to my grandpa and telling him about you and Andreas, and—"

"Wait." I stood up straighter. "You were talking to your grandpa about me?" Did people have those types of relationships with their grandfathers?

I felt a pang of longing for my own grandfather, but then immediately shoved it away.

"Yes. Anyway, just listen. So, I told him that you had gotten engaged to some chess guy, and he asked for his name, and so I told him, and he knew who Andreas was! Isn't that crazy? But then he reminded me that in his hometown, there are a ton of chess grand masters. It's a big deal there, as it should be honestly. But I'd forgotten and I love that. So, my grandpa says congratulations."

"Huh." I felt a sliver of unease at the realization that my friends were unknowingly spreading this lie I'd started. Was I making a liar out of Diya if she didn't know she was lying?

"Are you still there? Sam?"

"Yes! Sorry. Yes. I'm still here. Please, uh, tell him thank you for me." It was all I could think to say. I'd known and accepted that I would have to lie to my friends, but my stomach felt a little queasy at how large this lie had already ballooned.

After promises to see each other soon, we hung up. Lowering my phone, I thumbed through my notifications and saw that I'd missed two texts from Kaitlyn.

**Kaitlyn:** You're coming over for Thanksgiving, right? I'm counting on you to bring cranberry sauce and mashed potatoes.

**Kaitlyn:** And I saw a photo of you with your "fiancé" online. I guess that's happening???? Martin and I want you to bring Andreas if he's up for it. Be prepared to spill tea.

The first text made me smile. The second one made me break into a cold sweat. Not only did Diya's sweet grandfather now think we were engaged, my fake engagement was the subject of online speculation too. And possibly a meme. I'd never been memed before. *But Andreas has.*

This reminder did not improve my mood.

Uncertain how to respond to Kaitlyn, I placed my phone back on the nightstand and surveyed the damage in the bedroom. My sleepwalking self had been busy last night. The bin I'd just kicked was one of four that I'd stacked against the door, a barricade I vaguely remembered constructing before going to bed in order to keep myself from leaving the room. All four bins were now strewn around the room, the door wide open. My suitcase, which I'd propped as an additional security measure, now sat upright and open, clothes spilling out.

I was impressed. My subconscious had the strength and determination of a bison. For the record, I would take any opportunity to compare myself to a bison. Theirs is the most delicious of the red meats. Also, they are freaking majestic animals. So much more majestic than a cow or a yak.

While I ranked the majesticness of hooved animals, Andreas appeared in the doorway. He now wore a plush, navy blue bathrobe that looked like he'd stolen it from a five-star hotel, and man-slippers. You know, the tan ones with a wool-lined interior.

He peered around at the chaos in my room, then at me while I worked to quell the fluttering in my stomach. That same stupid electric hyper-awareness returned.

"You really did try to barricade yourself last night." His voice held unadulterated awe.

"I said I did." Not knowing what to do with my hands, I set them on my hips. "I honestly don't want to keep bothering you."

Ignoring this, he asked, "Where is dinner on Wednesday? I need to let the security team know."

"A place called Smokin Greens BBQ. My old roommate Kendra works there. It's vegan barbecue. Even the sauces. But you really don't have to—"

"Is it the one with the meditating, neon dinosaur in the window?"

"Yes." I sucked in a deep breath, wishing this awareness of him would disappear just as quickly as it had appeared. "Have you been there?"

"I have not. But Elio swears it is the best vegan barbecue in New York. Possibly the world."

"Good to know. I guess we'll find out on Wednesday."

He nodded but didn't leave. Instead, he lingered, surveying the wreckage of my barricade.

I tried to ignore the butterflies that hatched in my stomach as I watched him. He looked both cute and sexy standing there in my doorway. The bathrobe giving him both a boyish and grandpa-ish aura, which shouldn't have been both adorable and sexy but—God help me—it totally was.

"Do you need something else?" I asked, knowing it was best that he leave so I could quash the butterflies.

"Thursday is Thanksgiving. Do you have plans?"

I hesitated. Did I want Andreas to meet Kaitlyn? She and baby Joey were the two most important people in my life. Did I want Andreas to know them?

When I said nothing, Andreas prompted, "Your grandfather is still alive, is he not? Do you—"

"No. We don't speak." I turned my back on Andreas. The butterflies had evaporated at the mention of my grandfather.

My mom's dad was the only biological family left to me, which had certainly simplified my decision to allow the adoption with Andreas and therefore cut all legal ties with my biological family.

He still reached out to me every so often, but I just couldn't bring myself to return his calls and letters. He'd left my grandmother three years after my mom died, the month she was diagnosed with cancer. I simply couldn't forgive him for that.

"I see," he said from someplace behind me. "So, you have no plans? If so, I thought—"

"Uh, I do have plans. I usually spend holidays with my best—um, my roommate from college." Rubbing my forehead, I spun in a circle, looking for something to do, and nearly tripped over one of the bins I'd strewn about the room while sleepwalking.

"You two are close?"

Picking up the bin I'd almost tripped over, I placed it against the wall and then moved to pick up another bin to place on top of it. "We are close. Really close."

*Stop overthinking and just tell him. Invite him. Have him come if he wants. It'll be worth it to watch Andreas beat Martin at chess.*

"And you should come!" I straightened, suddenly decided. There was no reason for Andreas not to come. He'd been invited. Plus, watching Martin get absolutely destroyed at chess would pay the mortgage on any regret I might feel later.

Andreas had placed his hands in the pockets of his bathrobe, his usual mask of detachment in place. "I do not wish to—"

"She invited you, actually." I crossed my arms, like the matter was settled.

A crack appeared in his façade of indifference, his eyes widening just a tad. "She did? Your friend did?"

"She did. She saw a photo of us online, from the night of our engagement, and she said you're invited. So"—I lifted my hands in the air and then let them drop against my thighs—"you're invited. And if you don't have any plans, we'll go. But I have to make cranberry sauce and mashed potatoes."

He nodded, still inspecting me. "Then I am very happy to come with you, if you do not mind."

I felt warmth crawl up my neck. "I don't mind at all. And they have a cute baby."

His mouth twitched at the corners, his eyes growing again for a split second. "They have a baby?"

Inwardly, I groaned. Outwardly, I asked, "Don't tell me, you like babies?"

He looked abashed, scratching the back of his neck. "Of course. Who doesn't like babies?"

The butterflies re-alived themselves and performed a synchronized routine, then collapsed in a heap. For reasons I didn't want to examine, the fact that Andreas liked babies made me feel gooey and hot in equal measure.

A slightly hysterical laugh tumbled out of me at the whiplash of my own emotions. Enough. I needed to get ready for work. That wasn't an excuse.

"Okay, I have to clean this up and then get to work. Out." I gathered an armful of clothes from the floor in front of my suitcase and gestured toward the door.

He didn't move. Instead, he reached forward and caught my hand, pulling me up as I tried to shoo him away, his grip surprisingly gentle. I felt immobilized by the shock of warmth traveling up my arm at the contact.

"Do not worry about the bins. I will take care of it. But, what I wanted to tell you, I should let you know, I have to leave Thursday night for a trip."

This news broke through the haze. "What? Why?"

He still held my hand, his thumb tracing a slow arc across my knuckles. "I have a tournament in London. I have to fly out a few days before it starts to acclimate to the time change."

"Oh." I was surprised at how disappointed I sounded. My chest felt empty but tight, airy but hot.

"I will be gone just over two weeks."

The disappointment dug in deeper. "That's . . . obviously fine. Thanks for letting me know."

His gaze moved over my face and he licked his lips before asking, "Do you want to come?"

The question blindsided me. For a moment, I imagined myself in London—watching Andreas play chess, wandering city streets, eating scones and clotted cream, and perhaps wearing a bowler hat for some reason. The fantasy was so vivid I almost said yes.

But then reality swooped in. "I can't. I have too much to do, especially with my switch in PIs." With as much gentleness as he'd reached for me, I pulled my hand away. Going to London and playing house with Andreas wasn't an option.

Andreas leaned against the doorjamb, his features giving away none of his thoughts. "PIs?"

"Principal investigators," I explained. "Remember when Tobias came to my office and threatened to get me expelled from my program? Well, it appears he called in a favor and I had to switch PIs because Dr. Hauser— my original PI—her funding was frozen."

His face darkened and his eyes lost focus, presumably his thoughts turning inward. "I see . . ."

I shrugged and went to my suitcase, rifling through it for pants. "My new PI is—well, he seems okay now."

"This new PI, does he treat you well?" Andreas's voice sounded careful.

"Since I've been reporting to him, he's been fine." I tried to come across as confident, as if the whole thing was an upgrade and not a shakedown.

I felt Andreas's eyes on me as I gathered my stuff, then he said, "You have to tell me if he mistreats you."

I chuckled. "Why? What will you do? Challenge him to a duel?"

"Something like that," he said, his eyes flicking away. And his expression was strange.

Peering at him, I decided this was weird. He was suddenly acting weird. That statement from him, it was weird. He almost sounded like Tobias. And what could he do in reality if my PI was a dickhead? Stare at him with those judgy little eyes?

Crossing to the bed, clothes in hand, I said, "Okay. I'm getting dressed. So, unless you want a free show, close the door."

His eyebrows shot up abruptly—comically, actually—and he grabbed for the doorknob, stuttering, "Of course—sorry. I apolo—sorry, yes. Sorry."

As soon as the door clicked shut, I shook my head at his gentlemanly bashfulness. My opinion of him improved by at least twelve points this morning. Seriously, he needed to start spouting ignoramus opinions about the polio vaccine. And soon.

Just as I'd pulled off my sleep shirt, Andreas's voice drifted back from beyond the door. "Can I make you something for breakfast?"

My spine stiffening with the knowledge that he was on the other side of the door and I was both shirtless and braless, I called back, "I'll have whatever you're having. I'm not picky."

A pause. "I bought you eggs. How do you like your eggs?"

Distracted, I rushed to put on a bra. "I don't care. Whatever is easiest."

A longer pause. "But you must have a preference. Scrambled? I can make an omelet."

Glancing up at the ceiling, I called back, "I honestly have no preference."

It was quiet for a moment, then he said, "Do you like omelets?"

Why was he was so fixated on eggs? "Sure. I like omelets. But that seems like a lot of work. Hard-boiled is fine."

"I'll make you a spinach, tomato, and goat cheese omelet," he said, as though that were a perfectly reasonable way to start the day.

My mouth immediately watered. I had to swallow before responding, "Thank you. That sounds good."

I heard his footsteps pad away and I clutched my forehead in my hands. How did he know Florentine omelets were my favorite omelet? There was no way he could know that. It must've been a lucky guess.

Shaking out my limbs of nerves, I dressed, pulled my hair into a pony-tail, and decided not to think about how I'd sleepwalked into Andreas's lap last night, or how I'd slept in his bed the night before, or how his cheeks had turned pink both times, or how I felt when he held my hand just now and his thumb had rubbed over the back of my knuckles so tenderly.

I decided I would save all these fluttery feelings and this hyperaware-ness for later. Much later. After I inherited Genetix.

And hopefully by then, it would all have stopped for good.

## [ 5 ]

## PUBERTY

***Samantha***

I will say this about the world's friendliest bodyguard-slash-chauffeur, Tara knew when to give a girl space.

I sat in the back seat of the black Mercedes, hands clutched to my messenger bag, fighting the urge to ask Tara to just circle the block another twenty times. People streamed by on the sidewalk, many in heavy jackets, some in business casual, one or two in actual evening wear because New York is chaos, but all of them seemed to move with a purpose that I envied.

My former roommates were inside, likely with Andreas. Adjusting the engagement ring on my finger, I took a deep, bracing breath.

Unwittingly, I'd begun playing a perverse game of chicken over the last two days, where I tried to see how long I could go without making a total ass of myself in front of a man who had, for some reason, decided to be tremendously sweet to me. I'd constructed a meticulous schedule where our time at the apartment rarely overlapped, save for a critical intersection at breakfast. He was awake before me no matter what time I got up, had made himself some kind of perfectly balanced vegan meal, and was waiting for us to eat together—having made me an insanely delicious non-vegan breakfast—by the time I stumbled out of the hallway.

It was, objectively, the best living arrangement I'd ever had. Even better than rooming with Kaitlyn. She never cooked.

It also didn't hurt that, true to my planned experiment and hypothesis, I'd decided to dress for bed in a scandalous pink negligee on both Monday and Tuesday nights, just to see if my subconscious would be too uncomfortable to sleepwalk if it meant parading around the apartment in see-through lace. And, miracle of miracles, the system worked. Two nights, zero sleepwalking. My subconscious was more modest than me. Not necessarily a high bar, but still. Go figure.

Anyway. Tonight was the first time I'd see Andreas in public since his hug on the sidewalk after the incident with Henrik. It was also the first time I would see him since the Monday morning sleep-lap-straddle-cuddle encounter. There would be friends, food, and—God help me—conversation.

Checking the time, I realized I was now officially two minutes late.

I exhaled, gripping my bag, and pushed out into the cold. "Thank you, Tara," I said.

She gave me a little wave. I shut the door behind me. The Mercedes didn't pull away from the sidewalk. I knew she wouldn't leave until I was inside. I wondered if she'd already texted Andreas that I was here.

The wind had that metallic edge peculiar to late November, the kind that promises snow soon. Smokin Greens BBQ sat on the corner, its windows glowing warm and amber in the dusk, and every wall inside was papered over with concert posters and flyers for local events. In the window, a neon sign in the shape of a brontosaurus advertised plant-based brisket, which I found delightful.

Opening the door, I found the inside air thick with the scent of hickory smoke and something tangy—possibly kimchi?—and the place was so full that the noise of conversation pressed against my ears even before I crossed the threshold. Five tables, all packed. At table two, directly under a painting of a stegosaurus grilling presumably tofu kabobs, sat the entire population of my former apartment: Kendra, Diya, Nakita, and, in the seat with the best view of the door, Andreas.

None of them saw me come in.

Instead, all four were hunched over the table in a configuration that suggested a classified briefing, heads bent, shoulders overlapping. It was Diya who drew my focus first, because her hands were in motion, gesturing wildly with a fork in one and a napkin in the other, and some of her words carried over the hubbub of the room.

". . . skin dryness," she was saying, "you really can't go wrong with a retinol product as long as you're also using glycol and a moisturizer with vitamin C during the day. Oh! Don't forget the SPF."

The others listened like acolytes at the feet of a particularly attractive and knowledgeable prophet. Andreas had his phone out, thumb poised above the screen. Kendra and Nakita nodded with the seriousness usually reserved for our discussions about corruption in the federal government or campaign finance reform.

I stood there, momentarily invisible, and took the opportunity to stare at Andreas for a full, guiltless ten seconds. He wore a charcoal turtle-neck and what looked like slate-colored slacks, hair artfully messy, and a watch I would bet my student loan balance was handmade by horolog-ical monks in the Alps or something like that. His posture was impec-cable even though he leaned forward, and the line of his jaw was relaxed.

He was, infuriatingly, still extremely attractive. I sighed. I kept wishing that the next time I saw him, I would feel less mesmerized by him. It hadn't happened yet. So, I let myself enjoy ogling him for one more beat of my heart, then steeled my nerves and approached.

Halfway there, Nakita said something like, "And I think gardenia, because I have a hand lotion that's gardenia and she said it smelled really good every time I wore it."

Andreas, still typing, eyes on his phone, asked, "Was it a white floral, or more powdery?" There was the tiniest sliver of an accent in his voice tonight, which I only noticed because I was hyper-tuned to every aspect of his existence like an idiot.

Drawing to a stop beside the table, I cleared my throat and said, "Hey. What's going on?"

Four heads whipped around in unison, Nakita's braids swinging so forcefully they nearly knocked over the water carafe. For a half second, no one spoke, then all three girls shouted my name and surged to their feet.

There was a sequence of hugs. Nakita first with a squeal, then Kendra with a tight squeeze, and finally Diya who seemed to pat me down as though searching for injuries. Acutely aware of him, I felt and saw Andreas watch the whole rigamarole, eyes crinkling at the edges, waiting until the others finished before moving forward and drawing me in for a quieter, longer embrace.

"Hi," he said, and, without warning, took my hand and kissed it. Not a joke, not a flourish, just the faintest touch of lips against the back of my hand, then a gentle pull to lead me into the seat next to his.

I could not feel my knees.

Once seated, I tucked my legs under the table and placed both hands in my lap, partly to hide the trembling and partly because they were cold. Andreas reached over and grabbed my hand under the table, holding it between both of his as though to warm it.

My insides were rioting, my chest too tight, my brain in disorder at his closeness and casual touch. He likely had no idea what he did to me. Forcing myself to look around the table at my friends, and not him, I did my best to act normal, whatever that was.

For their part, my former roommates all grinned at me like they were lottery winners.

"Sorry I'm late," I managed. "How long have you been here?"

Nakita flapped a hand. "Please. You're right on time. Kendra and Diya only got here, like, ten minutes before you. Andreas was the early bird."

Diya, eyes sharp as ever, cut in, "How's work? How's the new PI? Do you like him? Do you want us to kill him?"

I laughed. It sounded weak.

"She's had enough excitement," Kendra said, saving me from answering. "Let's not give her a reason not to return our calls." She smiled at me, then leaned over to squeeze my arm. "It's so good to see you, babe. You look incredible."

"Agreed," Nakita said. "Is that a new lipstick? It looks bomb on you. You have to tell me the shade."

I glanced at Andreas. He simply watched us, still holding my hand under the table, a tiny smile on his mouth. I willed my heart to slow down. My neck felt hot.

"Uh, yeah. I guess I'm wearing makeup," I said. "Decided to dress up for the occasion."

"How's engaged life?" Diya asked, a glint in her eye.

I forced another laugh. "Exactly the same as unengaged life, only with more paperwork."

Andreas, without missing a beat, said, "You forgot about the breakfasts."

Nakita leaned farther forward. "Wait. He makes you breakfast? Every morning?"

I opened my mouth to respond but my brain couldn't immediately think of a single thing to say. An awkward pause passed. But before I could decide what to say, Kendra spoke. "I hope you guys are hungry. I already put in an order for the barbecue platter. But if you want something else, the cornbread is life-changing."

"I have never had vegan barbecue before," Andreas said, his tone dry and polite and gentlemanly. "Thank you for inviting me. I am looking forward to it."

"It's legitimately the best," Kendra said. "Every sauce is made from scratch and the owner is a vegan pitmaster legend."

"Andreas, I have a question." Diya took a sip from her glass. "What is your accent? You're from Norway, right? Is that Norwegian?"

Andreas made a short sound of consideration, tilting his head slightly to one side. "It is not. I am not really from anywhere, honestly. My mother was from Italy, and my—uh—father"—Andreas darted a glance at me, then back to Diya—"was from Norway. But I spoke English early, and many of my chess coaches from a very young age were Russian. We communicated in English and Russian. I think I must have picked up some of their pronunciation of certain words, as I most often get asked if I am Russian. Do I sound Russian?"

All three of my roommates shook their heads, with Diya speaking for the group. "No. Well, maybe. But sometimes you don't have an accent at all and sound like you're from the US. And sometimes I can hear the Italian, I think. I was just curious. I hope I didn't offend."

"Not at all," he said graciously. "I am a bit all over the place, yes?"

"What language do you think in?" Nakita placed an elbow on the table and set her chin in her palm.

I listened in as they asked Andreas questions about himself, attempting to slot myself back into the group's rhythm, but finding it hard with Andreas's hands still wrapped around mine. My brain kept snagging on where our skin touched, like a sweater catching on a nail, pulling me out of the flow. The warmth, the steadiness, the way his thumb traced idle, absentminded circles on my skin.

During a lull in conversation, and trying to snap out of my own awkwardness, I said, "So, what were you all talking about before I came in? I caught something about retinol?"

"Nothing really. Skin routines, that kind of thing." Kendra's eyes darted to Andreas's then away as she reached for the pitcher of water. She topped off everyone's cup, then held her glass up. "A toast! To Sam and Andreas. May your wedding be a destination one, preferably someplace warm."

Diya rolled her eyes, but Nakita said, "Here, here! And may we all be invited."

I joined in on the toast and sipped my water to buy time. I needed to recalibrate. This was my first dinner with a fake fiancé—a fake fiancé I had very real feelings for—and I should've come up with a game plan before walking in the door.

As the first round of vegan barbecue and sides arrived, the table conversation shifted to plans for Thanksgiving. Kendra was working a double at the restaurant; Nakita was doing a Turkey Trot in Queens then spending the day with her family; Diya had a rare Thanksgiving off and planned to spend half of it sleeping in and the other half at her brother's place in Connecticut.

Catching me off guard as the conversation turned to strange Thanksgiving side dishes, Andreas leaned close, voice low in my ear, and said, "You look beautiful tonight."

I choked on a bite of black bean brisket, which prompted Nakita to thump me on the back with enough force to realign my vertebrae. "Are you okay?" she asked, eyes wide.

I coughed, nodded, and gave Andreas a side-eye that I hoped would convey confusion. Why would he say that? They couldn't hear him. He could've whispered anything, nonsense, the recipe for hollandaise sauce. Why tell me I look beautiful?

Wait. Were we being recorded? Was there a bug at the table?

Meanwhile, Diya grinned, probably at the way my cheeks had just turned very, very red. "Okay, but you two are too cute. I mean, look at you. Sharing plates. Whispering. Kendra, are you seeing this?"

Kendra made a show of dabbing her eyes with a napkin. "It's true. I was skeptical at first, but the chemistry is undeniable."

Andreas didn't react, but I could feel his posture relax, like he was happy to let the girls run wild with the narrative. *Maybe we are being recorded right now.*

Surreptitiously, I glanced around at the other patrons, looking for someone who could be Tobias's spy.

After finding no one suspicious, it occurred to me belatedly that I was the only one not playing along. I was too busy second-guessing myself, filtering every word before I spoke it, afraid to say anything that might make me look foolish in front of Andreas.

WHO AM I RIGHT NOW?

Before I could answer this question, Andreas released my hand to pull out his phone. He frowned at the screen flashing with a number. "Sorry, I need to get this. It is about my trip tomorrow. I will be right back." Before leaving, he placed his hand on my shoulder and gave it a gentle squeeze, a gesture so sweet and old-fashioned I barely resisted the urge to follow him like a lost puppy.

As soon as he was out of earshot, Nakita leaned in and said, "Girl. I don't know what kind of magic spell you put on him, but I'm obsessed."

Diya chimed in, "Seriously, Sam. I've never seen you like this. So quiet, and calm."

Kendra snorted. "That's not calm. That's what it looks like when you try really hard to be normal for an hour."

"Shut up," I said, but I was laughing because she was right, and it felt good to laugh and be known.

Nakita tapped her glass. "I love the way he looks at you. It's like you're the only person in the room."

I rolled my eyes. "He looks at everyone that way. It's just the Italian intensity from his mom's side."

"No," said Diya, "it's the 'in love with you' intensity. Don't try to science this one, Sam."

I had no response to this, so I just drained my water.

The table fell quiet for a moment, and I felt, for the first time since I walked in, genuinely happy to be here, even if my entire romantic life was an elaborate legal ploy and I was lying to them. I hoped they forgave me, when it all became public.

Kendra nudged me. "You look like you need a drink. You want a drink? I can get you a shot of whiskey if you want."

"Yes," I said, too loudly, "please."

She flagged down the server, who took my order of a double without judgment.

When Andreas returned, he slid back into the seat next to mine and smiled at the group. "What did I miss?"

"We're drinking," said Nakita, winking at me. "Whiskey. Want one?"

He looked at me, eyebrow raised. "You sure?"

I pressed my lips together in a smile. "Positive," I said, then under my breath I added, "I think I need it."

[ 6 ]

# REPRODUCTIVE AGING

***Samantha***

Two hours after the first alcoholic beverages went down, the world had softened around the edges, the way it does after not enough sleep. Kendra's boyfriend, whose name I kept forgetting and replacing with "Keith" because I was convinced he looked like a Keith, had arrived about an hour ago with his work friends, and they brought reinforcements in the form of new energy and conversation.

By 9:00 PM, we'd annexed three-quarters of Smokin Greens and the party had metastasized from a catch-up dinner to a legitimate, full-scale celebration of everything that was and ever would be worth celebrating. Friendship, promotions, graduations, vegan brisket, selling a boat, good hair days, weddings, babies, vacations, and tofurkey that actually tasted like turkey.

I was more than tipsy, past the humming, happy phase and floating on that upper stratosphere where time is an accordion and entire conversations disappear into the memory foam of your brain before they even finish. I knew I was beyond tipsy because every time I blinked, the restaurant shifted a few centimeters to the left. I also knew I was past tipsy because I'd allowed myself to slouch sideways and press my temple against Andreas's shoulder. His arm was around me, holding me to him.

His other hand had laced with mine and was resting on my lap. I cradled our joined fingers with my free hand and caressed the bones of his like I was sculpting them.

Kendra and Nakita had long since abandoned our table in favor of the big round one, and Keith and his army of software developer clones (I think one of them was literally named Clive) filled in the remaining seats. Diya, ever the MVP of social events, was alternating between dispensing rapid-fire medical trivia ("Yes, you can die from eating too many carrots, but only if you're a rabbit") and aggressively setting up rounds of shots. Andreas, to my enduring amazement, took it all in stride. He seemed utterly unbothered by the chaos, never once glancing at the time, or at his phone, or at the door. Instead, he fielded questions, laughed at jokes, and every once in a while, when the noise level dipped, he'd turn to me and whisper some observation that made me want to go home with him and never come back out.

But that would never happen, because we weren't a real couple even though we played one on TV.

Also, he smelled unfairly good tonight. A new cologne, something expensive and alive, cedar and citrus. His hand in mine felt solid and generous and warm. I found myself repeatedly stroking his knuckles with my thumb, fascinated by the structure of them. Part of my brain was narrating a National Geographic episode: "Observe, the majestic male, perfectly evolved for the manipulation of chess pieces and, apparently, the hearts of emotionally unavailable women."

I tried to listen to the conversations at the table, but my attention kept circling back to the reality of my body, of how good it felt to be leaning against his chest and torso, and how I didn't want to escape my own skin. I was so at home in this moment, I would've signed a lease.

The group dynamic was better than I could have hoped. My friends, for all their varied credentials, were softies at heart and clearly delighted to have Andreas among them. Every time Nakita made a joke, he'd tilt his head and smile, the ghost of a dimple appearing at the edge of his mouth. When Diya, emboldened by her third vodka soda, challenged him to a game of speed chess using only soy sauce bottles and ketchup packets as pieces, he demurred with gentle grace. Kendra, ever the ringleader, decided Andreas should be in charge of the music for the table, which led to him requesting (with dry, deadpan conviction) the entirety of *ABBA Gold* as the only acceptable playlist for the rest of the night.

It was, by any metric, a flawless integration. Too bad it wasn't real.

And yet, through the haze of alcohol and noise, I could not stop thinking about the way his hand fit in mine. About how easy it would be to tip my face up and kiss him in front of all these people, and how absolutely zero percent of my pickled brain thought it would be a bad idea.

And, on that note, why was sober me so resistant to the idea of a real relationship? Why did every instinct in my sober body scream at me to run when all I wanted to do right now was stay, and maybe even—God forbid—let myself love someone for more than three consecutive business days? These were the kinds of philosophical queries you should not, under any circumstances, attempt to answer while three whiskeys deep and riding a contact high from your childhood turned adult crush. And yet, my brain would not stop circling the drain.

I kept thinking: If I don't tell him how I feel, if I don't propose right here at this table to make it all real, then what the fuck am I even doing? But then another voice, the one that was allegedly in charge, reminded me that I was drunk, that nothing I said tonight would survive the morning, and that this was precisely the kind of disaster my psychiatrist had warned me about. Emotional decisions under the influence of dopamine and alcohol were not, generally, sound or strategic.

So, I decided to wait. I would wait until tomorrow, or at least until I sobered up, to address the growing suspicion that I wanted, more than anything, to make this the last first date of my life.

At one point, Diya and Andreas got deep into conversation, just the two of them, and their voices rose above the clamor, a duet of quick, bright syllables and the occasional cross talk about chess and gene sequencing and the merits of kimchi. It was only when Diya leaned forward, her eyes lit with what seemed to be wild curiosity, that I tuned in fully.

"Half the chess grand masters in India come from Tamil Nadu. My uncle says it's the water, or the weather, or maybe the local Wi-Fi," Diya said, gesticulating with her dessert spoon.

Andreas nodded with a small, admiring smile. "Tamil Nadu is beautiful. I have visited many times for tournaments in Chennai. They study and make it their life, and they are very good at identifying and fostering talent. Your uncle is incorrect, however. It is not something in the water. But perhaps it is the food?" His tone had turned teasing. "The food is what really made an impression on me."

Diya grinned. "I'll have to take you to my aunt's next time she's in town. She makes a dosa that'll ruin you for life." Then, abruptly, her phone buzzed on the table. She checked it and her face changed; she excused herself with a quick apology, and slipped away to take the call.

With her gone, the table's conversation splintered into smaller groups, and I became aware that I was still, possibly for hours now, petting the back of Andreas's hand in my lap like it was a beloved pet.

I chanced a glance at his face. He watched the room with a serene detachment that made me wonder what was going on behind those eyes. Was he bored? Was he counting down the seconds until he could escape? Or was he as deliriously content as I was, just sitting here, being present, not needing to fill the air with words?

I couldn't tell. I'd never been able to read him well. But I wanted to. So, I squeezed his hand.

He looked down at me, and when our eyes met, he smiled in that slow, unreadable way. Then he leaned over and pressed a kiss to my forehead that made my heart spike with heat. It wasn't hurried, but not lazy, either. It was so out of nowhere, so gentle, that it fried my brain for a moment.

"How are you feeling?" he asked, his voice pitched for me and me alone.

I inhaled a shaky breath, registered the smell of him, and exhaled. "A little drunk."

He made a noise low in his throat, almost a laugh. "You had three whiskeys and a glass of wine."

"Yeah, yeah, yeah." I slouched even further, my cheek pressing into his sweater. "Don't let me drink anymore, please. I will do things I'll regret."

His arm tightened around my shoulders, just enough to let me know he'd heard. Then he kissed the top of my head again, sending my heart to my throat, and said, "Okay."

My eyes fluttered closed. I could've slept there, in the restaurant, if not for the crescendoing volume of the conversations around us and the small, persistent voice inside my head reminding me I needed to go to Kaitlyn's tomorrow, and that the next time I woke up, it would be Thanksgiving.

I felt the weight of his hand shift in mine, and then, slowly, he lifted my fingers to his lips and kissed the back of my hand. A simple, old-fashioned gesture, but when his mouth touched my skin, it sent a supernova up my arm and straight to my heart.

Opening my eyes, our gazes met again. This time he held my eyes, not letting me go even when my face went hot.

"Do you want to leave?" he asked, so quiet I almost missed it. "It is getting late, and we have your friends' Thanksgiving tomorrow."

I thought about it. I weighed the prospect of leaving this perfect, timeless, alcohol-glazed moment against the inevitability of waking up tomorrow. But if life had taught me one lesson, it was that all good things always, always, *always* came to an end.

"I think we should," I said, but didn't move to stand.

He nodded, then let go of my hand just long enough to help me up. He was so gentle, it felt like being picked up by a breeze. He pulled my coat from the back of my chair, helped me slide my hands through the armholes, and took a moment to button it for me while I stared at his mouth. His movements were slow and precise, almost ceremonial.

Andreas offered his arm, and I took it, which made everyone at the table pause and turn in our direction. Diya, who'd returned at some point and was now grinning, caught my eye and gave me a double thumbs-up. Kendra shouted, "Don't be a stranger!" and Nakita blew me a kiss. Or maybe she blew Andreas a kiss. Mostly probably, it was for both of us.

Andreas was the opposite of awkward as he made his excuses. So smooth. He thanked Kendra for inviting us, told Keith and Clive it had been a pleasure, and said something to Diya in what did not sound like English, Norwegian, or Italian. I didn't know what it meant, but Diya laughed so hard she nearly fell out of her chair. *What language was that?*

Diya must've caught my confused look, because she said, "It was Tamil. And I am very impressed."

So perfect, this guy.

Andreas escorted me to the door, pausing every so often to steady me when I started to veer off course. The outside air hit me like a wall, but instead of sobering me up, it made everything feel softer, like the world had been dunked in fabric softener. I clung to his arm and let him guide me down the steps and onto the sidewalk, where Tara waited beside the Mercedes, arms folded and eyes scanning the street.

"Hi, Tara. You're awesome," I slurred, but she just smiled and held the car door open for me.

Andreas ducked inside with me, his hand warm on my lower back as he helped me in. Once we were seated, he leaned across my lap and fastened my seat belt for me, the side of his face just inches from mine, the line of his jaw so crisp I wanted to bite it.

I closed my eyes as the car started to move, but then, because I was at that stage of drunkenness where all consequences are theoretical, I turned my face into his neck and planted a gentle, deliberate kiss just above his collar.

"Thank you," I whispered against the skin of his neck, "for being so great with my friends." It sounded embarrassing the moment it left my mouth, but I didn't care.

Andreas went perfectly still. I felt his pulse under my lips, fast and sharp.

When I pulled back and looked at him, his eyes were dark and focused, fixed on mine. He didn't move, not right away. Maybe he was waiting to see what I would do next. Or maybe I'd upset him?

But my head was heavy and my body was even heavier, so instead of parsing the tension between us, I let my cheek fall to his chest and curled up against him again, sighing in contentment.

After a moment, I frowned because he felt tense instead of yielding. I wiggled and shifted, demanding, "Loosen up! And let me cuddle your big, sexy body."

It sounded like he gave a short, stunned laugh. Or maybe he coughed. Then, after a pause, he wrapped his arm around my shoulders and held me as I fell asleep.

* * *

Thanksgiving morning, I woke up in Andreas Kristiansen's bed.

Correction. I woke up alone, in Andreas's bed. Both better and, paradoxically, worse than waking up sprawled all over him.

Worse, because I remembered, with spectacular—albeit, hungover—clarity, being carried by the man himself last night. The brutally vivid memory of my own idiocy played in my head. He'd physically lifted me from the sidewalk, bridal carried me through the lobby, into the elevator, and into the apartment. We'd paused at the bathroom as he helped me brush my teeth—*ohmygodIamtheWORST!*—and then he'd deposited my limp, drunk body onto my mattress in my room. I remembered all of it.

What I didn't remember was walking in here and taking over his bed. Again.

I groaned, kicked the air under the sheet, and tried to will myself out of existence. Failing that, I rolled over and attempted to die face-down in the pillow. This plan was immediately complicated by the sharp, masculine scent of Andreas that lingered on the pillowcase. Cologne and soap, plus the unmistakable base note of "damn it, why does he get me so hot."

I tried to reconstruct all the events of last night. We'd gotten back from Smokin Greens at, what, ten? Before that, we'd left the restaurant together and in the car I'd kissed him. Not on the cheek, but on the side of his neck.

I shot upright in bed, clutching the duvet to my chest, horrified.

*Oh no. Oh no no no!*

I'd kissed his neck, right under his jaw, and then—I groaned again, this time louder—called his body "big" and "sexy" in the back seat of the Mercedes. That memory, clear as HD, was followed by a blank patch. I'd probably fallen asleep in the car.

I groaned again, reached for the nearest pillow, and started whacking myself on the forehead with it.

"Stop sleepwalking into his bed. Stop sleepwalking into his bed," I chanted, punctuating every word with a fresh pillow whack. "Never drink around Andreas again. Never drink again, period. Never speak again, actually. Monastic vow, effective immediately."

I took a breath and surveyed the damage. Still in the clothes from last night: jeans, T-shirt, and—oh, I must've gotten cold, because I wore his enormous gray sweater, which was now stretched out from where I'd probably tried to cocoon myself. My hair, which I could only see by its shadow on the white duvet, was a haywire mass. My mouth, at least, tasted like peppermint toothpaste. But also regret.

The only logical solution was to strip the bedding and do his laundry as an act of penance. Hauling myself out of bed, legs shaking, I gathered the sheets into a ball while chastising myself.

I wasn't used to being a hot mess. I was used to being the chick who had her shit together, who others asked for advice, who showed up on moving day to help no matter what, and who visited friends in the hospital. I'd baked seventeen freezer casseroles for Kaitlyn after baby Joey was born, for God's sake! I'd done their laundry for over a month and cleaned their guest bathroom with a toothbrush. I was CAPABLE!

But now, I didn't know this person who drank too much and kissed necks and sexually harassed their revenge partner. *Get yourself together, Sam!*

It was only after I maneuvered the comforter off the duvet cover that my thoughts quieted down enough for the sound of voices in the living room to reach my ears.

Specifically, the low rumble of Andreas's voice, and the soft, polite laughter of someone else over the phone. The odds that Andreas had heard me pillow thumping my own skull were very, very high.

*Sigh.*

Well, that's just freaking . . . great.

[ 7 ]

# THE HUMAN SEXUAL RESPONSE

***Samantha***

Steeling myself and breathing through the bundle of nerves in my chest, I wrapped the sheets, comforter, and pillowcases into my arms, attempted to smooth my hair, and tiptoed out of Andreas's bedroom.

He sat at the big circular table in the living room, dressed in black lounge pants and a black T-shirt, hunched over a chessboard with a mug of coffee steaming beside his left hand. His phone was set next to the chessboard and was lit up with a call.

Andreas's eyes flicked up, pinning me in place for a long moment. His face didn't move, but his brow creased at the sight of me emerging from his room, arms full of bedding.

"I will call you later, Elio." Not waiting for a response, Andreas ended the call and leaned back in the chair, gaze moving down then up, giving me the sense he might be looking for injuries. "Good morning," he said.

"Uh. Good morning." Not recognizing the diffident quality in my own voice, I clutched the laundry tighter. "Sorry. I'm going to wash these."

Andreas continued to stare without giving any of his thoughts away, then returned his gaze to the board. "That is not necessary."

I didn't want to insist out loud. Actually, I didn't really want to talk to him at all since I felt so ashamed of myself. Thus, I swallowed and scut-

61

tled past to the laundry room. There, I deposited the sheets, started the load, and retreated to my own bathroom, avoiding my reflection in the mirror. I knew I looked like a meth-addicted raccoon, okay? I didn't need to actually see the evidence.

After a mercifully hot shower, during which I practiced my apology over and over, I emerged from the hallway, dressed in leggings and an oversized hoodie.

Andreas was still in the same position, giving me the impression that he hadn't moved. But the fresh pot of pour-over coffee sitting on a tray in the center of the table along with a second mug dispelled this assumption. In the spot next to Andreas was also a plate enclosed with a metal cover, a glass of water, utensils, and a linen napkin.

Approaching on light feet, I sat across from Andreas and folded my hands on the table's surface, preparing my speech and starting with "I apologize for last night." My voice emerged steady and even. Good.

Andreas took a measured sip from his mug, then glanced at me over the rim. "For which part?"

I exhaled a long breath and couldn't help but duck my head. "You're right. I have a lot to apologize for."

He frowned. "I did not say that—"

"But I'm saying it." I gave him a tight smile. "So, here's a list. I'm sorry for the unexpected hug, the neck kiss, for speaking to you disrespectfully in the back of the Mercedes, for getting so sloppy drunk you had to carry me up here and help me brush my teeth. And I'm sorry—once again—for sleepwalking into your room and invading your personal space."

He huffed and glanced away, his jaw ticking. "Samantha—"

I lifted a hand since I wasn't finished. "I will not drink alcohol again during our cohabitation. And I promise not to cross any boundaries from now on, as much as it is in my power to not cross them. But, the sleepwalking . . ." I held his gaze for a moment, a sense of real helplessness building within me.

Giving into the urge, I pushed my fingers into my hair and then covered my face with my hands. "Since this is apparently a chronic problem," I said, voice still steady despite the volcano of frustration beneath, "maybe we should talk about—uh—changing the doorknob on that bedroom to lock from the outside?"

Andreas blinked at me, then set his mug down. "No. Locking you in your room is not safe."

"I think it's a better option than to keep ending up in your bed," I said, trying to make it sound a bit like a joke even though it was serious. "What if one night I get even more creative? Sleepwalk into the downstairs neighbor's hallway? End up in the lobby?"

He appeared to consider this, steepling his fingers. "I can lock us into the apartment at night with a code."

I shook my head. "We both know I'd find a way around that. My subconscious is a criminal mastermind."

He tilted his head. "What if only I had the code?"

I laughed, because I couldn't believe we were now plotting against my unconscious brain. "You're leaving tonight. Am I going to be locked in the apartment for two weeks?"

"It is programmable and accessible remotely, and could self-lock between certain hours, which will keep you inside the apartment at least. And I can arm or disarm it from my phone no matter where I am."

"Then let's put a similar lock on my bedroom door—"

He shook his head resolutely, obvious frustration making the line of his mouth flat and grim. "No. I do not want you trapped in your room, that is nonsense. What if you have to go to the bathroom?"

I leaned back in my seat and crossed my arms. He had me there.

"Are you sure you cannot come with me to London?"

"There's no way. And besides, what would that solve? Is it better for me to sleepwalk into your bed at a hotel than it is in this apartment?" Scratching at the uncomfortable heat crawling up my neck, I looked away.

We sat in silence, the only sound being the intermittent drip of the pour-over coffee.

At length, Andreas stood and grabbed the covered plate, napkin, and utensils sitting next to him. He carried them over and placed them in front of me, seeming to arrange them carefully. Once everything was neatly set, he lifted the metal cover, revealing eggs Benedict.

My mouth dropped open even as it watered. "You . . . is this for me?"

"It is supposed to be good for hangovers." He set the metal cover to the side, then leaned over the table to grab the water glass he'd left behind.

"How did you know eggs Benedict is one of my favorites?"

He shrugged. "Is it?"

"Thank you." I swallowed and picked up the utensils. "This is very kind of you. You didn't need to, but I really appreciate it."

Andreas's movements stilled briefly, then he placed the water to the left of my plate. "No need to be so formal. I make you breakfast every day." An edge of annoyance had entered his voice.

I pressed my lips together to keep from saying something that might irritate him further. Given my wonky behavior and everything he'd put up with since I'd moved in, the man was basically a saint.

And here I was, a world-class succubus.

Andreas poured me a cup of coffee and set that next to the water glass while I stared at the plate. Then, with no dignity whatsoever, I dove in. The first yolk was perfectly runny, the sauce creamy and lemony, the muffin toasted to a golden brown. I made a small, involuntary moan-whimper of delight. "Ah. It's so good!" I forked and shoved another bite into my mouth.

"What time do we need to be at your friends' place? And should I prepare anything?" Andreas's questions sounded almost chipper.

The sudden change in his tone had me looking at him. He'd just poured himself more coffee and set down the pot. Gazing at me from across the table as he sat, the side of his mouth hitched, eyes warm.

I dabbed at my mouth with the napkin and waited to respond until I'd swallowed my bite, just barely refraining from moaning again. "We need to arrive around eleven and I've already made everything. The mashed potatoes and cranberry sauce are in the fridge. Again, thank you for the use of your kitchen."

"It is your kitchen, too."

"For the time being," I muttered under my breath. It was mostly a reminder to myself, which stung, but was necessary. Nothing about this was permanent.

He drank from his mug, watching me with that serene, analytical stare, eventually saying, "Since you cannot come to London, what if Tara slept here while I am gone? She could lock the exterior door to keep you from wandering, if you sleepwalk again." He made it all sound so reasonable, like we were discussing the logistics of traveling uptown rather than babysitting an adult woman while she slept.

"If Tara is up for it, then sure. I don't want to impose, but that's a good idea." Examining him, sensing that he seemed to be genuinely concerned for me, I decided to share something personal, hoping it would set his mind at ease. "Look, I did call my therapist. I have a virtual appointment with her on Monday. So, I'm working on addressing the root cause."

He nodded, seeming pleased to know this information, and added, "You should sleep in the main bedroom from now on. It is larger, and you —or, at least, the you who sleepwalks—prefer it."

I laughed, shaking my head and cutting into the second poached egg. "Sure, okay. That's very . . . generous of you." I wasn't sure if I would take him up on this offer. For obvious reasons, I preferred to sleep in my own bed.

Andreas mumbled something like, "It is not generosity," his attention on his coffee cup as he arranged it just so on the table.

I finished my breakfast while he fiddled with his chessboard. Once I drained the last of the coffee, I sat back, feeling marginally better about the day, if not the future. Glancing over at Andreas, I let myself watch him for a few moments, marveling at the intensity of his focused gaze, like perhaps he expected the chess pieces to shift squares if he so much as blinked.

Clearing my throat as a precursor to breaking the silence, I slowly stood and gathered my plate. "May I ask, are you playing against yourself?"

His eyes flickered to me then back to the board. "Replaying the Spassky–Fischer match."

I wasn't sure what that meant, so I made a mental note to look up "spasskyfisher," and carried my dishes to the kitchen. When I finished hand-washing them, seeing that Andreas had already cleaned up after making me breakfast, I wandered back into the living room. Still staring at the chessboard, Andreas rolled the black knight over his fingers, flipping it back and forth with his thumb.

I didn't want to interrupt his concentration, so I turned for the hallway, stopping short when he called out, "As I said on Monday, I am not bothered by you sleepwalking. The only thing I care about is that you are safe and comfortable."

There was something about the way he said it—no inflection, no humor, just absolute certainty—that made me want to believe him.

Fiddling with the sleeve of my hoodie, I faced him. "Andreas—"

He cut me off, dipping his chin and deepening his voice. "Do you recall when we were young? I would find any excuse to sleep with you. I slept in your bed most nights. Remember?"

I'm sure I looked confused, because what did that have to do with anything?

"Just consider this a repayment, if that will make you feel better," he said, biting his bottom lip while we locked eyes.

I tried to keep my thoughts from my face, which were mostly flavored by skepticism and bewilderment. The two situations weren't comparable. We'd been kids back then. He'd been seeking comfort from a friend. Everything between us had been innocent and platonic.

But now, we were adults. And my feelings for him? Well, let's just say, I'd be lying if I said my feelings for Andreas were innocent.

* * *

To say that Thanksgiving at Kaitlyn and Martin's was a circus would be an insult to circuses, which at least have OSHA standards they're supposed to adhere to. The only constant was the perpetual motion of baby Joey, who rotated from lap to lap like a hot potato with a self-destruct timer, pausing only to attempt suicide off the edge of the sofa or scream in protest when denied a third dinner roll. By the time we finished dessert, the entire apartment looked like an explosion in a bakery, with dollops of mashed potato welded to the hardwood, and what I prayed was gravy crusted into the tabletop.

Through it all, Andreas managed to monopolize Joey. I don't know how he did it. There were four adults and a baby in a palatial three-bedroom penthouse, but somehow Andreas spent the majority of the afternoon holding, soothing, or otherwise interacting with a seven-month-old as if he'd been training for it. He'd swing Joey with one hand while sipping tea with the other, bounce the baby on his knee as he and Kaitlyn discussed Italian composers (turns out, Andreas's mother was one of Kaitlyn's favorite composers), and when Kaitlyn needed to run to the bathroom, he wrangled Joey's diaper situation with a dexterity that suggested past-life experience as a neonatal nurse. The baby, for his part, gazed up at Andreas with starry-eyed worship, giggled when he made faces—oh my God, Andreas made so many adorable faces!—and fell asleep against his chest in a feat of trust I'd never seen Joey display toward anyone but Kaitlyn herself.

It was obscene. It was unfair. It was, on a molecular level, illegal to be that good with children while also being devastatingly attractive. My latent competency kink reared its ugly head and roared. The only saving grace was that Kaitlyn's husband, Martin, looked even more jealous than I was.

Right now, Joey was asleep in his crib. Andreas and Martin had vanished into the kitchen to wage war against the mountain of dirty dishes, leaving Kaitlyn and me on the couch with nothing but a throw blanket and our secrets.

She tucked her feet under her and used the remote to increase the volume of the stereo. Kaitlyn cast a glance toward the kitchen. Dishes clinked, water ran, the men were out of earshot. She leaned over, blanket slipping down to her lap.

"Okay, let's finish our discussion. You moved in on Saturday and then started sleepwalking into his bedroom? How did he react?" Her voice was a whisper.

I sighed, bracing myself for this part of my story. I'd been giving Kaitlyn the CliffsNotes version of my last week in scattered, five-minute bursts between rounds of vegetable roasting and diaper changing. The goal had been to keep her from dying of curiosity while also minimizing the odds of Martin or Andreas overhearing. It hadn't quite worked. She'd nearly asphyxiated on a carrot when I told her about the show Andreas and I had put on for Nakita at my old apartment. Martin had stormed into the kitchen when he'd heard her choking, sending me a vicious look, like I was trying to murder his beloved spouse.

Then, when I told Kaitlyn about the sleepwalking, she'd gasped so loud, both Martin and Andreas had run into the nursery to ensure nothing was amiss.

Now, with the evening winding down and only the kitchen as our buffer, Kaitlyn wanted the director's cut.

"He seemed a little bashful about it," I said, picking at the edge of the blanket. "Like, I woke up on his bed, and he just sort of blinked at me, then his cheeks got all red and he went full android. Very formal. Lots of 'It's no big deal' and 'Please, don't be embarrassed'—which, as you know, is the number-one way to make me more embarrassed."

Kaitlyn's eyebrows jumped high on her forehead. "Really? He told you not to be embarrassed?"

"Yeah. I mean, he keeps saying it doesn't bother him, but how can it not? I keep waking up in his room like a poltergeist with boundary issues. Even when I try to keep to myself, it happens anyway. He even tucked me in last night and, this morning, I somehow ended up nested between his sheets again."

She grinned. "He's not upset you keep sleeping with him?"

I shook my head, letting the memory replay. "He never says he's upset. He's just—stiff, sometimes? He'll get all quiet and his jaw goes tight. But then, if I apologize, he tells me it's not a problem, or says something so . . . nice that I want to die."

Kaitlyn nudged me with her foot. "Give me an example."

I exhaled. "Sunday night, I ended up sleepwalking and fell asleep on his lap. Like, literally, across his thighs. I woke up and he had his arms around me. Instead of making it weird, he just said, 'I want to be useful.' Which is simultaneously the most wholesome and the most unhinged thing I've ever heard from a man."

She reached over and gave my arm a gentle squeeze. "Sam, it's not like this is something you can control. You need to stop apologizing for existing. When I was in the kitchen with him earlier, he asked me all kinds of questions about your preferences, what you like, what you don't. And I've been watching him today, how he looks at you. It seems like he's really into you."

I made a face. "He's doing that to keep up appearances. Darn it, I should tell him the truth about you knowing so he won't feel obligated to pretend we're engaged."

Kaitlyn drew back. "'Darn it'? Did you just say 'darn it'?"

I groaned. "It's the strangest thing, but I find myself very much caring what he thinks of me. Like, actually caring. I don't even cuss around him because his manners are so good. I wore makeup to dinner last night. Voluntarily."

Kaitlyn's lips twitched, but she played it straight. "What does that— what do you mean? You care what people think."

I rolled my eyes. "Sure, but not like this. Usually, if someone doesn't like me, I'd think, okay, their loss, and move on. But with him, I keep nitpicking everything I do and say. Whether I smell good, whether I said something dumb, whether my laugh is too loud. I even find myself censoring my dirty jokes. Can you imagine?"

Kaitlyn snorted. "You? No sex jokes?"

"It's a tragedy. My therapist would say I'm repressing my authentic self."

She was quiet for a second, then suddenly made a face of discomfort, her hand going to her chest.

"What's wrong?" I leaned forward, inspecting her face.

Kaitlyn had been dealing with bouts of mastitis since Joey was born and had even been hospitalized for it once. When she first showed me her cracked and sore nipples, I'd almost fainted from friend-sympathy.

I knew she'd struggled with breastfeeding but had persevered, hiring a lactation consultant. Things had improved, but were nowhere near perfect. I would be forever in awe of women who breastfed.

Kaitlyn shook her head, giving me a reassuring smile. "It's fine. Just boob issues."

"Are you sure?"

She nodded. "I'm sure. Breastfeeding is not my favorite." She then studied me in that unique way she had when attempting to determine the truth of a matter. Kind but unsparing. "Sam. Do you think you might really like Andreas?"

I stared at the pattern of the blanket and, after a moment, nodded. "Yes," I said, and sounded extremely melancholy about it.

Kaitlyn covered her mouth, and her eyes glinted with suppressed laughter.

"Stop it," I hissed, smacking her shoulder. "It's probably just residual and unresolved crush feelings from when we were kids."

Kaitlyn cocked her head. "I don't know. He's pretty crush-worthy now. How many languages does he speak? That is some sexy shit."

I laughed, but it also sounded melancholy. "Well, he's leaving tonight for two weeks, so that'll give me some time to get my head on straight, at least."

She didn't let the topic drop. "Do you want to sleep here?"

I was touched by the offer, but I shook my head. "No. I told you about Andreas's brother Henrik earlier, right?"

"The scary guy who chased you into the biology building?"

"Yeah. I don't want him bothering you guys. And Andreas's apartment is like a fortress. I have security and everything, so I don't want to mess things up. Plus, Andreas can auto-lock the door so I don't sleepwalk outside the apartment."

Kaitlyn frowned. "I don't know, I feel like someone needs to stay with you."

"One of my bodyguards, a nice gal by the name of Tara, will probably sleep over while Andreas is gone."

She brightened. "That would make me feel better."

"Anyway," I said, eager to steer the conversation away from my train-wreck sleeping habits, "speaking of Henrik, he said something fishy when he was on the other side of the glass, trying to goad me out of the building."

Kaitlyn perked up, eyes wide. "What did he say?"

"He said my dad was a coward. But it was how he said it, you know? Like he had experience with my father, working with him, or some first-hand knowledge."

"Did they ever work together? At Genetix? How old is Henrik?"

I'd already done a little research on this, so I rattled off, "I think Henrik is not quite ten years older than Andreas, so that would make him something like thirty-five now, twenty then. I did a little digging and Henrik interned at Genetix while in college, under Oskar, who was the CFO at the time."

Kaitlyn's eyes narrowed. "That's something worth exploring. Do you think Henrik had something to do with the fraud charges against your father?"

"It's possible, right? But what could Henrik do as an intern? I've tried looking into the fraud charges before—if you remember, it's why I wanted to go to law school, to understand what happened—but since those charges were dismissed after my father died, the only resource for the proceedings are the board minutes at Genetix, when my dad was voted off the board and stripped of his shares."

"Let me tell Martin about this. He has *people* and can look into it without drawing any attention. Maybe he can reach out to Genetix about investment."

I grimaced. "I don't want you guys getting involved. These guys are dangerous. And you have Joey now and everything is so good between you two. I'll handle it."

Kaitlyn was about to say something else, but the click of a cabinet and the sudden clatter of plates announced the return of the menfolk from the kitchen. We exchanged a look that promised: to be continued.

Martin entered first, wiping his hands on a dish towel. He dropped onto the couch beside Kaitlyn and, with the world's least subtle body language, nudged and positioned her until she leaned against him—her back to his front—and his arms came around her torso. She didn't seem to notice, or maybe she was just used to it.

Andreas followed and as soon as he entered the room, my heart took an aching leap toward him. That same buzzing, electric tension ignited beneath my skin whenever we were in a room together and suddenly I was fighting to breathe normally. I was still mulling whether to warn him about Kaitlyn knowing the engagement was fake when he sat next to me, placed his arm around my shoulders, and pulled me closer to place a kiss on my forehead, the motion transferring a staticky jolt through the blanket to my skin.

"Andreas." Kaitlyn lifted her chin toward him. "I was wondering, do you own your mother's compositions now? Or, are they being held in a trust? A musician I work with tried to obtain licensing rights a while back but ran into a dead end of lawyers."

"Oh. Uh, I am not surprised." He gave his head a small shake. "My mother's music is part of my father's estate. When she died, as her husband, he inherited the entire catalogue."

"I see . . ." Kaitlyn's gaze shifted to me and she wisely let the matter drop. She knew my history with the Kristiansens.

"I am sorry to say, I have to be going soon." I looked at Andreas and found his eyes on me as he leaned back, gaze dropping to my mouth. Then, unexpectedly, he bent forward and placed a light kiss on my lips, stunning me momentarily speechless.

"Oh. That's too bad," Kaitlyn said, but her voice held a smile.

I turned my head to glare at my best friend. Her pretty gray eyes twinkled as they moved between us.

"My flight out leaves in three hours."

Finding my voice, I asked, "Do you need to go home first and grab your bag?"

He shook his head. "No. Elio has already collected it. He will call me when he is downstairs."

As if on cue, his phone buzzed. He pulled it out with his right hand, still keeping his left arm draped around me.

"That is him now," Andreas said, with a slightly apologetic tone. "I should go."

Martin pushed himself up, and Kaitlyn followed. I started to stand, but Andreas caught my hand and gave it a gentle squeeze, then rose to his feet with a grace I envied.

Andreas exchanged goodbyes, with Martin giving Andreas an actual hug instead of a bro-hug, which surprised me, and Kaitlyn embracing him with genuine warmth. When it was my turn, Andreas hugged me tightly and, into my hair, murmured, "Will you walk me down?"

I nodded, and he released me. To Kaitlyn, I said, "I'll be right back."

We walked out of the apartment, and when we entered the elevator, he faced forward. The ride down was spent in silence, my head all over the place. In the lobby, he grabbed my hand again as we crossed to the vestibule. A black Mercedes idled at the curb, headlights cutting twin blades of white through the early darkness.

Once we were outside the building, he stopped suddenly and turned to me. "Sam." His voice was quiet and almost swallowed by the sound of New York traffic, his eyes seeming to search mine. "We should kiss good-bye, just in case someone is watching."

Surprised by the suggestion, I opened my mouth to reply. But before I could, he kissed me. Not the kind of peck you'd give a fake fiancée, but the kind of kiss that made my toes curl in my boots and threatened to melt my knees into the sidewalk.

At first, his lips were warm and sweet, but the press of his hands on my back felt hot. Once the immediate surprise wore off, my brain told me to make the most of this moment, and so I did. I slid my fingers up into the back of his hair and kissed him deeply, wondering if he could taste my selfishness or the urgency in how my tongue sought his and explored his delicious mouth. He groaned, yanking me closer, and the kiss turned hungry as he angled his head to one side, chasing my mouth even though I wasn't going anywhere. Fireworks exploded in my stomach. I loved how tightly he held me, how every pass of his lips felt like a demand rather than a request, and how his hands shifted lower with each passing second until they completely palmed my backside.

When he pulled away, he didn't step back immediately. He rested his forehead against mine, breathing in, breathing out.

"I will really miss you," he whispered, so low I wondered if I'd imagined it.

And then he was gone, striding to the car, slipping inside, and leaving me on the sidewalk feeling like a pin had been yanked from some critical axis in my chest.

I blinked around the sidewalk, trying to get my bearings and not knowing what to expect, but nobody had been watching us. Or, if they had, they were pretending not to now. I spotted a couple guys in suits, loitering by a hot dog stand across the street. I recognized one of them as the security detail, which made me feel a little safer.

As the Mercedes pulled away, I watched the taillights for a long time, then turned back to the lobby, planning to squeeze a few more hours of friendship out of Kaitlyn before returning to my own fortress. And, maybe, to my own self, if I could figure out who that was anymore.

The elevator doors opened and I paused, thinking about what Kaitlyn had said. About the way I was acting. About how, even after everything, the person I wanted to talk to was the one who'd just left.

I pressed the button for the penthouse, and as the elevator climbed, I found myself grinning, stupid and secret, at the thought of seeing him again, already counting down the days until he returned.

It wasn't until I was right outside of Kaitlyn and Martin's door that the bubble burst on the fantasy.

*This is fake.* That was fake. *Everything about us is fake.*

Fighting to draw in enough air past the tightness in my chest, I couldn't help the traitorous thought: *Then why does it feel so real?*

[ 8 ]

# PROCREATION

***Samantha***

Sunlight filtered in through the heavy blackout curtains. It took me a minute to realize where I was.

*This is not my room.*

No, this was Andreas's room—the main bedroom—because of course. After only one day with Tara as my night watchman, I'd already failed at Operation Sleep in My Own Bed.

Though I had sorta agreed to sleep in the main bedroom when Andreas and I had discussed it yesterday morning, I'd started the night in my own room last night, hoping against hope that I would stay put.

Stifling a groan, I reached for my phone, which was perched on the marble-topped nightstand, and thumbed it to life. The notification bar was a record of my weakness. Six unread messages: three from Kaitlyn with photos of a happy baby Joey; two from Dmitry asking me when I planned to be at work on Monday; one from Andreas.

I stiffened, bracing myself before clicking to open his message.

**Andreas:** How did you sleep

No punctuation. No emoji. No appurtenance that might give me any insight or clue as to his intended inflection or thoughts. Typical.

I lay there, staring at the message, debating how best to respond and how much to admit. This indecision lasted maybe a full minute, then restlessness took over and my fingers began to type.

Before I answered, though, my brain—ever the helpful parasite—replayed the events of the previous twelve hours. After Thanksgiving at Kaitlyn and Martin's, Tara picked me up at exactly 8:01 PM, walked me to the car with the discretion of an off-duty Secret Service agent, and drove me to Andreas's apartment. No questions, no conversation. I'd been thankful for her silence since I'd still been trying to process Andreas's sneak-attack kisses.

At the apartment, Tara made sure the perimeter was secure, then explained that Andreas had arranged for her to sleep over every night for the next two weeks. "This way, if you sleepwalk again, I can help redirect you," she said, her voice a warm blend of casual and commando. She even offered to walk me through some basic jiujitsu moves before bed, should I wish to "relax" before hitting the hay.

I laughed at the time. But now, as I rolled over and found the empty, perfectly made side of Andreas's bed, I realized that somewhere in the night, despite my best efforts, I'd migrated like a very determined barnacle from my own mattress to his.

The only possible explanation was that my subconscious preferred this bed. *Yep. That's the only explanation.*

I disputed the pros and cons of a lie. I could just say, *Slept great, thanks!* and leave it at that. Or I could admit the truth, which was that I had once again invaded his personal space.

I decided to keep it vague.

**Sam:** I slept very well

There. A statement that was not a lie.

My phone buzzed, his reply instant, like he'd been waiting for me.

**Andreas:** Where did you sleep

I frowned at the screen. Was this a trick question? Had Tara reported back to him with a full incident report? Did Andreas know already and he was just baiting me into an admission? Was there a security camera I hadn't noticed? *Nah. He wouldn't place cameras around without telling me. That would make him a super creeper, and nothing about him broadcasts creeper.*

Technically, I fell asleep in my own bed. Also technically, I woke up in his. Not that I had any memory of the transition.

My fingers hovered. I tried to assemble my response and make it sound as non-sus as possible. Once again, I settled on not a lie.

**Sam:** I fell asleep in my own bed

Which was, for the record, true.

I watched my phone, waiting for his response. Five seconds passed, then ten. Then, finally, it appeared.

**Andreas:** Where did you wake up

I made a noise—a sort of compressed laugh-scream—and flopped back against the pillow, phone resting on my chest. The embarrassment was total. Apparently, technical truths had no effect on Andreas.

Reluctantly, but with *feeling* and while gritting my teeth, I replied.

**Sam:** In your bed

I punctuated the confession with a self-owning emoji that looked like the monkey covering its eyes. And then, just for good measure, a pile of poop.

The three dots appeared as he typed. Then they disappeared. Then appeared again. Eventually, I gave up waiting for a reply and rolled out of bed.

The apartment was as silent as a cryogenic freezer. The only sign of life was the faint click of the smart thermostat adjusting the ambient temperature to "optimal living conditions." I padded down the hallway, careful not to disturb Tara, who was supposedly sleeping in the guest room. I had no idea what time it was—my phone said 6:04, but the light outside the windows was the kind that only happened on winter Fridays, when the sun doesn't so much rise as it does negotiate with the clouds.

I peeked into the guest room, just to be sure. The door was open a crack and Tara was sprawled on top of the covers, one arm above her head, mouth slightly open. She looked peaceful, which was weird considering she could probably kill a man with her pinky. Deciding not to risk waking her, I crept down the hall to the bathroom and turned on the shower.

The water pressure was water-pressuring, which is how I liked it. As I soaped myself, I replayed every glance, every micro-interaction with Andreas since this whole thing began. The more I tried to categorize what we were, the less I understood it. We'd gone from mostly strangers to co-conspirators, to maybe friends, to . . . whatever this was. I didn't have the right vocabulary for it. I wondered if he did, since he seemed to know every single language.

After I finished showering, I dried off and headed back to my room, determined to at least get dressed before I had to interact with humans. I pulled on a soft T-shirt and jeans and my phone buzzed as I was twisting my hair into a bun.

**Andreas**: We should schedule date nights. We'll look more like an engaged couple if we go on dates.

I sat down hard on the edge of my bed and spent several minutes staring at the message. My thumbs hovered over the keyboard, not knowing what to type. The air felt electric, and for a minute, I just sat there, feeling my heartbeat echo in my chest.

After a long pause, I responded.

**Sam:** Okay

I stared at the word, then hit send before I could overthink it.

* * *

If you pumped all the world's agitation into a single floor of a university building, you'd get my department on the Monday after Thanksgiving. The halls smelled like burnt coffee and sadness, and every colleague I passed looked like they'd only barely survived their own family dinner. Some had the thousand-yard stare of people who'd spent the break explaining, for the fourteenth consecutive year, that no, they weren't going to be a "real doctor" but were in fact a "PhD," which was "different" but "still a doctor, Uncle Bob." Others had the hollow eyes of those who'd failed to meet a single writing deadline, or, worse, had met the writing deadline and now awaited the bloody aftermath of reviewer comments.

I, on the other hand, sat at my desk grinning like an idiot at my phone because I was, in fact, engaged. Not in the classic sense, but in the "I am currently engaged reading the plethora of texts my fake fiancé keeps sending me" sense.

Andreas had left for London Thursday night, but he texted me every day. Multiple times a day, in fact. He sent good-morning messages every morning. He sent me photos of London. He sent me photos of him around London. He asked me how I was, what I was doing, he asked my opinion about scarves, ties, gloves, jackets. He'd gone shopping on Saturday and

I'd participated via text message. At one point, someone took his photo while he modeled a suit and he'd asked me what I thought.

I couldn't text him back what I really thought—which was that, though he looked mighty sexy, I suspected he'd look even better out of it—so I responded with two thumbs up. Today, before I was awake, he texted me a photo of a pigeon eating a croissant off a chessboard in some park. The accompanying text had been "She's my main competitor here."

I'd snort-laughed.

It was exactly the right kind of dry humor and passive-aggressive adorableness that I'd always wanted in a pen pal, only this pen pal was in fact my fake fiancé. Who I missed, which was deeply concerning, but here we were.

I glanced around the office, making sure nobody was peering over my shoulder, and scrolled through our thread. It was almost exclusively photos and text plus a few emojis from me when I was at a loss for words. He'd only sent one emoji. It had been in response to a picture I'd sent of me after Tara's kickboxing class on Saturday at her gym, grinning while wearing a sports bra and black leggings, beet red and sweating like a pig.

The emoji he'd sent in response was of a queen chess piece. I'd spent well past midnight trying to decipher its meaning. Did this imply that I was a queen? Or powerful? Or . . . what was he saying?

Tara was, as it turned out, the perfect roommate. She got up early, made magical protein shakes, and coaxed me into self-defense practice every night before bed. When I'd attended her Saturday night kickboxing class, she gave me a "Hell yeah!" and within ten minutes had taught me how to break someone's nose using the heel of my palm. "Just in case Henrik shows up again," she said, not at all joking. I knew she wasn't joking because, after I got the movement right, she'd added, "I can't wait. The crunch of a nose breaking is incredibly satisfying."

Then, she'd winked.

I'd gotten used to having her in the apartment. More than that, I liked it. There was a particular comfort in knowing someone slept nearby whose main professional skills were violence and discretion. I also liked that, despite being a total badass, Tara had no shame in binge-watching British reality shows and giving running commentary on everyone's wardrobe choices.

Also, I'd given up sleeping in my own room after waking up in

Andreas's on Friday morning. Truly, I'd surrendered to sleeping in his bed every night. And let me tell you, I'd been sleeping like a wee little baby. Never better. Snug as a bug in a rug. Legit.

Thus, it was with a weird mix of well-rested contentment and adrenaline that I started my Monday, sipping the last of my sad office coffee, reading Andreas's latest message ("My tournament started today. I am free to talk after noon your time if you want a call"), and prepping for the day ahead.

I was mid-response to Andreas when Dmitry's pale, stubbled face appeared over the cubicle divider, a can of some indie-brewed coffee in his hand, complete with a sad little red bow on top.

"My dear future Dr. Jarlston," he intoned, voice like a melancholy cello, "I know you already have a JD, but I'm talking about your future PhD, my friend. How can I thank you enough for all your amazing help last week? You rewrote my methods section and now it isn't shamefully inadequate."

He held the can aloft like a tiny Olympic torch. "Please accept this can of gourmet coffee as a humble token of my gratitude. It is all I can afford."

I accepted the coffee. "Thank you, Dmitry. 'Twas nothing."

"In that case, may I have it back?" he deadpanned, hand over his heart. "I was late this morning and haven't had coffee yet."

I hugged the can to my chest. "Buzz off, ingrate. It's mine now."

Dmitry shrugged, unoffended, then peered at my hand, which still donned the diamond ring. "Wait. What's this? Are you engaged?"

"Oh, uh . . ." I glanced at my hand. "Well. Yes." Setting the coffee can to the side, I slipped the ring off and put it on the chain around my neck, tucking it under my shirt as I spoke. "I forgot to take it off this morning in the locker room."

He narrowed his eyes. "That's it? You're not going to give me any more details? Who is the guy? Or girl? Or non-binary human?"

Caught, I stared at Dmitry, wondering how much to say. It was one thing dragging my friends into this farce. I didn't like it, not at all, but I understood why it was necessary in order to enact revenge and sell this smoke screen Andreas and I had created. I hoped that they would understand my motivations once everything was settled.

But this was work. Dmitry was my colleague. I would never expect a work colleague—or ask a work colleague—to give me the benefit of doubt.

Dmitry seemed about to press for more details when Dr. Nieminen materialized in the doorway of my cubicle, his ever-flawless hair and jawline radiating influencer energy.

"Sam! You're back." His voice boomed across the whole aisle. "How was the holiday? Do anything fun?"

Instead of pointing out that I wasn't *back* because I'd been in the office and lab every day last week except Thanksgiving, I said, "Nothing of note." Lord help me, but I still didn't want to have a sharing kind of relationship with Dr. Nieminen. Something deep inside me still didn't trust the guy. "Did you receive my email with all the cross-checked citations? I sent it to the group."

"Yes! Thank you for doing that so quickly." Dr. Nieminen pulled out his phone to show me the calendar. "We're on track with the poster. Are we still on for our Friday evening meeting? I have it on my schedule. Does that time work for you still? No plans?"

I nodded. "That time works."

Dr. Nieminen grinned wider. "Awesome. Awesome. I have to run to a meeting, but let me know if you need anything, okay?"

He left as abruptly as he'd appeared, leaving behind a cloud of expensive cologne. Dmitry, perhaps sensing that I truly had no plans to return his can of coffee, tossed a thumb over his shoulder. "I need caffeine. Can I get you anything?"

I shook my head. "Thank you, no."

He waggled his eyebrows and left.

For a brief moment, I allowed myself to bask in the normalcy of it all. Office banter. Group projects. The comfort of old routines. I could almost forget that I was now a pawn in a multigenerational revenge plot.

*You're not a pawn. You're a bishop, at least.*

And then my desk phone rang.

"Sam here," I answered.

The voice on the other end was monotone but polite. "Ms. Jarlston, this is building security. We have a VIP visitor for you at the main entrance."

My heart stuttered. "Did they give a name?"

"Let me check." The line went quiet for a moment, then the security guy returned and said, "Tobias Kristiansen."

$$[\ 9\ ]$$

# GAMETE TRANSPORT AND FERTILIZATION

***Samantha***

I didn't even finish hanging up the phone before I texted Tara.

**Sam:** Come to the lobby. Kristiansen the Elder wants to see me. Can you be here in five? I'll let you in.

My compulsion to use humor wherever possible demanded that I include an emoji. Tara responded with a thumbs-up less than thirty seconds later. I pocked my phone, squared my shoulders, and tried to remember every breathing exercise I'd ever learned in thirteen years of therapy.

This was it, a showdown. The sequel nobody asked for but the universe, in its infinite sense of humor, had green-lit anyway.

On my way out of the office, I made a point of passing the coffee lounge and swiping the free mini-donuts on the counter, because if I was going to face Tobias again, I wanted to be heavily fortified by fried dough and sugar. I also considered taking the elevator, but decided to walk the stairs for the sake of dispelling my nervousness. Four flights down, my heart was pounding out a bossa nova in my chest and I had to stop, lean against the stairwell wall, and check my phone to see if Tara had replied with anything new.

She hadn't, but as I rounded the last flight to the lobby, my phone buzzed. It was her.

**Tara:** Andreas doesn't want you to meet with Tobias.

I stopped short, reread the line three times. Then, because I couldn't help myself, I immediately typed a reply.

**Sam:** I'm meeting him. Please come to the building and I'll let you in. I want you with me.

My finger hovered over the send button for half a second, but then I hit it. The message was direct and honest. A second later my phone buzzed.

**Tara:** Okay. On my way.

I slipped the phone into my pocket, trying to ignore the simmer of annoyance in my gut. Maybe Andreas had good reasons for wanting me to avoid Tobias. But he hadn't communicated them to me clearly. I saw no reason why meeting Tobias would be risky, especially with Tara present.

And if I was ever going to get closure on what happened to my dad—or even just a scrap of information that I could chew on—this was an opportunity I couldn't let pass.

I reached the glass doors that separated the lobby from the second badge-access area and stepped to the side, hiding myself from the main area. Through the doors, I spied Tobias waiting near some midcentury modern couches with the exact same bored expression as last time, except now he was scrolling through his phone and occasionally looking up to glare at the security guard on duty behind the desk. He wore a suit that was only slightly less well-tailored than Andreas's but made up for the sloppiness by being a loud shade of periwinkle.

I watched him for a second, and used the time to remind myself that Tobias Kristiansen was not the real threat. His mind games wouldn't work on me. He could threaten and cajole and I would remain unshakable. Unlike Henrik—who was unpredictable and unhinged—Tobias's penchant for manipulation seemed to stick to the established playbook of following up threats with behind-the-scenes machinations. Which meant that if I could just get him talking, he might let slip something useful about my father's fraud case.

Tobias walked over to the security guard and said something. The guard stood and gestured for Tobias to follow. I assumed they were heading to the same private area where we'd met the last time he'd paid me a visit.

Movement outside the building caught my eye. Tara pulled up at the curb and parked in a space that definitely wasn't legal. Seemingly unperturbed, she strode across the sidewalk. Making eye contact with me through the glass, she nodded once and waited for me to open the door.

I pushed open the second access door and jogged across the lobby to open the main entrance for Tara. She stepped in, pulled off her gloves, and eyed the scene like a SWAT team leader prepping to breach.

"You want me in the room?" she asked, voice low and calm.

"Definitely," I said, matching her volume. "You can punch him if he tries anything."

She grinned, and the energy in the lobby shifted in my favor.

I led her down the corridor to the side office where I'd met with Tobias previously, and we passed the security guard on the way. He didn't give us so much as a double take. It was like stepping into a time capsule of discomfort.

Tobias turned as we entered, and his eyes flicked over Tara, then back to me. "Bringing body doubles everywhere you go now?" he asked, his voice sliding off the vowels like they'd personally offended him.

"Actually, yes," I said, seeing no reason to sit down. "What do you want?"

He shrugged, then set his phone on the table in the middle of the room and crossed his arms. "It seems you didn't take my advice last time. Have you forgotten? I can make the rest of your academic career very, very uncomfortable."

I almost laughed, it was such a weak opening gambit. "How very innovative. This is the same threat you made last time, and see how well that went?"

He leaned back on his heels, lips twisting. "You don't think I'll do it?"

"I don't think it'll be any more effective this time," I said, deadpan, channeling the ghost of every grad school office hour I'd ever attended.

His face didn't change, but his eyes narrowed a little. "I haven't done anything yet. Don't test me. One phone call is all it takes."

This tripped me up. I was under the impression that Tobias had already made the phone call, already twisted the arms and greased the wheels that got Dr. Hauser's funding frozen. So why the veiled threat again? Why not just say, "I did it. Here's what you get if you don't play nice"?

Unless there was more leverage he could apply . . . ? Or maybe Tobias was just fishing for a reaction. I was about to confront him when he withdrew an envelope from his inside pocket and placed it on the table next to his phone.

I rolled my eyes so hard I worried I might detach a retina. "Are these more pictures of me with Andreas? Are you making us a photo album for our wedding?"

Tobias's mouth twitched. "This envelope contains a contract you might find interesting, but I do have some new pictures, from last week. I believe my younger brother paid you a visit, yes?"

I froze. *Henrik.*

The name landed like a barbell on my chest. Suddenly the world was too bright and every sound felt amplified, like my ears were trying to track every molecule in the room. Tara must have noticed because she shifted her weight next to me, shoulders tensing as if to intercept a thrown punch.

I managed to speak, but it came out hoarse. "Did you put Henrik up to that?"

Tobias shook his head, lips curling with what I assumed was mock disgust. "No one puts Henrik up to things. He has his little hobbies, and fucks things up all on his own."

The envelope sat between us like a land mine. I forced myself to look at it, to focus on the reality in front of me rather than the panic mounting in my throat at the reminder of Henrik's visit.

"What's the contract for?" I asked, keeping my voice steady only through raw will.

Tobias didn't touch the envelope, but he tapped the table next to it. "I can get Henrik under control, but I want control of my father's shares. I know about the addendum." His eyes crawled over me, evaluating. "Are you already pregnant? Henrik said he didn't think so, not yet anyway."

The blood in my body stopped moving. "What is the contract for?" I repeated.

He drummed his fingers on the table. "Walk away from Andreas, from our family, and I will make it worth your while. You could start your own company with the amount I'm offering you."

"That's what's in the envelope?" I said, letting the disbelief saturate my tone. "You're trying to pay me off so I'll leave Andreas?"

"That's an ugly way to put it, but yes," he said, not the least bit abashed.

I looked at Tara. She watched Tobias with a mixture of obvious professional disdain and plain personal contempt.

I turned back to Tobias. "I'm not interested."

He shrugged, like he didn't expect me to say yes anyway. "Don't blame me if Henrik's clumsiness makes you lose something precious." His voice had gone soft and creepy.

I took a step back, my body demanding that I escape. "This conversation is over."

I didn't wait for a response. I turned, grabbed Tara's sleeve, and practically ran for the door. Behind us, Tobias called, "My offer has no expiration date, come to me anytime."

Once we were around the corner and out of sight, I leaned against a wall and bent my head, trying to regulate my breathing. *Damn it!* I'd gotten nothing valuable from Tobias. Not a single thing.

Tara placed a gentle hand on my shoulder and asked quietly, "Are you okay?"

I wanted to say yes. I wanted to say I was fine, that none of this fazed me. But the truth was, the second Henrik's name came up, my brain stopped working and adrenaline had flooded my body. I'd meant to pump Tobias for information about the fraud, about the addendum, about what steps he was taking to stake his claim on the shares, but instead I'd let fear short-circuit my entire personality.

Forcing a smile, I pushed away from the wall and shook out my hands. "I'm fine. I should get back to work."

Tara eyed me for a long moment, then let her hand drop. "I'll be here when you're ready to leave. We can go at any time."

I nodded. And I couldn't stop the disloyal thought from creeping into my mind. *I wish Andreas were here.*

* * *

I decided to head home early and take the virtual call with my therapist from the apartment. There's a feeling I experienced sometimes, especially after a taxing day, where my thoughts were both tangled and muted, where silence sounded like background static and I wanted to escape it by doing something unproductive but engrossing, like an internet search for my fake fiancé to see if he was trending on the chess subreddit. Not that I was about to actually do that.

The call with my therapist had ended a while ago and now I was lounging in Andreas's bed, horizontal across the mattress with my laptop glowing at quarter-brightness, the room dark except for a pencil stripe of late-afternoon sunlight crawling in through the drapes.

I hadn't called Andreas today. I hadn't texted, either. For the entire afternoon, I'd done a spectacular job of not thinking about whether I should reach out, or if he was mad at me for meeting with Tobias, or if our goodbye on the curb last Thursday meant something to him. It had to, right? No one kisses like that without it meaning something . . . right?

Except, we'd kissed like that on the night of our fake engagement, and it had meant nothing then.

Instead of checking the subreddit, I spent forty-five minutes reading back through our text string and not spiraling over what it meant that he'd hearted the text message I'd sent yesterday wishing him good night, a fact I'd missed until this afternoon. For the record, it was a really good text. Funny, but not try-hard. Then, I'd spent another hour on a resale site for yachts, judging rich people for not having three full bathrooms on their ten-million-dollar floating McMansion.

Setting the laptop to the side, I rolled onto my stomach, resting my cheek against the pillow. There was no trace of Andreas's cologne or shampoo in the sheets. I'd made the mistake of washing everything the day he left, since I'd slept in his bed with my clothes on. Now I regretted it. If I could wish for one additional coping mechanism tonight, it would be the ability to smell a man who was several time zones away and pretend, for a minute, that everything was fine.

My therapist had been less than impressed with this wish.

Our virtual session earlier today started exactly on time, as always, and lasted precisely fifty minutes. When I'd told her a lot had happened since our last visit, Dr. Glass had blinked once behind her large, aggressively round glasses and said, "So you're not sleeping. Tell me about that. Let's start there."

I explained the sleepwalking. The relocation from my bed to Andreas's. The sense of being a passenger in my own body.

She wrote things down on her tablet, and then, when I was done, asked, "When did this first start?"

"The very first time was years ago, after my dad died," I said, and realized I hadn't rehearsed that answer at all. "I was thirteen. I'd get up, move things around the house. Sometimes I'd wake up in the backyard."

"Did your mother address it with a doctor?"

"She was, uh, a little busy being nonfunctional." My laugh was brittle. "But after a while, she put a lock on my door. She didn't want me wandering outside."

Dr. Glass digested that for a minute, then nodded. "There's nothing abnormal about stress manifesting in these kinds of dissociative episodes. Especially if you experienced a sudden trauma at a formative age."

It was so clinical I almost wanted to hug her. God, I loved her analytical approach. She always made me feel less broken in a critical sense and more fixable in a pragmatic one.

"Have you ever tried medication for it?" she asked.

"I'm already on sleeping aids," I said. "But I don't like to take them too much."

She nodded again, scribbling. "I agree. Sleepwalking while on sleep aids can be dangerous. Have you tried meditation? Or grounding exercises?"

I told her I'd tried everything: deep breathing, progressive muscle relaxation, counting sheep, counting backward from ten thousand, listening to classical music, binaural beats, actual brown noise, guided meditation apps, and once, in a moment of true desperation, those ASMR videos where women whisper compliments at you like you're a child in need of a sticker.

None of it worked. Or at least, not well enough to keep me from getting up in the middle of the night and sleepwalking into the bed of the world's sexiest chess master.

She said, "I think your current situation is unique in that you're dealing with multiple stressors. The inheritance. The security threat. The pressure to perform at work and academically. And on top of all that, you're living with a man you may or may not be in love with. And for the first time in your life, you're open to the idea—albeit, just a slight opening up—of a committed relationship with that person. This is a lot, Sam."

"Thank you. That's a relief to hear someone else say. I was worried it was all in my head."

Dr. Glass smirked kindly at my poor attempt at a joke and prescribed more self-care, less caffeine, and a list of meditation apps that I'd already tried but would try again. She also said, "May I suggest—since you said he's okay with it—you continue to start the night sleeping in his bed? Let's see if this reduces your sleepwalking. Keeping you safe is the top priority here. And give yourself time to adjust to the new normal. You are not responsible for fixing everything at once."

Now, as I lay in Andreas's bed, I opened my phone and flicked through the meditation apps, then gave up and typed "London chess tournament standings" into the search engine. The coverage was, as you'd expect, less than riveting. *The Chess Master* blog recapped each round like it was a boxing match for the criminally nerdy. Andreas was, of course, undefeated, but the write-ups focused mostly on his rivals' self-destruction. There were only a few candids of him, and in them all he was staring at the chessboard with that same intensity I'd witnessed Thanksgiving morning, like the pieces might move if he blinked.

I watched a video clip of his most recent game, not because I understood chess, but because I liked to watch his hands when he played. I discovered he had this habit of twirling the pieces between his fingers, never slamming them down but always moving with an economy that was so . . . Andreas. The video was annotated by some bespectacled British guy who talked a mile a minute.

"And you see Kristiansen here, arriving with less than a minute on the clock, which, frankly, you never see at this level—most players, you give them a thirty-minute clock, they'll use all of it—but Kristiansen, look at him, he sits, shakes hands with his opponent, stares at the board, and bang, bang, bang, executes the first ten moves in less than five seconds. It's like the man was playing from memory."

I paused the video, rewound it, and watched again. He did sit down late. He did shake the hand of his opponent. And then he just, almost absentmindedly, destroyed the guy.

I tried to imagine what it must feel like, to be so certain in your next move that you don't even bother to look up. To know, before anyone else, exactly how the game will end.

The phone was heavy in my hand. I wanted to text him, but what would I even say? How's the bird with the croissant? Try on any other suits? Please come home soon . . .

Instead, I set the phone aside and pulled the duvet up to my chin. It wasn't cold in the apartment, but I wanted the extra weight. I counted backward from one hundred, as Dr. Glass suggested, and I was halfway to fifty-six when a sharp rap at the door pulled me upright.

"Come in," I said, voice embarrassingly hoarse.

Tara entered with the confidence of a woman who'd once subdued a drunk hedge fund manager using only a plastic spoon and her own elbow. (True story. She'd told me about it on Saturday after our kickboxing class.)

The woman wore actual pajamas, a cartoon-print T-shirt and plaid pants, and held a box in one hand. She set it at the foot of the bed and said, "Something came for you."

I sat up completely, pulling my legs under me. "What is it?"

She shrugged. "It's not a bomb. I already checked. It's from Andreas. He texted me yesterday and said it was coming."

The box was heavier than it looked, and taped shut with precision. I picked at the tape, then gave up and used my keys by the bed to slice it open.

Inside was a blue-and-silver tin of Scottish shortbread, a box of herbal tea called Nighty Night Relaxation Blend, and, on top, a card. My name, written in Andreas's neat, almost typewritten print. No heart, no flourish, not even a "to" or "from." I opened it.

The note inside read,

*Thinking of you. I hope you have sweet dreams.*

*—A*

I stared at the card for a second, my face doing that thing where it tries to express seventeen feelings at once and lands on none. I wanted to laugh because it was such a short message for him to rush across the sea. I wanted to cry a little because he remembered that I liked shortbread cookies. Mostly, I wanted sniff the card just in case it held traces of his rosemary shampoo.

Tara watched me, arms crossed. "Cookies and tea?"

I held up the tin. "Want one?"

She narrowed her eyes. "No, Sam. These are for you, not us."

I frowned, confused.

She shook her head. "You're weird, Sam. Why would Andreas rush a package of tea and cookies? These are meant just for you. You're the one he's in love with."

Before I could formulate a response to that, she yawned and padded back out the door, leaving me alone with the parcel and the echo of her words.

I opened the tin. The cookies were arranged with geometric precision, three rows of four, each one stamped with a pattern. I picked one, then another, and arranged them into a triangle on top of the tin. I stared at them for a long time, thinking about what Tara said.

Andreas obviously hadn't told Tara or any of the other bodyguards about the nature of our arrangement. If one wants to keep a secret, the fewer people who know, the better.

And I knew that if I didn't come clean soon regarding how I'd consulted Kaitlyn and Martin about Andreas's proposal before I'd accepted it, I would start sleepwalking again. I felt certain I would. Thus, I resolved, right then, to call Andreas tomorrow and tell him.

I picked up my phone, debated for a second, then sent him a photo of the cookies, arranged in the shape of a smiley face. Underneath, I typed out a message.

**Sam:** Thank you for the cookies and tea.

I hovered over the send button, then pressed it, and immediately buried my face in the pillow. I should've called him earlier today instead of avoiding it after Tobias's visit. I shouldn't let Tobias—or Henrik—factor into my relationship with Andreas.

When I surfaced, there was a reply already.

**Andreas:** Let me know if you want bedtime company. For tea.

My heart did the thing, the swoop and fly thing. Was he flirting with me?

*I think so, yes. This is, what the kids these days call, the flirting.*

Before I could formulate a response, he texted me again.

**Andreas:** I need to go to sleep. Don't want to be late tomorrow. Call me when you're free.

I smirked at his reference to being late, then I exhaled a long breath. I liked this. I liked his check-ins and I liked knowing about him and what he was up to. Setting the phone on the nightstand, I lay down and stared up at the ceiling, imagining a chessboard there, all the pieces in their perfect rows, waiting for someone to move.

I would call him tomorrow. I would tell him the truth. But for this evening, at least, I could let myself rest, and dream of the one man who, for better or worse, always seemed to be five moves ahead of me.

$$[\ 10\ ]$$

# REPRODUCTIVE HEALTH

***Samantha***

The next morning I woke up with my alarm, before the sun had managed to brighten or color the sky, and rolled out of bed. The thick wool carpet beneath my feet felt plush and warm, making me wish I didn't have to traverse the wood floor between Andreas's room and my bathroom across the living room and down the hall. But I did.

Tara was probably already gone. Regardless, I decided to tiptoe to the bathroom. Then I ran through a shower, brushed my teeth, and stood for a solid three minutes trying to decide what to do with my hair. There was no reason to do anything with my hair. And yet, my hair existed. Thus, the question remained. Bun? Ponytail? Down? I split the difference and left it a damp mess around my shoulders. There, decision fatigue solved.

I used Andreas's fancy espresso machine. It felt more approachable than his pour-over contraption, and I sipped it standing at the kitchen counter, staring at the digital clock on the oven. It was 5:18 AM East Coast time. In London, it would be just after ten in the morning. He'd probably been up for hours, already destroying some unfortunate international grand master, or whatever it was they did during the early rounds of chess tournaments. He hadn't texted me yet, but that was normal; he always waited until after 7:00 AM my time.

The knowledge that every time I'd texted him so far, he'd sent a near-instant reply, felt oddly . . . comforting. Like a safety net. Maybe that was why I felt nervous about calling him today. Because I was about to cut that line, or at least threaten it, by telling him what I'd put off saying since Thursday.

I paced the apartment for twenty minutes, then padded back to the kitchen for a second shot of espresso. I opened the fridge, looking for the oat milk, and was greeted by a single row of vegan yogurts, each container organized with military precision. How did he even do that when he wasn't here? Had he called Tara and asked her to alphabetize the fridge? Had he bribed the cleaning service? Did the food arrange itself when he left the room, like *Toy Story* but with probiotics?

*Stop stalling and just call him!*

I shut the fridge and drank the coffee black. The bitterness helped focus my thoughts. Grabbing my phone, I went to his bedroom, which I still couldn't enter without a fluttery, dumb feeling in my chest. Shutting the door, I sat cross-legged on the edge of his bed, and opened our message thread. I stared at the last text he'd sent.

**Andreas:** I need to go to sleep. Don't want to be late tomorrow. Call me when you're free.

I smiled despite myself, then forced my face back to neutral. I needed to focus. I needed to be honest. I texted,

**Sam**: Hey, can we talk later today? Not urgent, but I'd like to call you.

Less than sixty seconds later he responded,

**Andreas:** I can be free whenever you need me to be free.

That was so him. An immediate, all-in commitment to my whims.

**Sam**: How about now?

There was a brief lag—maybe a minute—then my phone rang, and there he was: ANDREAS KRISTIANSEN calling.

I let it ring twice, just to take a deep breath, then answered.

"Hello?" My voice sounded rough. I cleared it and tried again. "Hello."

He was somewhere busy; the background was a low thrum of voices and the tinny sound of plates clattering. But his voice was calm and immediate. "Hi. Are you okay?"

I hated that this was the first thing he asked, but also, I loved it. No hello, no small talk, just a direct line to my internal status.

"Yeah, I'm fine," I said, swallowing. "I . . . I wanted to tell you something. Before I lose my nerve."

He made a small hum, not impatient but maybe a little wary. "What happened?"

"Nothing bad," I rushed to clarify. "It's not bad. I—well, it's something you should know. About Kaitlyn and Martin."

The line was silent for a beat. "Yes?" he prompted, when I didn't immediately continue.

"I told them," I said, all in a rush. "About us. Before I agreed to anything with you, I needed to talk it over with someone, so I talked it over with them. Or, well, Kaitlyn, but Martin was in the next room and he eavesdropped, so he found out, too."

There was another silence, but it was longer this time. It didn't feel like an I'm-about-to-yell-at-you silence, but more like an I'm-recalibrating-my-assumptions silence.

I hurried on, "They haven't told anyone, I promise. But I feel bad for not telling you sooner. It was bothering me. I wanted you to know. I trust them completely. But I should have told you before."

I heard a sound like a door close, and then all the background noise suddenly stopped. His side was so quiet I wondered if the call had dropped.

I gripped my forehead. "Are you still there?"

"Let me see if I have this correct." His tone was calm but struck me as precise. "They knew about our arrangement, even when I came for Thanksgiving?"

"Yes, they did." I gave into my urge to wince. "Are you mad?" I asked before I could chicken out.

His response was quick. "No. No, I am not at all mad." He let out an audible breath, then added, "But why did you not tell me when we were there on Thursday?"

This, I had rehearsed. "Because it completely slipped my mind, honestly. And then you were there, and you started pretending—kissing my forehead, holding my hand—and that's when I remembered—that I hadn't told you—but I didn't want to make you self-conscious about it, not when we were already there. It's been really bothering me since, that you still didn't know. I want us to be honest. That's why I'm telling you now. I didn't want to wait any longer. I'm sorry."

He was quiet again, but—thankfully—this time the silence felt less loaded. "It is fine," he said. "Thank you for telling me."

I let out a breath. "You're really not upset?"

"No. I am glad you have friends you trust. To be honest, I am somewhat glad I did not know on Thursday. Meeting your good friends, I was already very nervous. But being your fiancé gave me a good reason to be there. Otherwise, why would I deserve a place next to you?"

His tone sounded matter-of-fact, but something about the way he said it made my insides tighten. "What are you talking about? Kaitlyn is the best. She wanted you to come. You were invited. You don't need to be my fake fiancé to have a place at the table. You're my friend. That's enough."

He was very, very quiet. Then, softly, he said, "It is good to know you consider me a friend now."

I blinked. "Of course we're friends! Do you not want to be my friend?"

There was another pause and it struck me that Andreas had paused and considered his response for a significant period of time nine out of ten times so far on this call. Whereas, I hadn't paused and considered my responses at all. Usually, I wasn't this reckless. Only with Kaitlyn, who I trusted completely.

Eventually, he said, "Knowing one's position on the board is imperative before making the next move."

I snorted, and the tension that had been coiling in my gut all morning started to unwind. "Everything is chess with you."

"It is what I know," he said.

"I'm so glad you're not mad. It's important that we trust each other completely, right? We're in a very precarious situation. If I couldn't trust you, I wouldn't know what to do." My confession, and therefore vulnerability, settled around me with a hush. I'd stopped short of admitting to Andreas that the level of trust I'd decided to place in him was monumental for me. It felt scary, but also strangely good. I found myself smiling at my phone screen like an idiot.

Again, he said nothing for a while, and the silence didn't feel awkward at all. It felt like the inside of a snow globe, muted by something gentle and invisible.

"Are you sure you're not mad at me?" I asked again, because I needed to hear his assurance again. I'd really done a number on myself this morning, twisting my worries into a noose.

"No," he said, his tone intoxicatingly gentle. "I am not mad at you, Samantha. Not even a little."

But there was an odd edge in his voice this time, something almost sad.

Instinct demanded that I try to cheer him up. "Is everything okay there? Any challenging matches? You sent me cookies and tea from London, and all I can do is sit here in your apartment and eat them without you. I wish I could send you something in return."

"All is well here, but . . ."

I gripped my phone tighter, waiting with anticipation. "What? What can I do?"

"You could send me more photos."

I laughed. He must be joking. "Of what? You live here. You already know what New York looks like in winter."

He cleared his throat. "You could send me photos of what you are doing. You do not have to, of course, but . . . I spend a lot of time at the tournament waiting. It can be boring."

His voice was weirdly gruff, like he was embarrassed by the request. My stomach did a weird summersault at the reemergence of his bashfulness. "Then I'll send you photos meant to entertain."

"As long as you are in them."

I tried to ignore the way his words made my chest tighten, and endeavored to dispel my body's reactions with a joke. "I'll dress up in a clown costume and have someone record me juggling petri dishes."

He laughed, the sound low and lovely. "By the way, I meant to say, thank you for helping me pick out the suit. You know, I can also help with that kind of thing, if you want."

"Helping me pick out clothes?" I asked, amused.

"Sure," he said, like it was the most natural thing in the world.

"Is this your way of saying my wardrobe needs an upgrade?"

"I am saying, your style is very American."

I cackled. "I'll have you know, half the girls in my department consider my ten-year-old skinny jeans awesome cosplay."

"You deserve better than a costume." His voice held a smile. "We should revisit this. It would not be strange for a fiancé to buy his beloved clothes, do you not think?"

"Do not buy me clothes, Andreas."

"Why not?"

"Because I'll have to reimburse you, and you have expensive taste. It's a slippery slope from one nice sweater to a closet full of cashmere."

With supreme confidence, he said, "You will be able to afford my taste and more once you inherit. And I am not going to listen to you on this. Expect clothes."

"Andreas!" I said, half laughing, half warning.

I heard a new voice on the other end, someone saying his name. Andreas's line fell quiet for a minute.

Then he returned and said, "I have to go. I am fifteen minutes late for a match."

"What?!" I stood from the bed. "Then why did you call me?"

"I only need five minutes with this guy," he said, dry as the Atacama Desert. "We will talk again soon, okay?"

"Okay," I said, smiling like a doofus as he hung up.

Sitting back down on the edge of his bed, I hugged my knees and let my feelings simmer without trying to name them. I didn't have the right vocabulary anyway.

Eventually, I got up. I made breakfast for both Tara and me. She drove me to work. I spent several hours in the lab, catching myself staring into space and grinning. And when I returned to my desk, every time I glanced at my phone, I again smiled like a dope, replaying the words, the tone, the laughter of our call.

I hadn't ruined anything. We were more in sync than before.

* * *

The first Friday—and first snow day—in December, and I was still at work at 6:45 PM, listening to Dr. Nieminen enumerate my own accomplishments like he'd been the catalyst for all my success. Not even the anticipation of knowing that, at this precise moment, Andreas Kristiansen was likely past security in Heathrow and would soon be on a flight home from London, could save my mood.

The tick of the conference room's analog clock sounded disproportionately loud for some reason. Perhaps because it was the countdown to my freedom. I'd been sitting in this chair for forty-three minutes, and the two most meaningful things I'd managed to accomplish—really, the only two things—were not falling asleep and not losing my temper.

"Your time logs are thorough," Nieminen said, flipping a page. He wore a navy quarter-zip and, as always, looked like he'd just come from a corporate retreat where the team-building activity was silently judge your subordinates. He had a stack of papers at his elbow, the top one marked in his fine blue pen: "Jarlston, S. – November."

Nieminen flipped through two more pages and gave a tight nod. "You're quite productive for someone who's lost their funding and was saved by a new PI in the middle of the semester."

"Thanks," I said, though it didn't feel like a compliment. The way he'd said the words, he'd put the emphasis on "lost their funding" and "saved" as though to remind me that my place here had more to do with his generosity than my ability.

*Or maybe you're just reading menace into his words where none exists because you simply do not like the man.*

It was a possibility. Nothing he'd said was false, even if I didn't like the words.

*Stop assuming the worst of Dr. Nieminen!*

I'd tried. I'd really, really tried. Honestly, he'd done nothing tangible I could object to since taking over my funding.

Yes, over the last two weeks since Thanksgiving break, he would frequently and randomly check in on me during the day, something Dr. Hauser never did. And he would lean over my shoulder to peer at my computer screen while I showed him evidence of my progress. In our smaller department meeting last week, he'd said "we" instead of naming me specifically when giving credit for the fast turnaround of the poster presentation, a la, *We were able to confirm all the citations before the break.*

I was a junior member on *his* team. Thus, he could technically say "we" and take public credit for all my work if he wanted. That was how academia worked. Dr. Hauser never did that, she'd always given the specific person credit for their contributions, naming them in public. Sadly, Dr. Hauser seemed to be the exception.

Presently, biting my tongue, I tuned him out as he continued reciting out loud all the tasks I'd completed in November, and let my mind drift to more pleasant thoughts. Namely, my reunion with Andreas and the ever-expanding collection of gifts he'd mailed to the apartment since leaving New York.

The collection was, in a word, absurd.

Every night for the last ten days, I'd come home to one or more surprise parcels. After the tea and cookies, the next package contained a pair of Italian-made pajamas, a lady version of his gentlemanly suit of sleepwear. The next day brought a tiny, perfectly wrapped box of perfume that smelled absolutely divine—like fresh gardenias at first, but then with a dark, velvety scent after, one I couldn't quite place, like sweet cedar but better. I'd considered bringing it into the lab and running an analysis on its chemical composition.

After that, a stationery set so beautiful I couldn't imagine ever using it, along with an actual fountain pen that wrote smoother than any pen had the right to and felt magnificent in my hand. Next, a beautiful new scarf in the exact shade of my eyes, with a note that read, "To keep you warm while I'm away." And I'd gasped upon opening an antique copy of Darwin's *On the Origin of Species*. He also sent an entire suite of skincare items that even Diya would've approved of.

To my surprise, some of the gifts originated from close by. A kombucha brewed locally that I quickly became addicted to. (I didn't even know I liked kombucha.) Pickled vegetables from the Bronx that I started putting on everything because they were so spicy and tasty. A crusty sour-dough loaf from Queens that Tara and I polished off in two days. He'd even sent a yummy charcuterie spread last Saturday night with olives, almonds, fancy cheeses, cured meats, and a bottle of Italian red.

I felt so spoiled. The only people who had ever given me gifts like this were my parents and grandparents.

And then came the clothes, always with a note requesting I send a photo of me wearing the item. "To ensure they fit," he'd explained in his note. "If they don't, I can send a new size."

More than once, usually after unwrapping that evening's box and marveling at how much I loved whatever was inside, I would wonder why Andreas was sending me gifts at all. He'd explained them away on the phone as expected since the world thought we were engaged, but that excuse didn't fully explain his constant and effusive lavishing. Every item was thoughtful, personal, and indulgent, clearly chosen specifically for me. If he'd simply wished to put on a show, then he could've sent the same item every day. Or jewelry. Or flowers. Why go to such trouble?

Not quite understanding the impulse, I began leaving work on time and stopping by shops on my way home. Visiting four different vintage resellers and two antique shops, I found myself searching for something Andreas might like, trying to find the right thing, only to walk away empty-handed, except for a tiepin shaped like a rook that I worried he'd think was tacky.

It wasn't until the night before last, standing in the back of a dusty used bookstore on East 12th, that I found it: a complete, signed set of Bobby Fischer's chess writings, the spines brittle but the dust jackets intact. I'd nearly fainted when I opened the first volume and saw the signature, because I suspected what it would mean to Andreas. Based on his library, he obviously loved books, and I'd snooped around his collection enough to know he didn't have signed versions of these.

Using grandma's account to pay for the—ahem—extremely expensive set didn't even faze me. It seemed like something she would want me to do, like an expense she'd heartily approve of. I'd wrapped it in tissue, hidden it under my bed, and planned to present it as casually as possible so as not to seem too eager.

Apparently, I was more concerned with the appearance of chill than reality. But what could I do? I'd never given a man I was interested in a gift before. This was new territory for me.

". . . and the rest looks good," Nieminen said, yanking me from my thoughts as he loudly set down his pen. I blinked the room back into focus and found him giving me a faint smile. "There are only a few weeks left in the term. Your project proposal is strong. Let's just make sure you keep hitting your time benchmarks, okay?"

"Will do," I said. I began packing my laptop away, a move he either didn't notice or chose to ignore. I had half a mind to ask if he needed anything else, but I was worried he'd find something.

Instead, as I slowly stood and zipped my bag, I waited for him to say, "Thanks for coming in," or "Enjoy your weekend," or, God willing, "You can leave now." He didn't move, simply kept watching me. Since I'd finished packing my things and he still hadn't spoken, I decided to take that as implicit permission to skedaddle.

I'd just placed my backpack on my shoulder and reached for the door when he said, "Oh, yeah—"

"Yeah?" I turned to face whatever Dr. Nieminen's "one more thing" was.

Dr. Nieminen, standing now on the other side of the table, reached into his bag and pulled out a thin blue folder. He slid it across the table to me. "I got us two tickets for the show tonight," he said. "If we hurry, we can get a quick bite to eat before curtain."

[ 11 ]

# FERTILITY AND ITS CONTROL

***Samantha***

I stared at Nieminen, then at the folder. His words didn't compute.

"A show?"

He smiled again, a flash of white teeth and cleft chin. "I overheard you mention to that guy in the cubicle next to you that you haven't been to any Broadway in months, and I had an extra connection with the box office. It's Company, at the Bernard Jacobs. The reviews are excellent."

I picked up the folder. Inside were two tickets, row J. I was so confused. "This is for tonight?"

"Of course," James Nieminen said, like it was the most normal thing in the world to randomly spring a Broadway show on an colleague less than an hour before curtain, let alone a *boss* springing it on an *employee.*

I blinked, then tried to recover. "Uh, Dr. Nieminen, I can't. I have other plans tonight."

He cocked his head to the side, lips pursed. "You have other plans? But I thought—when we scheduled these meetings, you said you didn't have other plans on Friday nights."

I stifled a strangled bark of laughter. "I agreed to meet you in the conference room, not to go to a Broadway show."

He frowned. "You said you were free. You didn't mention anything else."

"I'm not—I mean—" I glanced at the wall behind him. "I am free Fridays, but only for this meeting. I have plans after work." My face was getting hot. With anger.

James exhaled loudly through his nose, shoulders going rigid. "Sam, I wouldn't have bought these tickets if I'd known you weren't available. Are you telling me you can't change your plans?"

The phrasing, the sudden shift from genial to weirdly controlling, made the inside of my skull itch. "No. I can't."

James's face went flat, the smile gone. "Fine. With whom do you have plans that can't be canceled, if you don't mind me asking?"

This was too much. Even my least chill hookups had never interrogated me like this. I summoned every ounce of petty I had, which, to be fair, was enough to run a midsized petty kingdom where petty trees were logged and made into petty paper at a petty mill.

"I'm having dinner with my fiancé."

James stared at me, unblinking. "You have a fiancé?" The way he said *fiancé* told me he thought I was lying.

Which I was technically, but still. Whether I had a fiancé was none of his business.

"Yes." The lie came so naturally, it shocked even me. "And he can be very jealous, controlling, so I don't like to provoke him." Internally, I wondered why I'd never made up a jealous, controlling fiancé before now. Fictional controlling men were so hugely handy in a pinch.

James's eyes dropped to my hands, which, to be fair, were empty of rings of any kind. "Where's your ring?"

"In my locker," I said, without missing a beat, because that was the truth. I took it off on days I knew I'd be in the lab.

For a second, I thought he might laugh or otherwise let it drop. Instead, he just stood there, staring with a sort of clinical dissatisfaction, like I was an unexpectedly recalcitrant cell culture.

James eventually shook his head. "I didn't know you were seeing anyone. You never mentioned it before now."

I shrugged, wanting to leave and never think about this again. "I keep my personal and professional life very separate," I said, which was not just true, it was extremely true.

James was silent for a moment, then asked, "Are you sure you can manage the increased responsibilities of your position, Sam? I'm not convinced you can keep your commitments. Or that you're being completely truthful with me."

I didn't know whether to laugh or smash his face into the table. Instead, I could only look at him blankly and try to keep my voice pitched as detached as possible. "I'm happy to continue meeting the obligations you set for me, as long as we keep things professional."

"I'll think about it." His voice was tight and cold.

Not bothering to smile or offer a parting salutation, I placed the tickets back on the table, turned, and walked out of the room, hearing him huff loudly just before the conference room door closed behind me.

I left the corridor as quickly as I could, taking the side stairs to the women's locker room. The building felt empty now, each echoing step in the cinder-block stairwell rebounding back at me in a hollow, rattling syncopation. Once I made it inside, I sat down on a bench and put my face in my hands. My cheeks were burning, and my heart was pounding so hard I could feel it in my throat.

I wondered how many other times James had tried this move on other grad students. I wondered how many of them had given in, terrified that they'd be blacklisted or kicked out of the program if they said no. I thought about the way James had looked at me, the sudden withdrawal of praise, the veiled threat about funding. I thought about his postdoc who everyone whispered about and dismissed as *dramatic* because he'd said so. I thought about how little control I would have over the narrative, how easily a man's expectations could be treated as fact. I thought about the last fifteen years of my life, about watching my father be destroyed by liars, about my mother's body wasting away, her giving up because no one would listen to the truth.

When she'd denounced the Kristiansens publicly, would people have taken her more seriously if she'd been a man? My father had died before he'd been allowed to plead his case, before he'd even made a public state-ment or given an interview.

But if he'd lived, would he have been believed? Would his word carry more weight because of his chromosomal arrangement and phenotypic sex? *Yeah. Probably.*

Standing from the bench, I walked to the sink and splashed cold water in my face, certainty taking hold in my bones. Discovering the truth about my father and the charge of fraud against him now felt more important than securing Oskar Kristiansen's shares upon his death. Proving that my dad had been framed wouldn't only absolve my father, it would also vindicate my mother, show the world she hadn't been hysterical or lying about the Kristiansens before her death.

Thank God for Andreas. Thank. God.

Thank God he'd pushed me to take revenge. Thank God he'd found a way to make it happen that didn't involve bringing an innocent child into the situation. Even if I discovered all of their secrets on my own, I would never be able to confront Oskar and Tobias and Henrik openly with the truth or go to the press, not even with rock-solid proof. Without Andreas to back me up, I'd have to use some other surreptitious means. Because women weren't believed. Somehow, I'd have to trick them into confessing, or otherwise trick them into destroying each other.

But with Andreas, he'd arranged the pieces masterfully, our subterfuge with the engagement making me appear like a pawn instead of the queen.

*They will find out soon enough*, I promised myself as I glared in the mirror. They would all find out soon enough. Including Dr. James Nieminen.

* * *

I zipped my parka all the way up after waving goodbye to the dude at the security desk in the lobby. As I approached the glass doors of the main entrance, I scanned the street for Tara's Mercedes beyond. I never left the building until Tara arrived. Per protocol, she generally showed up ten minutes after I texted her, which I'd done in the locker room right after placing the engagement ring on my third left finger.

Pulling my hand out of my pocket, I studied the twinkle of the large stone in the dim light. I honestly didn't know precisely why I'd put it on my hand. Usually, I wore it on a chain around my neck if I wore it at all. But for some reason, after telling James that I had a fiancé, wearing it on my ring finger just felt right.

Faint sound and movement beyond the glass doors had me lifting my head. I spotted Tara's Mercedes pull up to the curb, hazard lights blinking. That was my sign that it was safe to leave.

I had barely reached the first step down when a voice said, "Where are you going?"

James Nieminen materialized from behind one of the columns. Apparently in full stalker mode, dressed in a dark wool coat and leather gloves, he looked me up and down.

"Just heading out," I said, faking cheer. Then, because I'm a petty queen, I couldn't resist adding, "You should get going if you want to make that show."

*Ah. Sam. You are your own worst enemy.*

I shifted my weight and looked past James toward the waiting black car, which had just been joined by a second SUV. From the passenger side of the Mercedes, Tara climbed out, eyes locking on mine. I gave my head a faint shake, hoping she'd stay put. The last thing I needed was James claiming that he'd been harassed by my security team, then I'd have to explain why I had a security team. He was a dipshit, but I didn't consider him a physical threat. I didn't need Tara this time.

Meanwhile, James smiled, and I didn't like how much teeth it showed. "I realized we didn't finish discussing the distribution of tasks for the conference poster. There's a lot to do, and I decided I want you to draft my section."

"You want me to draft *your* section?" Quickly, I scanned the sidewalk and I spotted two other security detail people who I recognized. Both glanced at me, then at Tara. Obviously, they were following her lead, hands in pockets but stance alert. They fanned out, silent as bats, and started inching toward us as though they were simple strangers passing by.

"That's right," James said, leaning closer, "you draft it, I'll edit it. That'll save me time." He stepped fully into my personal space, the gap between us narrowing to "intimate conversation" range. I could smell his cologne, citrus and chemical, and the tang of it made me want to sneeze.

I backed up a half step. "Sure," I ground out. "I can send a draft tonight."

He smiled even wider. "Good. I know you have a lot on your plate, but this is something you should've proposed to me, not the other way around. I need you to be more proactive if this is going to work."

I stared at him, my anger suddenly sharper than the cold. "In that case, if this is going to work, you'll need to give me more of a heads-up before assigning major tasks like this. I would've thought, as the lead for the poster, you would've already created a first draft of your section. Especially since mine is done and it's due for everyone else on Monday."

He shrugged, all faux casual. "Things change. You can work on it tonight, or wake up early and do it. I don't care. But it has to be done by tomorrow."

I opened my mouth to tell him where he could put his poster, but in that exact moment, approaching movement caught my eye at the curb.

Andreas walked toward us, long strides, hands in the pockets of his camel-colored cashmere coat. Underneath, he wore a blue sweater and dark gray pants. His hair was perfectly styled, his jaw shaven, and his skin much more hydrated than I would expect for someone who'd just flown in from England.

Currently, Andreas wasn't looking at me. The entire weight and force of his glare was on James. He wore the same flat, predatory stare that he'd employed during the chess matches I'd been stalk—er, watching online from the London tournament.

He'd won, by the way.

He'd won the tournament. He'd barely smiled when he'd been presented with the £750K check, and his short interview afterward had made me laugh.

Because when the interviewer had asked, "Are you relieved that you won?"

He'd said, matter-of-factly, "No. It was expected."

Drawing even with us, Andreas stopped beside me and his gaze shifted to mine, suffusing with warmth. "Are you ready, Samantha?"

*Dear. Lort.* His voice was deep and smooth and gentle and just magic.

Not waiting for a response, Andreas reached out, took my backpack off my shoulder, and slung it easily over his arm, the side of his mouth tugging adorably to one side. "Where are the mittens I got you? Your hands must be cold."

I felt my eyes narrow with confusion because—as far as I knew—Andreas had never bought me mittens.

Regardless, using his teeth, he tugged off his left glove and fitted it over my fingers, his thumb giving the ring on my third finger a little twist as he did so, his smile growing more obvious the moment he spotted it.

I couldn't speak for a second. Despite being irrationally angry mere seconds prior, my brain was now busy rerouting all available blood to the part of me that was in charge of appreciating how utterly, dangerously hot Andreas looked and how overwhelmingly happy I was to see him.

I finally managed a weak, "I am ready to go."

Giving me one last warm almost smile, Andreas turned his attention back to James, who was now blinking rapidly and trying to recover his composure.

Andreas extended his gloved right hand. "Andreas Kristiansen," he said, in a tone so incredibly flat and unfriendly. After a beat, he added, "Samantha's fiancé."

James stared at him, face slack. "Kristiansen?" he repeated, the word a croak.

Andreas's handshake was brief but obviously punishing; I saw James's knuckles blanch, and when Andreas let go, James cradled his hand for a second before hiding it in his pocket.

I cleared my throat. "This is James Nieminen. My new PI."

James was still looking at Andreas, and his skin had lost all its color despite the cold. "Are you—uh—by any chance, are you related to the Genetix Kristiansens?"

"I am."

There was a moment of silence so thick it felt like the world had been soundproofed. I didn't want to laugh and ruin it, so I rolled my lips between my teeth and bit down lightly, wishing I could snap a photo of James's face.

Nieminen licked his lips, eyes wide. "Nice to meet you. I—" He broke off and cleared his throat, likely needing another minute to collect himself. At length, he repeated, "Nice to meet you."

Andreas's lips curled at the edge, but not in a way that suggested humor. "I could not help but overhear that you want Samantha to finish a task by tomorrow morning? Assigning work on a Friday night, after hours? Seems like poor planning." Every word was cut with ice.

James's face went red, then white. "I was just—" he said, then caught himself. "I was joking. Obviously, she can do it on Monday."

Andreas stared at him for a moment longer, then nodded, as if dismissing him from the conversation.

James stood there for another heartbeat, looked at me, then at Andreas, and then said, "Have a good evening, Samantha. Nice to meet you, Mr. Kristiansen."

He turned and left, shoulders hunched and pace just shy of a jog.

The moment he was out of earshot, I said, "That was . . . I'm not sure what that was."

Andreas didn't look at me, just watched James's retreating figure. "He is your new PI?"

"That's right."

"Does that man bother you at work?"

I hesitated, then shrugged, not really wanting to talk about James Nieminen, not when Andreas was finally home. "I should be able to handle it."

Andreas said nothing, but I saw his jaw clench. Then, finally, he looked at me, eyes scanning my face. "If you want, I can get rid of him."

The way he said it, so calm and practical, made me laugh out loud. "That's not necessary. Besides, I think you just inadvertently solved my problem for me. He's terrified of you."

He seemed to consider my words, then nodded. "Good."

I felt like laughing again, but this time with frustration. No matter how competent I was, no matter how good of a job I did, all my efforts were nothing compared to the power of the Kristiansen last name. *Sigh.*

"Shall we?" Using his left hand, Andreas reached for my right one and entwined our bare fingers together, bringing them both into the pocket of his coat, the movement smooth and natural.

I couldn't believe he was here, and so the question slipped out of me. "When did you get back?"

Andreas didn't break stride. "I took an earlier flight. I came here from the airport. Are you hungry?"

"A little." I caught myself staring at his profile and grinning, thus I rapidly tore my gaze away.

"We will go on a date."

"A date?"

"Yes. You agreed last week. We should go on dates, as an engaged couple. I saw you are wearing the ring."

"Aren't you tired? The time zone shift must be brutal."

"I want to go and I already made a reservation." Andreas stopped short and turned to me, his forehead wrinkling. "Wait. Are you tired? We can go home if you are tired."

Shaking my head, I gave his hand a little reassuring squeeze. "I'm not too tired. We can go on a date."

He seemed to study me, as though to ascertain whether I told the truth. His forehead clearing, he turned back to the car and we walked the last few feet. Tara stood at the hood and sent me a small smile, but I noticed when her gaze shifted to Andreas the smile evaporated.

He opened the back door for me, and I slid inside. Instead of following me in immediately, he leaned down in the open door. "Give me a moment please, I need to speak with Tara."

Wondering what he wanted to discuss that either couldn't wait or had to be discussed without me, I nodded and settled back against the bench seat. *I'll ask him during our date.*

With a quick smile and a promise to be fast, Andreas shut the door, leaving me in the quiet car with my own thoughts, which consisted mostly of replaying the incident with James over and over in my head. Most especially, I enjoyed the look on James's face when Andreas had introduced himself, and the particular shade of white—ghostly white—when James confirmed Andreas was one of the Genetix Kristiansens.

But then my mind snagged on a particular detail of the interaction and I frowned.

Andreas had given me his left glove, leaving my right hand and his left hand without any protection from the weather. And then Andreas had used his right hand—which was still gloved—to shake James's hand.

*Hmm.*

The glove musical chairs hadn't all been a calculated maneuver so Andreas could hold my bare hand, but avoid touching James, had it?

*. . . Nah.*

Who thinks so many steps ahead? Just to ensure we held hands but also to avoid touching James?

That would be truly diabolical.

[ 12 ]

# BRAIN SEX

***Samantha***

Fifteen minutes after Tara pulled away from the biology building, Andreas and I were in a booth at Del Vino, one of those Lower Manhattan wine bars where the walls looked like they'd been imported from Tuscany and the food menu consisted of "lite bites." Even though this place was only a block from Andreas's apartment, I'd never entered it or any other wine bar in New York before. Wine bars weren't in my budget.

The host had shown us to the most public booth after confirming Andreas's reservation. Located right up against the window, it was practically a diorama for the passing parade of New Yorkers. Andreas seemed immune to the idea of passersby watching us, and he had his jacket, scarf, and glove off, already rolling up the sleeves of his cable knit sweater as soon as he slid in across from me.

*Forearms.* I tried not to stare as I took off his other glove and passed it to him.

A server materialized to take our order for "something to nibble," and gave us our wine-dispenser cards. I barely registered what Andreas ordered—some kind of cheese and nuts, roasted olives, charcuterie? Sure, all of it sounded like food. The reason my brain was on vacation was

115

because, less than three feet away across the table, Andreas Kristiansen's eyes settled on me with a focus and intensity I hadn't mentally prepared for. Because he wasn't supposed to be back until tomorrow.

Presently, he was trying to deduce my taste in wine, a subject about which I was both ignorant and, apparently, also abysmally unprepared for.

"Italian?" he asked, hands folded on the table. "Or Argentinian? Or New Zealand, perhaps?"

I shrugged. "The last time I drank was with you, house red at Smokin Greens." After a brief period of internal debate, I decided to stop censoring myself and just tell the truth. "Usually, it's in a box and cost six dollars. I'm not sure I have a region."

*Ugh. I just admitted that.* But I had to stop pretending to be someone I wasn't whenever we were together, like I'd done before he left for London. So what if I embarrassed myself? I was embarrassing. Plus, it's not like this was an actual date.

Andreas considered my words with a faint smile tugging at his lips, his eyes feeling warm as they moved over me. "You paint quite a picture."

"I don't know how to paint unless it's with my fingers," I said primly, picking up my water for a sip. There. Another honest answer. *I'm a plebeian. So sue me.*

Andreas's grin instantly claimed his mouth, and his laugh surprised me. Entranced, I watched him and slowly set my water down. I found myself smiling in response to his smile, basking in his twinkling green eyes, his features soft and unguarded.

"Come now, you must have a preference," he pressed, voice low and ridiculously sexy.

"Honestly? No." I lifted my hands, helpless. "If it's red and doesn't taste like battery acid, I'll drink it. If it's white, I'll also drink it, but less happily. If it's rosé, I'm just as clueless as with the other two." I shrugged. "I've had good wine before, just not often. And I did like the rosé we had for our engagement dinner, which I actually recognized because Martin once ordered it when I went out to dinner with him and Kaitlyn."

Andreas stared at me, his smile lingering, then stood and held out his hand. "Come with me."

Before I could respond, he reached for my hand with his, pulling me from the booth. Predictably, I fought a jolt of hot awareness as Andreas took my hand, not in a let's-go-couples-bowling way, but in a very deliberate, fingers-laced, this-is-mine way. Aware that we were being observed (by both the host and the three women at the next table who were definitely ogling Andreas, but who could blame them?), I tried to walk like a person who belonged in expensive restaurants and not like an imposter lost in a Neiman Marcus while searching for the bathroom.

He led me through the open corridor that separated the main dining area from the wall of wines. There were racks and racks of bottles, arranged by country and varietal. Opposite the racks, a row of glass-doored dispensers with little digital readouts and shiny metal taps, like a self-serve soda fountain but with—you know—alcohol. The aroma of cold, damp stone and wood mingled with the acidic perfume of three dozen open reds.

Andreas guided me to the middle bank of dispensers. Bringing me with him, he slowly paced the row, perhaps cataloguing the options. The light was dim and golden. The way it caught in his hair reminded me of candles and firesides and all the other things I associated with fictional romantic rendezvous.

"Do you like robust flavors?" he asked, not breaking his relaxed stride. "Or softer, lighter?"

I considered the question. "I like my coffee black. Does that help?"

He almost smiled, head tilting as he read another label. "What about fruit? Berries or citrus?"

"Uh. Berries."

"Cherry, blackberry, raspberry, blueberry, or strawberry?"

"Cherry . . . ?"

"Dark chocolate, right?"

I nodded. "Yeah."

"And on pancakes, maple syrup rather than honey or powdered sugar."

I leaned back, giving him a suspicious side-eye. "How do you know that?"

Andreas grinned at me, his gaze sweeping over my face before he leaned close and whispered, "Let us try something bold, then."

*Yes. Let's.*

His words paired with the intonation of his voice had me imagining all sorts of dirty and delightful things. Making out behind a row of wine dispensers; his hand down the front of my jeans at the end cap; sex against the imported Tuscan wall.

Sadly, Andreas was clearly talking about the wine. But he did lift my hand and press his lips to the back of it, holding my eyes as he did so.

Then, he turned a bottle for me to read. I was instantly, irrationally aware of how much I'd missed this over the past two weeks, our pretend PDA, the way he invaded my personal space. My body felt lit from within and my hand, which should have been limp and dignified, instead twitched and then gripped his.

He seemed not to notice my hand spasm. Or if he did, he was very gracious about it. "This is a Brunello. Sangiovese grape. It is high in tannin."

I nodded, as if those words meant something. "Great. Let's try it."

He dispensed a tiny pour into a stemless glass and handed it to me. "Tell me what you taste."

I sipped. It tasted like wine. Like, a little more sophisticated than the six-dollar box, but still—wine. "It's fine."

He arched one brow. "Fine? No leather and tobacco?"

I tried another sip. Now that he'd said "leather and tobacco," it was all I could taste. "Huh. You're right. That's exactly it."

He turned to me. "Do you want me to pick a few different kinds of wine that are representative of different flavor profiles? Then you can eliminate the ones you do not care for, and we can narrow down which might be your favorite?"

It was adorable that he wanted to optimize the process for my enjoyment, but I wasn't really here for that. "We could do that," I said. "Or, we could just pour two glasses of random wine and compare notes."

His eyebrows lowered a smidge. "What if you select a wine you do not like?"

"I'll just drink it. No big deal."

Andreas seemed to stand straighter, as though taken aback by my words. "You should never have to accept something that you do not like or want, Samantha."

His tone was so earnest that I nearly snorted a laugh. I mean, come on. It was just wine.

And yet, I held back the laugh. His face was all gravity, as though I'd confessed to a grave personal failing.

Instead of saying exactly what was on my mind the second it occurred to me, I took a page out of his book and I let the moment breathe, gathering my thoughts before responding. "Andreas, it's not feasible to only go through life having exactly what I want. That's impractical and impossible."

He frowned, like I'd said something in need of urgent correction. "So, you drink the bitter wine? That is not acceptable, you deserve so much better than that."

His oddly touching statement was also vaguely annoying. "It's not that I want to drink bitter wine." I lowered my voice. "But if that's the drink life serves me, shouldn't I make the best of it? What would you have me do, throw the wine out and not drink at all? Isn't that like cutting off your nose to spite your face?"

He took the stemless wine glass from me and set it down on a nearby tray. He then gathered my hands in his and, frowning, his gaze somewhere between determined and concerned, he said, "Let me bring you all the wine."

Now I did snort laugh. "*All* the wine? You're going to bring me every bottle of wine that ever existed?"

"Yes." He nodded once firmly. "You do not deserve to make the best out of a situation, you only deserve the best situation. And then you choose which you like, and accept only those. You only drink the best wines, and the ones you actually want, from now on."

I wanted to argue that always getting exactly what one wanted eventually led to never being happy with anything. Humans needed struggle, we needed discontent, we needed something to strive for and rally against. Otherwise, where did character come from? And humor? Especially dark humor.

Andreas stepped closer. I felt the heat from his chest and the subtle pressure of his thumbs on the backs of my hands. The scent of his cologne and his rosemary shampoo invaded my senses, making my heart ping and my head light.

"Please," he said, not a demand but an entreaty. "Please let me do this for you. I want to do this for you."

I didn't have the vocabulary for the feeling that swept through me, but I nodded. "Sure," I said, voice steadier than my pulse. "Sure. I'll try your wines. But don't let me drink too much unless you want a repeat of what happened before Thanksgiving."

Andreas flashed a half smile. "These will be very short pours, so you can taste them. You do not need to drink them. There is a container on the table for those you do not wish to swallow."

I immediately censored a dirty joke about spitting and swallowing. Yes, I wanted to be more my true self without editing my words before I spoke them. But that didn't mean I needed Andreas to enjoy every single irritating thing about me.

A little bit of self-censoring goes a long way, and if more men understood this concept, the "male loneliness epidemic" in this country wouldn't exist.

But I digress.

"Return to the table." He released my hands after one last quick squeeze. "And I will select the first flight of wine for you."

Resigned to my fate of sampling expensive wine hand-selected by my incredibly hot, smart, and thoughtful fake fiancé—*woe is me*—I made my way back through the labyrinth of tables to our booth. Awareness prickled at my skin, and I scanned the other patrons as I passed, finding at least two parties watching me with a sort of fascinated detachment. Maybe they'd recognized Andreas? Or maybe wine people were like birders, always scanning for an odd species.

As I slid into the booth, my mind wandered, and I ended up replaying the tense car ride from the biology building to the wine bar.

When Tara and Andreas had returned to the car after their little talk on the curb, both had been stone-faced. At the time, I'd decided whatever business they'd discussed was best not brought up in the frosty air of the Mercedes. I figured I'd ask about it later, maybe after a glass of wine, when Andreas's tongue was looser and his inhibitions adequately marinated.

I liked Tara. A lot. I'd been attending her kickboxing class three days a week and loving every session. I'd also decided, once Andreas and I were no longer living together, I'd ask Tara if she wanted or needed a roommate. Obviously, if I inherited Oskar Kristiansen's shares of Genetix, I would be able to afford a place of my own. But I liked having roommates. I didn't like living alone.

Andreas appeared at the table with the same ease he did everything, this time trailed by a server holding a long tray with twelve stemless glasses of wine, each filled to the level of a swallow or two. The server set the tray on the table with a flourish, handed us a small notepad for tracking our favorites, then melted away.

Instead of sitting across from me, Andreas slid into my side of the booth, his body angled so his thigh pressed against mine, which made my heart twist. Before I'd recovered, he picked up my hand, thumb stroking my knuckles, and then, as if it were the most natural thing in the world, kissed the back of my hand. Again.

The effect of this touch paired with his closeness was chemical and immediate. I fought the urge to squirm, instead forcing myself to focus on the wine tray.

Once more I found myself asking what this was. Was he pretending still? Or was this real? I was so confused. And every time I convinced myself that Andreas was flirting, or truly interested in me, I'd gain a little distance and perspective and talk myself out of that belief.

Was this what other people did when they really liked someone? And if so, how did one exit this spin cycle of surging hopes and soul-eating self-doubt?

Cutting into my disordered thoughts, Andreas started with the first glass, describing it in a way that made me wonder if he'd studied as a sommelier. "Pinot noir from Oregon. Silky, with notes of black cherry and spice." He handed it to me, then watched with rapt attention as I sipped.

The flavor of the red wine burst over my tongue, though I lacked words to describe it. Peeking at Andreas's expectant expression, I sighed, setting it down. "It's good, I like it. But if you're waiting for me to tell you what it tastes like, I'm going to say 'good wine.'"

He smiled. "That is great, that is what I am hoping for. You tell me, good or bad. And that is enough."

I narrowed my eyes. "Are you sure? Because I can pretend."

His grin widened and he bit his bottom lip, eyes dancing over me. "What would you say? If you were going to pretend?"

Effecting a snooty and very bad pseudo-British accent, I cleared my throat and sat taller in the booth. "Notes of ripe candied melons sifted with pickled pepper residue and bee's anus dusted with honeysuckle pollen."

Andreas's eyes widened as I spoke and so did his grin, his features betraying his expectant anticipation. When I finished, he tossed his head back and laughed *heartily*. I mean, the man chortled. I set my elbow on the table and covered my mouth with my hand while I watched him, barely holding in my own laughter while also enjoying his.

When he gave his eyes back to me, they were shining, and he wiped away tears of hilarity while sniffing. "Oh my goodness. You are—I love how funny you are, Samantha. I love it so much. Please, never change."

Inhaling deeply to stave off the wave of nervous happiness, I shrugged, but discovered I had nothing to say to his praise because my brain was stuck on the word *love.*

He loves me!

*No, doofus. He loves how funny you are.*

. . . or, was this also part of the act? Was this still part of a performance?

I deflated, my confusion circling the drain of my confidence. I really hated this, not knowing what was real and what was fake between us. I needed to talk to Kaitlyn. I needed a sounding board who wasn't my therapist.

My therapist would tell me to be brave. SQUARE!

But Kaitlyn could be counted upon to advocate for caution. She'd been in a similar situation with Martin before they'd married. They hadn't fake dated, but she'd felt confused about his feelings for her, whether they were real or imagined. I now had newfound sympathy for my friend and her plight.

While I stewed in my whiplashing mood, Andreas moved on to the next wine, and the next, and over the course of an hour, we'd sampled all twelve wines. Sometimes I could catch a hint of whatever note he described—"graphite," "earth," "stone fruit"—but other times it was simply "good," "bad," "sour," or "sweet."

At some point during the second flight, my inhibitions dropped just enough for me to stop overthinking whether Andreas's behavior was fiction or nonfiction. I allowed myself to observe the apparent ease with which Andreas had settled next to me. His hand, still entwined with mine, remained on my thigh throughout, except when he needed it to refill my water or jot down a quick check mark next to a favorite on the notepad. I realized, with a slight start, that I hadn't felt this warm or this cozy in a long, long time.

Even if it was all ultimately for show, it was nice.

At the end of the second flight, Andreas ordered a glass of my favorite

—some big, juicy blend from Paso Robles, which I promptly forgot the name of but remembered for its immediate, heady effect—and sat back to let me savor it. I nursed the glass, cheeks warm, pleasantly buzzed but not even close to drunk.

"I'll drink this glass slowly," I said. "In fact, I should probably have more water."

He reached over, topped off my water glass from the bottle, then handed it back. "It is good to hydrate."

I smiled easily, then watched as his face shifted from what looked like playful to intent.

Andreas angled his body more toward mine and, with a gentle seriousness, asked, "So, this James Nieminen who is now your PI. Why is he your PI?"

I froze, not out of fear but because I wasn't expecting the pivot to Real Talk. But it was clear Andreas had been turning the question over in his mind for a while.

I took a steadying sip of water. "I've already told you this."

He frowned. "You did?"

"Yeah."

His frown increased. "I apologize, but could you tell me again, please?"

Sighing, I fiddled with my wineglass. "Do you want the short version, or long?"

"Start with the short," he said, voice soft.

I reminded him of Tobias threatening me at the university; how he'd then pulled strings to freeze Dr. Hauser's funding; how, with Hauser's accounts on hold, I'd been transferred to Nieminen's lab because James had the only opening and was willing to cover part of my funding.

Andreas listened, features composed and unreadable, though his eyes seemed to darken when I mentioned Tobias and James. Or maybe his eyelids just seemed heavier.

When I finished, he took a sip of his own wine, then set the glass down with a quiet finality. "I am sorry."

I was thrown by the apology. "Why are you sorry? You didn't freeze Dr. Hauser's funding."

He shook his head, the smallest smile at the edge of his lips, but not a happy one. "I am sorry you have to deal with Tobias and Henrik and this

Nieminen, and that my actions and wishes instigated all this trouble for you." He glanced around the bar, then back at me. "Samantha, let me know if you want me to get rid of him. I will leave it to you."

Now I frowned, blinking once. The way he'd said "get rid of him," I didn't know what he meant.

"Are you—" I shook my head, trying to clear it of wine and the cobwebs induced by my proximity to Sexy Andreas. "Are you saying you'll get rid of Dr. Nieminen if I ask you to? Like, remove him from his position in the department? Is that what you're saying?"

He nodded, his mouth opening, giving me the sense he wanted to say more. But then he pressed his lips together in a flat line. I watched his chest rise and fall with a deep breath before he finally settled on, "You let me know. I will do whatever you want."

# [ 13 ]

## ADULT FEMALE AND MALE REPRODUCTIVE SYSTEMS

***Samantha***

We left the wine bar and walked through the lightly falling snow, neither of us in a hurry. The air felt more like powdered sugar than ice; it didn't bite so much as dust and then vanish. The only sound was the click of my boots on the concrete and Andreas's steady, careful pace beside me. I wore his left glove, which swallowed my hand, and he gripped my right hand in his bare left, tucking it deep into the pocket of his coat. It was possibly the most effective means of preventing frostbite ever invented, and it was also unfairly cute.

Most of the world had clocked out for the evening. Rows of apartments stretched above us, with windows like little yellow beehives, people moving and living inside each frame. For blocks, it was just us and the odd taxi, the hum of the city distant and muted by the snow.

We didn't talk. I kept waiting for Andreas to say something, but his eyes were on the street, like he was trying to memorize the shapes of the shadows or the traffic cones, or maybe he was playing some internal game of urban chess, seeing moves no one else could. He only broke the silence when we turned onto his block, pausing to scan the avenue up and down.

"Is it too early to put up Christmas decorations?" he asked with a seriousness that made me look twice.

I followed his line of sight to the lampposts, which were now draped in silver garlands and had huge, cartoonish snowflakes affixed at the tops. Every other building had pine wreaths or string lights over the awnings. Now that I took a moment to notice, it struck me as magical.

"It's the first Friday in December," I pointed out. "Christmas is less than twenty days away."

He nodded, absorbing this information with an almost anthropological interest. "What do you want to do for Christmas?"

It wasn't the kind of question I'd expected. "Do you not have any family you want to spend it with?"

He shook his head. "No."

I studied his profile. *No lie detected.* "Not even on your mom's side?"

Andreas considered this for a moment, then shook his head again. "No."

We crossed the street in tandem. I tried to remember if I'd ever actually spent Christmas with anyone in my adult life, or if it was always a hodgepodge of roommate dinner parties and Skype calls with Kaitlyn. "I go to mass on my own," I said. "And then, not much. If any of my roommates are around, we'll have dinner together. Kaitlyn is usually in California with her parents."

"What do you think about getting a tree for the apartment?" He made the words sound like he was proposing a research collaboration.

The last time I'd had a Christmas tree was when Kaitlyn and I lived together in our first off-campus apartment. I'd made gingerbread cookies and burned half of them, and Kaitlyn had decorated the tree entirely in purple tinsel, mostly because she'd gotten it for free. We'd even tried to make eggnog from scratch.

I'd forgotten how much I missed that, the precious little rituals.

I squeezed Andreas's hand inside his pocket. "Sure. Yeah. Let's get a tree."

His smile was small but instantaneous. But then he tore his eyes from mine and wiped all expression from his features while clearing his throat, eventually saying, "Then we will."

We arrived at the glass-and-steel awning of his building. Mr. Costa, the doorman on duty, held the door and smiled as we passed.

"Samantha. Hello," he greeted me warmly.

I returned his smile. "Mr. Costa. I hope you're staying warm."

Shifting his attention to Andreas, he offered a more formal sounding, "It is good to have you back, Mr. Kristiansen."

Andreas gave the man a small nod and responded with a simple, "Thank you."

We walked through the marble lobby and waited for the elevator, Andreas still holding my hand in his pocket as he glanced over his shoulder toward the front of the building. "Do you know the doorman?" he asked me.

My cheeks were warm, and it wasn't just the change in temperature. "Yes. Well, sort of. I introduced myself to all of them over the last two weeks and brought whoever was on duty hot tea and cookies in the morning when I left." Lifting my chin toward the building's entrance, I explained, "That's Mr. Costa. His wife works at the United Nations and he's a sixth-generation New Yorker. He gave me some good tips on the best Puerto Rican bakeries near our—I mean, your apartment."

Andreas nodded lightly, as though absorbing this information and deconstructing it into pieces. His gaze grew unfocused as he did so and he repositioned our hands in his pocket, fitting our fingers together more tightly.

When the elevator arrived, we stepped inside. Still, he kept my hand, holding it in his, our threaded fingers tucked in the pocket of his coat like we were smuggling contraband affection.

"Will you help me decorate the tree?" Andreas pressed the button for our floor.

"Yes." I smiled despite myself, and my reflection in the elevator's mirrored wall looked almost deranged with how wide the smile was. I couldn't remember the last time I'd felt so thoroughly flustered by someone simply standing close to me.

"Do you get any time off around Christmas?" he asked, tone conversational.

"Yes. The week between Christmas and New Year's."

"I have a tournament right after Christmas." Voice neutral, he glanced at me, then away. "In Rome."

There was a catch in my chest. I tried to ignore it, but it was there. A twinge of discomfort. "Oh?"

He didn't say anything more. But he did remove our joined hands from his pocket and look at them, as if calculating the odds of something he didn't want to say aloud.

The elevator deposited us at his floor, and as we exited. My palm had suddenly gone sweaty at the continued discomfort in my chest. I gently withdrew my hand, telling myself I'd done it so he could unlock the apartment. He did with his thumbprint, then gestured me in first, ever the gentleman.

Inside, the air was warm and smelled faintly of the cookies I'd made earlier in the day for the morning doorman, Mr. O'Brein. Andreas wordlessly helped me with my coat. Then I unzipped my boots, also without speaking. The mood between us suddenly felt introspective instead of comfortable.

"Thank you for letting me borrow your glove," I said, trying to mimic his good manners. Pulling off the borrowed glove, I handed it over to him.

Eyes on the offering in my hand, he took it, holding both gloves in one hand. "You should come with me. To Rome."

Looking up at him, I inspected his features. That mask he wore when we were alone together was now firmly back in place. Stoic and bored.

"For the tournament," he went on as though to clarify. "Since you have time off work, would it not look strange for you to stay here alone? We need to be careful and convince my brothers this is real between us. I do not think you want to open the door to suspicion. If you were my fiancée, you would travel with me." He set his jaw, the line of his mouth slanted downward.

The change in his demeanor from friendly to standoffish knocked the wind out of me. Not only that, but his reason for suggesting that I go to Rome with him—not because he wanted me there, but because we needed to keep up the charade—made my stomach turn cold. I'd been feeling so light, so comfortable in my little holiday fantasy, and now the idea of being together with Andreas in Rome simply to perpetuate our fake engagement sent all those swirling hopes straight down the drain.

*This is all fake. And everything tonight, all the touching and joking and closeness, has also been fake.*

My throat felt tight and I didn't trust myself to speak quite yet, so I made a short humming noise and stalled by lining my boots up neatly in the closet. Needing space, I then walked to the kitchen, filled a glass of water, and sipped it slowly. I wasn't drunk, but the leftover buzz from the wine made everything feel dreamlike, a little less real.

To put it bluntly, I didn't trust myself not to say something I'd regret.

A moment later, I sensed Andreas enter the kitchen behind me. A quick glance over my shoulder revealed him hovering at the entrance and leaning against the doorjamb.

He waited until I finished the glass, then said, "I am sorry."

I twisted at the waist, inspecting him again. He still wore the same expression, eyes half-lidded, gaze unreadable.

I faced the sink again. "What are you sorry for?"

"I overstepped, asking you to come with me to Rome. Of course, you should spend your free time as you see fit."

I laughed, a short, confused sound. I was too tired to keep up with him, his offers and apologies. So, I made another humming noise, hoping he would interpret my "Mmm" as he saw fit, and I rinsed out the water glass.

I didn't know how to exist in this gray area between what was pretend and what was real. No matter how much of a crush I had on Andreas, the constant confusion wore on me. What was performance and what was genuine?

*Some of it has to be genuine . . . right?*

Muddled and too much in my own head, I walked past him into the living room, plopping down onto the couch. He followed but didn't sit, instead standing at the edge of the rug, hands shoved in his pockets. I sensed his eyes on me, but this time I didn't glance at him to confirm.

It was strange, this behavior from him. Andreas was the picture of confidence and charisma in public, a master of social and literal chess, every move and every word calculated yet perfect. But in the privacy of his own apartment, when he had no audience, he withdrew into himself. He was quiet, almost sullen. The difference gave me whiplash.

Eventually, he spoke. "What are you thinking?"

Not wishing to share my actual thoughts, I searched for a subject change. My gaze snagged on the errant remote on the coffee table and I picked it up. "What does this remote go to? Both Tara and I tried using it and nothing happened."

He crossed to me and extended his hand. "May I?"

I gave him the remote, careful not to touch him. Andreas pressed a series of buttons and the large glass window that overlooked the city instantly went from clear to solid black, a privacy setting I didn't know existed. He pressed another button and a TV lifted from the floor, rising smoothly until it faced us.

I stared. "Whoa. So that's where the TV is." *What else is hidden in this apartment that I cannot see?*

In my peripheral vision, I saw him nod, then set the remote back on the table. He finally sat down on the sofa, albeit several feet from me. The distance felt like a gulf.

Again, I sensed him watching me before he spoke. "I would like to get a tree with you, for the apartment."

I looked at him then, confused by the repeated request. "Didn't we agree we would? Downstairs?"

Andreas set his elbows on his knees, leaning forward, and studying his hands. "It is hard to know what is true when we are in public. I did not know for certain if you meant what you said, or if it was for show."

A tingling heat disrupted my blanket of numbness and I turned, drawing my legs up. I felt a flicker of hope. He'd just broached the topic I hadn't been brave enough to bring up, and now I felt like he'd given me the perfect opening to clarify things without sacrificing too much of my pride.

"I'm actually really glad you said that." Staring at the pattern on the pillow, I attempted to choose my words wisely. "I—uh—feel the same. It's hard to know, when we're in public, what's real and what's not. I'm not sure if—for example—when you held and kissed my hand at the wine bar, was that something you felt like you had to do? Or was it something you, uh, wanted to do . . . ?"

A blush rose over his cheeks, giving off that same bashful aura from weeks ago, and he peeked at me. "If I do anything you do not like while we are in public, I hope you would tell me. And if I have made you uncomfortable, I am sincerely sorry. It is never my intention. I know we are being watched, and it is important for us to be convincing. But if it bothers you, or feels too real, I can—hmm—dial it back."

I examined him as he spoke, and the coldness returned in my stomach, extinguishing the earlier tingle of hope. My heart fell through my ribs. *Ah. I see.* I'd misunderstood. This was a warning, right? To remind me that all the flirting and touching was just for show, that I shouldn't read into it.

I breathed a short sigh that probably sounded like a laugh, but it was actually a sort of melancholy relief. At least now I knew. "Don't worry, Andreas. I know you're a gentleman. And furthermore, I know it's fake and you see me only as a friend. I won't get carried away with the fantasy or whatever."

He visibly stiffened, his eyes snapping to mine. "I—pardon? I only see you as a friend?"

I busied myself by standing and refolding a throw blanket unnecessarily. "What? Are you saying you don't even see me as a friend?" I tried to sound teasing, but the ache in my chest made it come out brittle.

He stared at me, wide-eyed and lips slightly parted, like my statement or my reaction was something he couldn't compute. I immediately regretted speaking.

Scrambling to break the tension, I wracked my brain for a joke. Eventually, I shrugged and said, "I guess you believe fathers and daughters can't be friends, hmm? The moment that adoption paperwork was filed, you turned into an authoritarian parent. Figures. *Yeesh.*"

Andreas stood abruptly, as if propelled by a sudden jolt of electricity. He was suddenly all nervous energy. Staring at me, he tore his gaze from mine, turned away, then back.

Finally, he blurted out, "It would not be a good idea for us—for you—to get involved for real. Not now. You shouldn't be—you should not think of getting involved with me that way."

The words hit me hard, and the rejection clothed as a warning stung like a motherfucking hornet. "I understand. No worries." My throat was full of rocks and I couldn't speak any further without risking stupid tears. Thus, I grabbed my phone and headed for my bedroom.

I heard him follow, his footsteps soft but determined. He stopped at the threshold of my room. Meanwhile, I found someone—Tara probably—had brought my backpack into my bedroom. She'd likely dropped it off after taking Andreas and me to the wine bar earlier. I assumed she'd then collected her things and gone home to her own apartment now that Andreas had returned. No need for her to babysit me anymore.

I picked up the backpack and dug inside it for no reason other than to focus my attention somewhere.

*A pack of tissues.*

*That pen I thought I'd lost.*

*A ruler. Why do I have ruler? How long has this been in here?*

"You do not want to be with me," he said, voice low and rough from behind me. "Please, trust me on this."

I nodded, not looking at him. "Got it. Message received."

He made a strangled sound, something between a sigh and a groan, and stepped into my room and into my side vision. He seemed to struggle with the words before settling on, "You should not be my friend. I am not worthy of even that. Samantha, you deserve—you deserve everything. I am not good enough for you."

He reached for my fingers. Reflexively, I yanked them away. "Okay. Like I said, message received. You can leave now."

He covered his face with his hands, then let them fall, the movement drawing my attention. His eyes were red-rimmed, his jaw set in a way I'd never seen. When he looked at me, I saw a storm of emotion. Maybe longing? Definitely pain and regret. And something else I couldn't name. Or maybe none of it.

Where correctly deciphering Andreas and his motivations were concerned, I didn't trust myself.

He seemed to wrestle with himself for a long moment, then said, "I want to be your friend, of course, and I have wanted you—to be your friend again—for so long. But if I am allowed to be honest and selfish, I want to be so much more than that to you, for you. You are—you are my —I know you will never—my father and my brothers—and I would never ask you to—I would never ask that you make any commitment to me when you do not—when I am—"

I tried to parse his broken thoughts and sentences, the words a stop-start rush of what appeared to be completely unplanned statements. What I could gather: He did like me; he wanted to be with me, but he didn't think he was good enough for me? Because of his family, because of what his family had done to mine.

I took a step forward, swallowing around my own surging hope, and lowered my voice, a counterweight of calm to his chaotic speech. "Andreas, I know you are not like your family. I know you aren't one of them. You're trying to help me."

He grabbed my hands, holding them tightly, and closed his eyes. Andreas shook his head, his jaw tight, but didn't let me go.

I kept talking, hoping my words would make a difference. "I would never put you in the same category as your family."

He looked at me then, his face etched with misery. "I do not deserve you."

I sighed. "Well, I'm not giving myself to you. It's not like we're really engaged. And, to be clear, I'm not asking for a commitment from you, nor am I offering one. In fact, I'm not sure I'll ever want a committed relationship with anyone. I never have before. But, allow me to be just as honest here, I am *extremely* attracted to you."

Andreas grew very still, his eyes searching mine, wide and frantic. They seemed to be filled with hope and reluctance in equal measure.

So, I added, "I like you. *A lot*. I think about you all the time. I missed you when you were gone and checked my phone obsessively for your messages. I've never felt this way about anyone. And, so, the idea of a romantic commitment is frightening to me. So, if you're not ready for one, that's a relief."

He seemed to stop breathing, and the raw desire in his gaze made my heart soar.

"We don't have to commit to each other," I said soothingly, lifting my hand to cup his face. He leaned into my touch, his cheek hot. "But we are here in this apartment together for the foreseeable future, and I don't see why we have to torture ourselves by holding back what it seems like we both want."

His breath came shallow, his gaze fixed on my mouth. "What are you proposing?" he asked, voice barely above a whisper.

I took a deep breath, sent a quick prayer upward for emotional bravery, and told him the truth.

"We both agree, we'd like to be friends, right? And we both agree, we want more than that. So how about we try something low pressure? How about being friends with, you know . . . benefits?"

[ 14 ]

# SEXUAL DIFFERENTIATION AND DEVELOPMENT

***Samantha***

Andreas stared at me as though he waited for me to continue, as though *friends with benefits* couldn't be the entirety of my proposal. The way his eyes roved over my face, my neck, my chest—where my heart was hammering—left no ambiguity as to what he was thinking. Or, rather, what he wanted.

*Say yes.*

The air between us felt thick with tension, the silence heavy. It elongated, pulling the moment taut, stretching it until my nerves began to singe with anticipation. And, honestly, lots of lust. LOTS OF LUST!

Andreas was so sexy, so epically attractive in every possible way. I wanted him, all of him, so badly. I recognized my suggestion had been a tad reckless. Feelings—clearly, on both sides—were already involved. But he didn't think he deserved me and I was afraid of commitment. Thus, other than a no-strings, friends-with-benefits situationship, what was left? Walk away from each other? Call the whole thing off?

I was about to say something—anything, a joke, a question, a dumb comment about snow—when Andreas swallowed hard and rasped out, "I have never done that before."

He said it like a confession, every word precise and heavy.

135

"You mean friends with benefits?" I kept my voice gentle, like I was talking to a nervous undergrad on their first day of lab.

He nodded, very slowly.

"What about a one-night stand? Or hookups?"

He shook his head. I felt a jolt of affection for him. He looked both vulnerable and a little resentful. The admission about his lack of experience with noncommitted relationships had obviously cost him something.

Since he'd been vulnerable, I figured the least I could do was meet him halfway. Tilting my head, I studied him and asked, "Are you interested? With me?"

His answer came so fast, so automatically, that it had to be true. "Yes. Of course."

I smiled, I couldn't help it, the tension breaking for just a second. I genuinely hadn't expected that level of urgency or conviction, not from him. Perhaps he'd been restraining himself even more than I had.

Andreas watched me, and I thought I detected—no, I was sure I detected—a note of disbelief as he asked, "Are you interested? In me?"

Instinct, or maybe bad habits, wanted me to tease him. To drag it out, say something about how he was obviously the sexiest thing in a thousand-mile radius and he knew it. But if he currently felt even a tenth as brittle as I had moments ago in the living room, I didn't want to contribute to prolonging his suffering.

So instead, I stepped close and dropped my voice to just above a whisper. "Absolutely. So, why don't we give it a try? Hmm?" Unable to help myself, I pressed a light, teasing kiss to his lips, aware that this was our very first kiss without an audience. My stomach filled with rainbows and unicorns when Andreas swayed forward upon my retreat, as though his mouth were magnetized to mine.

"We're both adults," I continued, whispering, wanting this to be the real secret between us. "I want you. You want me. We already live together."

He remained silent. But in his defense, he looked entirely overwhelmed. I got the sense he half expected me to take back the offer, or say, "Kidding, this is a joke." Or maybe he thought this moment might be a dream and he was doing his best to stay asleep a little longer.

I reached up and cupped his face, pulling him gently into another kiss —just a brush, a soft invitation, nothing more. But when my lips caught his, he gasped, and then he took my hand in his, squeezing and pressing it to his jaw as though to anchor himself.

When I broke the kiss, his eyes were wide and raw with emotion and such visceral longing, my heart stuttered. He wanted this. Clearly, he did. So why was he still hesitating?

"Do you want me?" I asked. Perhaps he needed to say it out loud.

"Yes." It was a whisper, but it might as well have been a roar. "Very much," he added, as though he couldn't help himself.

The thrill that shot through me was electric. I wanted to laugh, to leap into his arms, to do every stupid thing I'd always made fun of in romantic movies and TV shows. Instead, I withdrew my hand from his face and brought it to the first button of my shirt. I unbuttoned the first button, then the second, then the third.

He watched my hands with a predator's focus. Abruptly, with a shake of his head—like he was physically shaking off restraint—he caught my wrists and stilled them. "May we—do you mind if we go slow?" he said, voice rough and uncertain.

My fingers went still on the fourth button. I looked up at him, searching his face. "Not at all."

His eyes dropped to my mouth again. "May I kiss you?"

"Please do," I replied, and this time it was me who leaned in, arms going around his neck. He responded instantly, his hands slipping to my hips, then my lower back, and then he pulled me to him, tight enough that I could feel the heat of his body everywhere we touched.

The kiss was different than the ones we'd performed in public. Softer, but also somehow more desperate. Desperate in the way one is desperate for air after being underwater for too long. He cradled my face in both hands, thumbs brushing my cheekbones as though trying to memorize the shape of me. And I realized there was nothing, absolutely nothing, fake about the way his mouth moved over mine, or how he shivered when I pressed up against his chest. Nor, I further realized, had there been anything fake in our previous kisses. He'd wanted me just as much then, and my heart cracked a little at how he must've suffered, waiting for me, pretending it was all pretend.

I felt his cock grow and lengthen, hard and insistent against my stomach, and couldn't help but smile into the kiss. When he pulled away for air, his breathing was ragged, his eyes glassy.

"I'm—I'm sorry," he stammered, as though his body's response was something to apologize for.

"Don't be," I said, and with one smooth movement, I reached down and slid my palm against the front of his pants.

Andreas's mouth felt open in obvious and silent shock and his entire body shook. His eyes fluttered closed, and for a second, I thought he might actually pass out.

"Do you want me to take care of this for you?" I murmured, grinning at the honesty and intensity of his response, fingers pressing lightly against the ridge beneath his zipper.

His eyebrows pulled together in something close to pain, and he nodded once, dazed.

He was so hot, so wound up, I wondered if it would take nothing at all for him to reach climax. I felt a rush of heady power at the thought, at the evidence of his desire for me. But I didn't want to overwhelm him; if anything, I wanted to see just how slowly I could make him unravel.

Dropping to my knees was not a move I'd ever considered especially romantic, but for some reason, doing it for him, in this context, felt like doing it for *us*. A particular kind of intimacy, one I'd never experienced, where giving meant receiving. Slowly, I unbuckled his belt, looking up at him as I did, and when I popped the button of his slacks, he flinched, like the sound was a gunshot.

"Wait," he said, voice strangled, eyes the size of quarters. "What— what are you doing?"

I grinned. "Taking care of this," I said, echoing my earlier words.

"You don't need to—you shouldn't—" he started, but I cut him off with a gentle tug at the waistband of his boxer briefs.

"Give you a blow job? What if I want to?" I teased, stroking my hands up and down his thighs. The fabric was expensive and soft, but the muscle beneath was hard as stone.

He said something then—something I didn't understand, a series of rapid syllables that sounded distinctly not English. Italian, maybe. I liked the way it sounded, dark and desperate.

Andreas bent down and forced me to stand, pulling me gently by the elbows until I was back on my feet. His face was red, his jaw clenched tight, and he covered his face with both hands again.

This was not the reaction I'd been expecting. This was beyond shy, beyond bashful. This looked like shame.

Holding my hands close to my chest, I asked haltingly, "Are you okay?"

He nodded, but didn't move his hands. "I have never done that before, either," he admitted, voice muffled.

I stared at him, stunned. "What? You've never received a blow job?" It came out louder than intended, but I couldn't help it. I was genuinely shocked.

Andreas shook his head, still not looking at me.

Who were these women who weren't giving Andreas blow jobs? I mean, maybe one or two of his previous relationships would've deferred, sure. No shade, no judgment. But *all* of them? Every single one? How was that possible?

I frowned, unable to let the question go, and was about to ask how many girlfriends he'd had, when another thought occurred to me.

I stiffened, suspicion smacking me across the face like a brick to the brain. "Andreas," I said, feeling unaccountably breathless. "Andreas, are you a virgin?"

His fingers speared violently through his hair, then laced together behind his neck. He dipped his chin, hiding his face. Silence.

I didn't know what to say. But now I understood what he'd meant by going slow. He didn't mean no intercourse. He meant kissing. Making out. Over the clothes. Eventually rounding bases, taking our time like we were new to this.

Because he was.

"I get it now," I said, softly, stepping closer. "I am sorry. I will go slow. *Actually* slow this time. Not, Mustang slow, but Cadillac-Fleetwood-75-driven-by-my-grandma-in-the-left-hand-lane slow."

He didn't answer but he did huff a laugh. It held humor, but it also held a fair amount of bitterness. He was so tense, so plainly mortified, that I felt a pang of protectiveness.

I reached out and pulled his hands away from his neck, encouraging him to lift his head. His cheeks were flushed, and his eyes were bright with what looked like frustration. I pressed a kiss to his cheek, unable to help myself, and then another featherlight one to his lips.

He immediately chased my mouth and kissed me back with a hunger

I'd never felt from anyone before. He grabbed me, held me tight, and for a moment, the world spun. It was dizzying, the way he kissed me. No hesitation, just pure, unfiltered need. Like he wanted to hide himself in the kiss, escape his feelings.

But I did break away first, gasping for much-needed air. But I also broke the kiss because my knees felt wobbly and I didn't trust them to hold my weight if he kept kissing me like that. I backed him up until his legs met the bed. He followed where I led, hands grasping on my body. And when I encouraged him to sit down, he did, eyes never leaving mine.

Straddling his lap felt normal and natural, perhaps because we'd already found ourselves in this position twice. "We're going to go slow, okay?" I said. "I'll go real slow. We're just going to make out."

He nodded, eyes wide, so full of trust it made my heart ache.

"If at any time you feel uncomfortable, or I'm going too fast, just say —uh—checkmate. Okay?"

Some of the haze of panic cleared from his eyes, replaced by a tiny flare of amused confidence. "Should be easy for you," I added, "since you say it so often."

He gave a miniscule smile, finally meeting my gaze fully. There was so much in his face—relief, gratitude, hesitation, concern, and something that looked suspiciously like awe.

Settling more firmly onto his lap, I kept my hands light on his shoulders and kissed him softly, then trailed a line of kisses down his neck, lingering at the pulse that pounded just below his jaw.

He groaned, the sound vibrating through his chest. His fingers dug into my lower back, strong but tentative, as if he were afraid I might break. Or disappear. Or change my mind.

He slid one hand up, slow and hesitant, to the back of my head, threading his fingers through my hair and pulling me back to his mouth. The kiss was again urgent, teeth and tongue, but always gentle. Always careful.

I could feel his hands drifting toward my chest, then diverting at the last moment to my hips, my back. I got the sense that he was strategizing every touch, trying to calculate the optimal sequence.

Pulling back, breathless, I said, "Just do what feels good. You don't have to plan every move. I want you, okay? And I'll tell you if I want you to stop. Trust me."

He stared at me for a moment, and in those seconds I saw every flicker of worry, every strategy, every last-ditch plan run through his mind and get torched by the pure, incandescent need that was currently holding him hostage. Then he surrendered to it, to me, with a short, helpless sound, and kissed me again. Deeper this time, but no longer frantic.

I let him take the lead for a while, marveling at the way he seemed almost shocked by his own desire, the way his hands gripped my waist tighter than before, as if anchoring himself to a reality that was quickly coming apart at the seams. But curiosity—and maybe a little cruelty, and horniness—compelled me to see what would happen if I just . . . nudged things along.

I took his hand, which was clinging to my hip like a lifeline, and guided it upward, sliding it over the curve of my rib cage and settling it directly onto my breast, over the fabric of my shirt and bra. He froze, eyes wide, mouth parted in a stunned little O. For a long, silent moment he simply stared at where our hands met, as if he'd never quite believed this was something I would allow him to do outside of his daydreams.

But then, with a cautiousness so at odds with the ferocity of his earlier kisses, he began to move. His palm flexed against me, fingers curling, thumb gently tracing slow, painstaking circles that set every one of my nerve endings on high alert. The sensation was at once infuriatingly gentle and almost unbearably intense. I couldn't help it. I shivered, and my own hands clamped down hard on his shoulders for balance.

He watched that reaction, catalogued it, and then started to experiment. Testing out a firmer squeeze, a change in pressure, the migration of his thumb along the edge of my bra. I realized, with a stab of something strangely tender, that he was learning me, in the same way you'd learn the layout of a new city or the steps of a complicated dance. He was methodical, deliberate, but never cold. It was the chess genius at work, except instead of pawns and bishops he was strategizing flesh and bone.

It shouldn't have been so hot. But it was. *Fuck.* It was.

He tilted his head, eyes still on my chest, and then looked up at me as if seeking permission before adding his other hand to the equation. I gave an encouraging nod, just to see what he'd do next. The answer was a lot. He slipped both hands under my shirt and ran them up my back, fiddling with the clasp of my bra.

I was about to offer to undo it myself when I felt it unhook. And then, after a moment's hesitation, he glided his hand back around front, under my shirt and bra, skin meeting skin for the first time. He sucked in a sharp breath, almost a gasp, and swore in what I assumed was Italian—another one of those dark, beautiful series of liquid words that made me want to bite his mouth just to taste the sound of it.

Perhaps he was cursing at how good it felt, how badly he wanted it, despite all his previous restraint. I was suddenly, weirdly proud of myself, for being so tempting that this tightly controlled mountain of restraint had crumbled. I wanted to push him farther, just to see how far he'd go, but I held back. *Go slow.*

He kissed me again, softer now but less careful, like he'd decided to stop analyzing and just experience. His hips rolled, the movement plainly involuntarily, pressing his hardness against me. There was nothing tentative about it, nothing shy. The move was pure instinct, and the sound he made—low and ragged, vibrating up from deep in his chest—was the hottest thing I'd ever heard. Period.

My own body responded on autopilot, pressing down, grinding into him, and I could feel the wetness gathering between my thighs, slick and hot and insistent. The tension in the room spiked, and I could tell from the way his hands shook that he was fighting a losing battle with himself.

I bent my head, mouth tracing a line from his jaw down the column of his neck, pausing at the hollow of his clavicle just to see if he'd shiver the way I had. He did, and then some, his hands tightening at my sides, dragging my shirt up high enough that the cool air hit my bare skin and made everything sharper, more urgent.

He muttered something in Italian, and I laughed, feeling drunk on the entire situation. I licked the pulse at his throat, tasting salt and adrenaline, and he groaned again.

His hands roamed, greedy now, cupping my breasts, kneading and stroking until I was practically vibrating. And when he slid his hands under my bra again and roughly pinched my nipples, I gasped so hard, my cheeks flooded with heat.

He paused, panic flickering briefly across his face, but I shook my head and kissed him hard, reassuring. "Don't stop," I whispered, and the relief in his eyes was almost comical.

The next few minutes (hours? years? time was a flow state) were a blur of hands and mouths, skin and heat, the two of us tumbling and rear-ranging ourselves until I straddled him, shirtless and flushed.

He was still in his slacks and sweater, but barely—his belt was off, button undone, zipper halfway down. I hooked my fingers in the waist-band, tugged, and he lifted his hips automatically to help me slide them down, never letting me go. He wore black boxer briefs, and the sight of him, tented and straining against the fabric, made me lick my lips.

*One day,* I promised myself, *one day you will be my popsicle and I will lick you like there's a heatwave.*

"Is this okay?" I asked, pausing, giving him one last out. Because with so few layers between us, an orgasm was coming for one of us. Actually, probably for both.

He nodded, breathless, eyes gone pitch-black with want.

I leaned down and kissed him, slow and deep, while my hands slid lower, exploring the cut of his hips, the sinew of his thighs. He trembled under my touch, every muscle in his body taut as a violin string.

I pressed my palm against him, over the cotton, and he arched up into my hand, gasping. I stroked him through the briefs, gentle at first, then harder, and he clung to me, one hand wrapped in my hair, the other digging into the flesh of my back, his mouth on my breast, wet and sucking.

He whispered my name, not once but over and over, each time softer, more desperate. "Samantha, are you—are you sure? Samantha . . ." It was like he was terrified this moment would vanish if he let go, and the sound of it did something to me that I couldn't quite articulate.

I slid my hand under the waistband, a new skin meeting skin, and wrapped my fingers around him. He was hot and hard and already leaking, and the way he shuddered when I stroked him was the purest thing I'd ever felt.

He tried to reciprocate—tried to unzip my jeans, to touch me, to explore—but I batted his hands away with a grin. "Let me take care of you," I whispered.

I worked him with slow, deliberate strokes, watching his face the whole time. Every hitch of his lungs, every flutter of his eyelids and eyebrows, every muttered curse or prayer in a language I didn't speak—it all added up to more *real* intimacy than I'd never experienced before. There was no performance here, no script. Just raw, unfiltered feeling.

Within what seemed like seconds, he was panting uncontrollably, hips bucking up to meet my hand, jaw clenched as if he could somehow will himself to last longer. But he was too new, too overwhelmed, and I knew the end was close.

"Samantha," he gasped, his voice breaking. "I think we should—have to—"

But before he could finish the sentence, his entire body went rigid. He grabbed my waist, holding on with an almost bruising intensity, and buried his face in my breasts as he came, hot and sudden, spilling across my hand and his stomach and my jeans.

The sound he made—half groan, half growl—ripped right through me, and the sight of him undone like that, so completely lost in sensation, made my own climax snap tight and sharp. I ground down on his hard thigh, seeking friction, and finished with a reckless, greedy desperation that was nothing like anything I'd done or felt before.

It was wild. It was messy. And it was—*he was*—completely perfect.

# [ 15 ]

## SEX DETERMINATION

***Samantha***

I didn't know how long I clung to him, maybe a minute, maybe an hour, maybe the half-life of a radioactive isotope. Time seemed irrelevant. There was only Andreas's heartbeat under my palm, the slick press of his arm at my back, and the warmth of our foreheads knocking gently together.

He was still breathing hard. As was I. My lungs were desperate for air. Every breath felt like it might be the one that reminded me of who I actually was, as opposed to who I became when he touched me. Or maybe this was who I actually was, a person with needs and feelings and a desire for this man that was so strong, it terrified me.

He lifted his chin and we kissed, slower and softer now, the rhythm of it tender and sustained. Then, some part of my rational mind—buried under the volcanic crust of post-orgasmic bliss—remembered the basic facts of anatomy and causality, namely that Andreas had come, spectacularly, and it was all over his gorgeous sweater, my hand, and my jeans.

Romantic, I know.

I shifted my weight to the side and managed, with an awkward crab-scoot, to avoid smearing even more of the evidence across my chest. It was only as the dopamine started to ebb, as my heartbeat began to slow, that a particular sensation rushed in. Not shame, not exactly, but a sort of dread, like a cold front arriving out of nowhere. The voice in my head piped up. *What have you done? You just made out with your fake fiancé like a desperate, horny teenager and it was the most fun you've had since . . . FOREVER.*

My previous hookups—such as they were—had all been transactional and efficient. Maybe a few minutes of foreplay, then straight to the business, because why drag it out?

With Andreas tonight, going slow had definitely been hot, but it had also been . . . deeper, somehow. It felt less like eating fast food in a parking lot and more like feasting at a table with endless gourmet courses, each one better than the last, and finishing with the knowledge that I hadn't yet sampled the full menu yet.

*Oh crap. Did this—did we just—did this mean something?!*

It did. It had meant something. I hated that it meant something. I hated even more that I was terrified of what it meant.

I felt his arms squeeze me a little tighter, and I could tell he wanted to say something. The words seemed to vibrate in his chest, just waiting to be expelled. But I was not ready for words. I was not ready for analysis or debrief or, God forbid, a check-in about feelings.

"Here," I said, my own voice embarrassingly raw. "Let me go so I can clean up."

He flinched as though he'd just remembered I was naked from the waist up and covered in bodily fluids. "Oh. Yes. Of course."

I peeled myself away from him—careful to keep the mess corralled—and scuttled toward the edge of the bed, my hand held away from my body. "I'll just go take care of things," I mumbled, grabbing my discarded shirt with my clean hand and trying to cover myself.

I did not look at him. I could feel something like panic spreading from my chest to the tips of my ears and the backs of my knees. I did not want him to see it. In the hallway, I clutched the shirt to me, wrapping my clean arm around my torso in a vain attempt to feel less exposed. Hurrying into the bathroom, I locked the door and went straight for the sink.

For the first twenty seconds I did nothing but stare at my hand under the running water and try to catch my breath. Then I washed my hands thoroughly, and the memory of his voice in my ear, his hands on my breasts, the way he'd come apart under me—like I'd done something powerful and beautiful—came rushing back. It returned so bright and urgent it made me dizzy. I gripped the edges of the sink for balance.

When my pulse returned to something resembling a resting state, I splashed cold water on my face. Only then did I glance in the mirror. My hair was a disaster, a horizontal comet tail. My cheeks were blotched with red, and my chest and neck bore the unmistakable evidence of our love-making, a constellation of love bites and handprints covered my skin, and—

*AHHHH!*

*Lovemaking?!*

I scolded myself for calling it lovemaking, even in my own brain. It was not love. It was friends with benefits.

*Yeah, yeah. That's the ticket.*

I stripped off my jeans and climbed into the shower, setting the temperature to hot but not scalding. The water felt amazing and I washed everywhere, twice, even though there was nothing left to wash away except the memory of his skin against mine. While I stood under the spray, I realized that the thought of facing him again made me more nervous now than I'd been before we'd taken things to sexy town.

Why? Why would seeing him be so much scarier now? I tried to puzzle it out, tried to analyze my feelings the way I would a bizarre result on a gel electrophoresis, but the answer eluded me. All I could do was focus on the fact that, in a few minutes, I'd have to see him again.

After the shower, I dried off and wrapped the towel tight around my chest, tucking the corner in so it would stay put. Peeking out of the bathroom, I saw no sign of Andreas in the hallway; he must've retreated to his own room. I sprinted the short distance to my bedroom and shut the door. Rifling through my drawers for the baggiest, most amorphous sweatpants I could find, I tugged them on plus my old undergrad hoodie with the paint stains on the sleeves.

Dressed in full emotional armor, I sat on the edge of the mattress— which Andreas must've stripped of covers—and tried to steady my breathing. *You are fine,* I told myself. *This is the ideal scenario. Friends with benefits is exactly what you said you wanted. No strings, no feelings, no expectations. It's a system that has been mathematically proven to work for you. I have an adequately powered sample size!*

So why did it feel like my heart had just been scooped out and left to air-dry on the radiator?

I stared at the ceiling, debating the merits of remaking my bed, crawling under my covers, and—

That was when I heard it. The soft thump of footsteps in the hall.

Andreas's voice, quiet but clear, called out, "Samantha, may I talk to you?"

The sound of my name in his voice was like a defibrillator to my insides. Instantly, every nerve ending buzzed. I pressed my hand to my chest, wishing I could forcibly slow the arrhythmia, and tried to compose myself. I had a job to do. I had to be cool, calm, and at least plausibly collected.

"Yes," I called out, voice only shaking a little. "Be right there."

I took a few deep, centering breaths, then patted my cheeks to see if the flush had faded. It had not. That was fine. I could be pink. There was nothing wrong with pink.

Walking out of my bedroom and down the hall, I found Andreas in the living room, seated at the black table with a notebook open in front of him. When he looked up at me, his features weren't masklike and detached, nor were his eyes weren't cold or unreadable. They were full of warmth and interest and anticipation.

I melted. I straight-up, puddle-on-the-floor melted.

I stopped a few feet away and managed a small, shy, "Hi." The word sounded alien coming from me. I was not a person who said hi in a small or shy way.

Andreas stood up and crossed the distance between us. "Hi," he said, his voice not at all shy. It was deep and loaded with meaning.

He took my hand and kissed the back of it, eyes holding mine, the faint smile on his lips never quite leaving his mouth. I felt like I was living inside a classic romance, the kind where the guy is tall and dangerous and very European, and the girl is . . . not me.

He didn't let go of my hand as he asked, "Where are you sleeping tonight?"

I blinked at him, caught off guard. "I mean, should I sleep in my room? Now that you're back? Right? Or—"

He interrupted, "You should sleep in my bed. Since you do not sleep-walk when you start the night in my room."

"Oh," I said, voice a little high. "Then where will you sleep?" I bit my lip to keep from adding, *I hope it's with me.*

He seemed a little uncertain, like he hadn't anticipated the question. That made two of us.

I blurted, "Sleep with me." The words hung in the air for a beat before I realized how they must have sounded. "I mean, just sleep. Obviously. Because we're going slow. And I've already showered."

I cringed so hard my soul left my body and hovered near the smoke detector.

But Andreas grinned, his shyness from the before-sexy-times replaced by something both confident and sweet. "If you do not mind, then I think we should sleep in the same bed."

I squeezed his fingers, smiling so widely I was sure my face would be sore tomorrow. I had never, in my entire life, felt anything quite like this.

As we stood there, close enough for the heat from his chest to reach me, I realized the truth. I was in so much trouble. I was definitely falling for Andreas Kristiansen.

Or maybe, I already had.

* * *

The next time I opened my eyes, it was because something hot and heavy was pressed against my bottom, and there was the soft sound of breathing in my ear. For a luxurious, floaty moment, I lay still and allowed the sensation to register. The weight behind me was not, as I'd half dreamt, a particularly dense body pillow. It was a person—a six-foot-plus, brilliant and sweet, abnormally considerate Norwegian-Italian specimen—and that specimen was spooning me with the kind of thoroughness normally reserved for vacuum sealing.

Andreas's entire body was a study in contrasts. His arms were wound around me, one under my neck and the other slung lazily across my chest, hand splayed against the fabric of my hoodie, which I'd slept in and which now, thanks to entropy, was rucked up almost to my rib cage. His body radiated heat, and his leg hooked over mine, pinning me in place. The rest of him pressed to my backside, and—yep—there was something unmistakably hard nudging into the soft curve of my ass.

It was the textbook definition of being trapped in a good way. I didn't even try to move. If I so much as twitched, I risked shattering the illusion that this was a perfectly ordinary thing to wake up to. But the only thing I felt, aside from the urge to never ever move again, was the smallest, tiniest spike of pure, uncut bliss. And possibly something else, but I refused to identify it without a second opinion.

Andreas was still asleep. His breath was warm on my neck, the slow, deep kind that suggested total relaxation. But then he shifted and his hand slid up, finding its way under my hoodie. He cupped my breast, skin to skin. My nipple, traitor that it was, gradually went stiff as an ice pick in his palm. I was half tempted to reposition him, or at least see if I could nudge his hand back to a more neutral territory, but instead I lay still, eyes shut, and tried to see how long I could go without doing anything to disturb the moment.

Not long, as it turned out.

Andreas moved behind me, stretching just enough to arch his back and press his erection more firmly against me. I sucked in a breath. Quiet, but not imperceptible. He must have felt it because the hand on my breast flexed, then relaxed, then resumed its gentle, absentminded hold. I could not, for the life of me, remember ever being this turned on before. Even the memory of what we'd done last night paled in comparison to the feeling of being pinned beneath him, helpless and wanted by his subconscious.

That's when his breathing changed, the rhythm of it, and I knew the precise moment he awoke. Furthermore, I knew the precise moment he knew I was awake. His body went rigid, and the air around us went from languid to charged.

"Are you awake?" His voice was a whisper, still thick with sleep and just a little rough.

I meant to say, "Yes," or maybe, "Barely." Instead, what came out was an incoherent, "Mmm-hmm," that sounded an awful lot like a moan.

There was a beat of silence. I could feel the indecision, the hesitation, in every muscle of his body. I decided to shortcut the deliberation by shifting my hips back, just enough that the hard line of him slipped between my thighs, pressed up against the warm spot where I was already embarrassingly wet.

I expected him to freeze again, to say something polite, to maybe roll away in a fit of virginal moral fortitude. What happened instead was that his fingers tightened on my breast, and then he pulled both hands away from me at once, as if burned, and rolled onto his back with a groan of what sounded like genuine torment.

"Sorry," he said, voice muffled as he scrubbed both hands over his face. "I did not mean to—"

I rolled onto my back, stretched languidly, and reached for his hand. "You can touch me," I said, trying to sound casual and maybe missing by a few octaves. "I like it. You don't have to—"

He caught my wrist before I could finish and, in one smooth move, rolled on top of me, pinning my hands to the mattress above my head. His face hovered inches from mine, eyes searching, alarmingly hungry, but still so full of restraint I could've screamed.

"You like it," he repeated, voice soft and curious. "How much do you like it when I touch you?"

Feeling heat rush to my cheeks, I admitted on a squeak, "A lot."

His smile was immediate and he bent his head, brushing his lips over my throat, my jaw, my earlobe. The smallest, most calculated touches. It was like being edge-of-orgasm tickled with a feather dipped in liquid nitrogen.

"I do not want to hurt you," he whispered against my ear, his breath sending a shiver straight down my spine.

"You won't," I promised, and I arched up to kiss him, hard, messy, desperate. I wanted him to lose control again. I wanted both of us to lose it, at least for a little while.

For, you know, science.

He groaned into my mouth, and I felt his hips grind down, his cock pressing into me through the layer of my sweatpants and underwear. I moaned again, louder this time, and wriggled my hips, teasing him, urging him on. In a move that was both infuriating and deeply sexy, he shifted his weight to the side and brought his hand to my waistband, watching my face as he slowly, torturously, slid it down and inside.

"Okay?" he said, his eyes locking on mine.

I nodded several times.

He took his time, fingers gliding over my clit, then lower, then back, barely touching, making me feel crazy. For a minute or an hour I just lay there, panting, not even pretending to have chill.

Andreas watched my reactions, studying every shiver, every shift of my hips, and seemed to adjust his approach accordingly, switching from delicate to rough, slow to fast, until I writhed on the bed. He slipped a finger inside me, then two, pumping slowly, curling at just the right angle, and I nearly blacked out from the sensation.

He moved faster, mouth coming down to my neck, nipping and licking, and the combination of pleasure and tenderness was too much.

"I'm gonna—" I started, and then the orgasm hit. My back arched off the bed, and I clung to his arm, not trusting my body to stay anchored to earth. It was a full-body, brain-melting climax and the man had barely touched me. As I came back to myself, I realized I'd grabbed his hair at some point and currently held his face tightly against my neck.

"Oh my God," I managed, voice shaky as I released him. "I am so sorry—can you breathe?"

As he lifted his head, Andreas grinned at me, wide and delighted, his hair wild from my clutching. "I can breathe," he said, and he looked so genuinely proud of himself I started laughing, shaky and a little hysterical.

"You are so sexy, I 1—" I stopped myself just in time, but I felt my face go nuclear. I hadn't finished the sentence. Even so, I wondered if he'd caught the implication. For me, it hovered in the air like a hazardous chemical cloud.

Andreas's smile softened, and he leaned down to kiss me, slow and sweet, then trailed his lips down my neck, lifting my hoodie as he went, and encouraging me to sit up just enough for him to take it off. I complied and was immediately rewarded with his mouth on my breast.

Not only that, his fingers returned to my underwear, gentle now, stroking, teasing. "Do you think you can go again?" he whispered, voice low and reverent. "I want to taste you."

"Mmm-hmm," I said in my now-signature moan of acquiescence. If he'd asked for a kidney, I would have handed it over, no anesthesia required.

He coaxed my sweatpants and underwear off, leaving me naked to his gaze, and propped himself up on one elbow to look at me. The way he did it—no smirk, no arrogance, just awe—made me shiver.

Andreas kissed his way down my stomach, hands tracing over my ribs, my hips, and then he spread my thighs, holding them open and wide.

The anticipation was unbearable, an ache, a static, a humming in every nerve. Andreas met my gaze from between my spread thighs, and for a split second, the world froze. Soft orange-pink light streamed in through the curtains, the sharp scent of his soap and sweat, his eyes on mine full of emotion I didn't dare name. Then he broke eye contact, his lashes lowering as he ran a single finger up the inside of my thigh, slow and gentle. My breath caught. He pressed a kiss to the side of my knee, then another, traveling closer, each one hotter, rougher, more deliberate.

The first pass of his tongue was tentative, exploratory, as if he were mapping the landscape of my desire in case he needed to draw it later from memory. I twitched, unable to stifle the gasp, and in response his hands tightened on my inner thighs, anchoring me, making it clear—without a syllable—that there was nowhere else I was allowed to be.

The second pass was nothing like the first. He licked me with greedy, unapologetic hunger, his tongue slick and soft and then, suddenly, hard and pointed, tracing circles around my clit with precision. The sensation was overwhelming, a scramble of pleasure flooded my thoughts and left me clawing at the sheets, at his hair, at my own skin. I became aware, in the most abstract sense, that I was making noises—unladylike, undignified, almost animal—and that Andreas was moaning in concert, the vibration of his voice making me lose my mind.

My body rebelled against the rules of muscle control; my thighs clamped tight around his head; my heels dug into the mattress; and my hands, acting independently of my brain, twisted into his hair and pulled, hard.

He sucked my clit between his lips, and the sound I made was so loud I was momentarily embarrassed, but then his hand pressed flat against my stomach and he groaned, "God, you're perfect," and I didn't care about anything except coming apart in his mouth. He repeated the word—"Perfect, perfect"—between licks, like he was programming it into my DNA.

The orgasm hit me sideways, unexpected and sharp, a heat-lightning strike that started at the base of my spine and radiated outward until I was nothing but aftershocks and stardust. The world went out of focus. I felt myself dissolving, my body a field of fireworks and trembling muscle, and I didn't even realize I'd sobbed out his name until his grip on my hips loosened and he nuzzled his face against my thigh, humming proudly.

I was still floating, unmoored, when he started again, this time with more patience and less urgency, as if he was savoring the slow, inexorable buildup for its own sake. He drew out the sensation—long, teasing strokes, punctuated by gentle bites that made me shudder. My third orgasm of the morning was nothing like the other two. It was slower, but more intense, like a wave lifting me higher and higher until I lost all definition, until my vision fuzzed at the edges and the only thing I could see was the flash of his eyes every time he looked up to see what he was doing to me.

I lost track of my limbs, lost my grip on everything but the sheets. My entire being reduced itself to one point of contact, one axis of pleasure, one spiral of sensation that kept climbing, kept fracturing, until I was babbling his name and clutching at his shoulders just to be sure I hadn't floated away altogether.

He slowed, finally, and rested his cheek against the inside of my knee, hands rubbing gentle circles up and down my thighs, as if he was coaxing me back into my body, reassuring me it was safe to return. I felt emptied out, like a glass flask rinsed clean and left to dry.

Damn. What a frickin' overachiever.

When I finally came down, Andreas slid up the bed and gathered me against his chest, kissing my hair and murmuring soft nonsense in my ear in a language I didn't understand. I'd never been held like this before, post-orgasm. It was weird, but in the best way.

I pressed my face to his collarbone and tried to slow my heart rate, aware that I was one careless word away from confessing something dangerous and irreversible.

I did not, under any circumstances, want to be in love with him.

But God, did it feel like that's exactly what was happening.

[ 16 ]

# PHENOTYPIC SEX

***Samantha***

Two hours after I'd sworn off ever moving again, I was moving—down Fifth Avenue, hand in Andreas's. Manhattan in December was its own kind of Grimms' fairy-tale setting. Wool coats in every Pantone-neutral shade, the low and ceaseless whine of traffic, and the hint of holidays floating through the exhaust haze like cinnamon sprinkled on a garbage fire. My lungs burned and my thighs prickled from the cold, but I walked on. I wanted to make a joke about Brownian motion and city particles, but honestly, I was still processing the fact that, not an hour ago, I'd straddled the most brilliant mind in chess and tried (and failed) to convince him to let me reciprocate his boundless oral enthusiasm with at least one—ONE—act of service.

Nope. Andreas wanted to spend the entire morning making it about me, which sounded hot in theory but was, in practice, deeply aggravating. Every time my hand wandered below the waistband of his fancy pajamas, he'd detour me with kisses, or nuzzle my stomach, or grip my wrists and pin them above my head. He was too strong for my cleverest work-arounds.

I'd even tried logic. "You do realize this is supposed to be a two-way street, right?"

155

He'd just smiled, then gone back to methodically mapping my erogenous zones with the kind of attention to detail you only see in astrophysics or, well, chess.

By ten, I'd called it. "We need to leave this apartment or I'm going to combust."

He'd nodded, still panting slightly, and stiffly stated that he needed to shower. Then he'd rushed off to his bathroom. I did not peek to see if he went cold or hot, but I had my suspicions.

Presently, Andreas and I were headed north, our destination Central Park. I didn't bother to ask if there was an end goal. I was just happy to have this, whatever it was.

At the corner of 74th and Madison, we waited for the light, the pedestrian swarm eddying around us like we were a couple of decorative bollards. I took the opportunity to check his profile, the sharp nose, the gold-shadowed cheekbones, the hair that looked tousled and deliberate. He stared at me, too. Actually, he stared at me so intently that I felt myself grow self-conscious under the scrutiny.

"Is there something on my face?" I asked, which was a fair question. I'd skipped makeup and gone for a hat that could generously be called elf adjacent.

Instead of answering, he stepped forward, hand warm at my elbow, and bent to kiss me on the mouth. Not a peck. A real, intent, you-will-think-about-this-at-inappropriate-times kind of kiss. It lasted through the red light, past the walk sign chirping, and into the next cycle of traffic. Pedestrians flowed around us in an indifferent stream.

He only broke the kiss when a wet, heavy snowflake splatted on his cheekbone and began to melt down his neck. Andreas blinked, then produced a sleek black umbrella from the depths of his coat like a magician. He snapped it open and tucked me under his arm, both of us shielded in the bubble of warm breath and umbrella fabric.

"You realize this is the world's worst snow," I said, glancing out at the wet-ice downpour. "It's not even snow. It's acid slushy."

"I do not think it is so bad," he replied, leading me off the curb and onto the crosswalk. "It gives me a reason to keep you close."

I let that pass without comment, but I did slide my arm around his waist, snaking my hand under his coat and looping my thumb through the nearest belt loop.

We walked for several blocks, the city becoming progressively whiter and slipperier. The avenue ahead looked like it had been glazed with cornstarch. After a while, Andreas leaned his head toward mine, so close that his breath made the fuzz on my hat stand at attention.

"I apologize," he said quietly.

I cocked an eyebrow up at him. "Why are you apologizing?"

He answered, stone-serious, "We agreed we would discuss public displays of affection before engaging in them." For a second, I thought he was genuinely worried he'd broken our agreement, but then I caught the twitch at the corner of his mouth. Andreas, the king of the deadpan.

I slid my hand down beneath his coat and pinched his butt, hard. His eyes went cartoonishly round. Looking down at me, mock-offended but actually clearly delighted.

"That was before we agreed to a friends-with-benefits situation," I said, not even trying to hide my grin.

He considered this, head tilting, then asked, "Does that mean I do not need to ask before kissing you?"

"If you're uncertain, feel free to ask. And I'll do the same. Otherwise, just kiss me."

He nodded solemnly. "What about when we are alone," he asked, "can I touch you without asking?"

I waggled my eyebrows. "Again, if you're uncertain, just ask. Otherwise, just touch me."

He mulled this over as we crossed into the park, where the grass was still that eerie, too-green-for-winter color but the trees and railings had already been decked out in blue and silver Christmas lights. A massive menorah and a giant blow-up dreidel stood next to a line of wire-frame reindeer. *Only in New York*, I thought.

Or maybe just in the USA? I had no idea. I'd never traveled outside the country.

The path narrowed, and the snow got deeper. Andreas shifted the umbrella so that it covered more of me, which meant he had to lean down, almost folding himself in half to fit under the dome. We walked like this for a bit, not talking, and I realized I liked the silence. It was soft and companionable, not the awkward kind.

After a few more yards, he said, "What is the difference between what we are doing and actual dating?"

The question startled me so much that I nearly tripped on an icy patch. "What?"

"I mean," he clarified, "if we are friends, but we also have benefits, but we are not dating—what is the difference?"

I was about to say something glib, like "It's marketing," but instead, a more interesting question slipped out of my mouth: "Have you ever dated anyone?"

He nodded. "Yes. I have dated a few people."

This was not the answer I expected. "But you never went all the way with them?"

He shook his head, matter-of-fact. "No. But they were long-term, committed relationships. However, my traveling got in the way, and so . . ." He let the words trail off, as if the rest was both obvious and irrelevant.

I couldn't help myself. "How far did you go with them? I mean, in the sex department."

He answered easily, without embarrassment, "Just a few kisses."

I frowned, trying to line up my understanding of him with the data I'd just been given. "Your decision or theirs?"

He thought for a long time, lips pursed, eyes squinted. Then he said, "Mostly mine, I suppose. I am not . . . I am not a very affectionate person, I think."

I had to bite my tongue to keep from bursting into laughter. I was currently being held, umbrellaed, and generally coddled within an inch of my life. He'd spent the entire morning worshipping my body like it was the lost ark. But he considered himself "not very affectionate"?

"Yeah," I said, "you're a real cold fish." I didn't bother hiding the sarcasm.

He glanced down at me, as if to see if I was joking. I grinned back up at him. His eyelids lowered, his expression looking half annoyed and half smiling, and then he bent his head to my ear and whispered, "That is not what you said earlier."

I nearly tripped again, but this time it was because my knees gave out a little. The way he said it was so low and intimate I could feel it in my teeth.

"I surrender," I said, laughing but also gasping a little when he nipped the edge of my ear. "We are in public. You have to behave."

He looked at me, eyes bright and hot. "We should have just stayed in bed all day."

I tried not to smile, but it was impossible. "We should change the subject," I said, more to myself than to him.

He sighed, as though the effort of talking about something that wasn't us in bed was genuinely painful. "Fine. Then tell me, what is the difference between dating and what we are doing?"

I glanced up at the skeleton trees and the gray sky, trying to organize my thoughts. "When you date, it's my understanding that you're in a monogamous—unless discussed and agreed to be otherwise—emotionally committed relationship. But friends with benefits means you're not in a relationship other than a friendship and there is no expectation of genuine feelings developing between the two people. It's just for fun."

He listened closely, brow furrowed. "So we should not develop feelings for each other, right?"

I nodded, because my throat felt suddenly tight.

Andreas mumbled something I didn't quite catch.

Neither of us spoke for a while. We walked deeper into the park, the snow collecting on the umbrella, weighing it down so that Andreas had to occasionally shake it off with a flick of his wrist. I was grateful for the break from talking, but I also wanted desperately to say something that would lighten the mood.

So, after wracking my brain, I settled on a subject I'd let drop last night. "Hey, I've been meaning to ask, when I got in the car last night, you spoke to Tara on the sidewalk before we left for the wine bar. What was that about?"

He kept his gaze forward. "I wanted to make a slight change in your security coverage and wished to discuss it with her before I forgot. That is all."

I nodded, not sure if I believed him but not wanting to press.

He looked over at me. "Do you have any other questions?"

I thought about this. Did I? There were so many, it would take a lifetime to answer them. But one rose to the surface, a little buoy of curiosity in the murk of my self-doubt.

"Yes. Actually, I do."

He smiled, just a small one, and said, "I will tell you anything."

I took a deep breath, not sure how to start. "Tell me about you."

He blinked, surprised. "Me?"

"Yeah. After my father's funeral, I never saw you again, not until you showed up outside my department building. Tell me, what was your life like? Did you go to college? Or what was high school—or secondary school—like for you? Where did you live?"

He looked at me for a long time before responding, "This information about me is available on my Wikipedia page, I believe. Are you saying you never looked me up?"

I dodged the question, because of course I'd looked him up. But just once. "I want to hear about it from you. Will you tell me?"

He met my eyes, inspecting me. Eventually, he nodded, serious and open.

"As I said, I will tell you anything," he said. "You only need ask."

* * *

On Monday morning, I'd showered at home, washed my hair, shaved, exfoliated, and then—on a lark—put on a swipe of eyeliner and a hint of mascara. I even did the thing where you blow-dry while holding your head upside down, so my hair actually had some volume. By the time I'd eaten breakfast with Andreas, laced up my shoes, and stepped outside into the cold December rain, I decided that Mondays were underrated.

This feeling persisted, even as I badged into the biology building and took the stairs instead of the elevator up to my floor. Exiting the locker room still feeling fantastic, I did not walk; I sashayed, twirling the chain of my necklace as I walked, the engagement ring strung on it clinking against my sternum with a very faint, satisfying thwack. I hummed as I made my way down the gray cinder-block hallway to my cubicle, and the tune wasn't even from the radio or my phone, just a musical outburst from unknown origins.

A postdoc in the hallway looked up, startled, as I chirped, "Good morning!"

She blinked twice, then replied with, "Good morning. And congratulations!"

I did a double take but kept walking, only faltering for a half step. "Thank you?" I called over my shoulder, because I had no idea what she

160

was talking about. Maybe it was a general congratulation, like, "Good job, you showered!"

As I approached the grad student bullpen, I passed two more people in the corridor, both of whom gave me the exact same look. A bright smile, eyes up and down my body, then a nod and a "Congratulations!" One of them even tacked on, "That's so exciting!" before turning into a copy room.

Now, I was really confused. Had I won some kind of grant lottery? Was there a rumor that I'd been awarded a Nobel? (Haha, as if.) Was there a secret plot among my colleagues to haze me with relentless praise? Or had someone uncovered my supersecret weekend activities, and this was the department's passive-aggressive way of expressing their jealousy?

Thinking about the weekend made me blush. Not just a little, but all over. In point of fact, the weekend was the single greatest forty-eight hours of my adult life. Saturday and Sunday mornings had started with mind-blowing and multiple orgasms. On Sunday, we'd transitioned into a few hours of nearly naked cuddling and eating breakfast foods in bed while we watched cartoons or random old chess matches on YouTube. Andreas did disappear for an hour or two to do, presumably, chess grand master things, and then came back to the apartment.

On Sunday night, he'd convinced me to try strip chess, which turned out to be less a contest and more a rapid-fire exercise in undressing me with maximum efficiency. I was naked after less than five minutes, but I didn't mind. In fact, I'm not sure I'd ever been so thoroughly, blissfully owned in my life.

He did *not* go easy on me. Not on the board, and definitely not off it. But for reasons beyond my comprehension, he was obsessed with making me come as many times as possible. The only thing that bothered me was that he barely let me reciprocate; any time I tried to make it about him, he'd just flip us over and start again. The man had stamina. I, meanwhile, walked around the apartment Sunday night on legs that felt like very tired Twizzlers.

But I'd lost count of how many cold showers he'd taken. I didn't want to push him to do more than he felt ready for. And yet—perhaps for the first time ever—I couldn't wait to make a man orgasm. I thought about it, making him come apart like he'd done to me over and over, all the time.

Andreas, his body, and especially the parts of himself he withheld, felt like they were starting to become an obsession.

*Maybe I need a hobby. I should learn to knit.*

I was still a little sore when I reached the open office. Three people glanced up from their monitors as I entered. One raised a coffee cup in salute. Another said "Good morning!" and the third nodded and muttered, "Morning, Samantha." These were people who usually only offered a faint nod.

Confused, I made my way to my desk. Except—someone was already sitting there. Dmitry.

He slowly spun in my chair to face me, elbows on the armrests, fingers steepled, giving him an air of Bond villain meets mafia consigliere. "Good morning, Samantha. I have been waiting for you."

"Good morning, Goldfinger," I replied, lifting an eyebrow at his theatrics, and dropped my backpack at the foot of my desk. "Do you know why everyone is offering me congratulations this morning?"

Dmitry stood, tilting his head slightly to the left then right as though considering my question. "Hmm. Well, it could be one of two things as far as I'm aware, unless you also won the lottery. It could be—" Before he could finish, a shadow loomed over the cubicle divider. James Nieminen. He looked as though someone had rung him out like a wet sock.

"Congratulations, Sam," he said, voice so clipped it could have doubled as a surgical instrument.

I stared at him for a beat, eventually saying, "Thank you," and doing my best to sound pleasant and unbothered, which seemed to infuriate him.

He made a sound like he was going to spit, but held it in. "Since I'm no longer your PI, I'll need you to hand over all the projects you've been working on by the end of the day. You can just leave anything that's hard copy with my secretary and everything else can be emailed directly to me." He waited a second, for what purpose I had no idea.

I nodded, saying nothing, because I didn't know what he was talking about. Since when had he ceased to be my PI? My nonresponse seemed to disappoint him. He turned on his heel and stalked off, the back of his white coat flapping behind him.

I watched him depart for a full three seconds before looking at Dmitry, who was blinking at me with a mixture of compassion and high-quality-gossip hunger.

"What is he talking about?" I asked.

Dmitry shrugged, not quite meeting my eyes. "So, that's the first thing. It's all over the department. Dr. Hauser's funding was restored and her accounts were unfrozen over the weekend. You're now her number one researcher and teaching assistant extraordinaire again. She's not in town today, so she asked Carter with the administrative pool to tell you when you arrived. But Carter's such a gossip, he told everyone he saw on his way here and asked me to fill you in when you got to work."

It took a second for this to sink in. When it did, I lost all semblance of chill. "What? You're kidding. That can't be—that's—oh my god, that's—"

I hugged Dmitry. I literally leaped into his arms. He didn't reciprocate, but stood stiff as a post and offered a tepid "Yay."

I didn't care. I did a little dance in place, hugged myself, then threw my arms around Dmitry again. "Yay!" I squealed, unable to contain my exuberance.

He let me hug him but offered no further reaction, just looked vaguely to the side, as if waiting for me to finish.

I did, eventually. "Sorry, sorry. I got carried away." Folding my hands under my chin, I grinned at him. "Thank you for letting me celebrate. Now, what's on your mind? You seem preoccupied."

He squinted at me, as if weighing whether to ask what he wanted. After a second, he grabbed my upper arm and pulled me a half step closer, lowering his voice to a conspiratorial hush. "I thought you would never ask. Is it true that you are engaged to Andreas Kristiansen?"

I flinched back, nearly upsetting a mug of pens and pencils. "Who told you that?"

"James Nieminen," he said, shaking his head in disgust. "He's been circling around your desk for the last hour like a pickpocket. And when Carter came by to tell me about the funding restoration with Dr. Hauser, Dr. Nieminen snidely told us that the reason Dr. Hauser's funding was restored was probably because you, Sam, are engaged to the youngest son of the Kristiansen family, billionaire endowment supporters and controlling shareholders of Genetix. Is this true? Please tell me it's true. Even if it's not true, tell me it's true. But prepare yourself. Because Carter is definitely going to tell everyone that too."

I groaned and rubbed my forehead. "It's very complicated. Let's just say I understand why James believes that. But I have no idea why Dr.

Hauser's funding was restored, and I certainly didn't have anything to do with it."

He nodded sagely. "But what about the other part? About you being engaged to Andreas Kristiansen. Is that true?"

I opened my mouth to respond, but before I could, Dmitry grabbed my hand with both of his and locked eyes with me, wild and intense. "I am a huge fan. I have followed Andreas's chess career since I was in middle school. Do not judge me for my parasocial relationship desires, but I have always wanted to be his best friend. If you are engaged to marry him, then you have to set us up so we can become best friends and I can live out my childhood fantasy of playing chess with Andreas while we sip martinis and him telling me I'm not a terrible player just before he beats me resoundingly. Can you do this for me? Will you make my dreams come true?"

I held back the urge to laugh admirably. Truly, I deserved a metal. With my free hand, I patted his. "I do know Andreas, and I will introduce the two of you. He is picking me up today after work, so you can meet him as early as today if you want. But whether or not you become best friends is entirely up to your sparkling personality."

Dmitry made a face I couldn't interpret, but I was a little worried it was his O face. Then he said, tone as flat as a pancake, "This is the happiest moment of my life."

I covered my mouth, again trying not to laugh, and he must have noticed because his grip on me tightened for a second before he let go and composed himself. "Thank you. I am so glad I never talked bad about you behind your back."

This time, I did laugh.

[ 17 ]

# HUMAN REPRODUCTIVE BIOLOGY

***Samantha***

The rest of the day passed in a blur of grant paperwork. By four o'clock, my email inbox had been ambushed by no less than nine congratulatory GIFs, including a dancing gnome and a Mariah Carey that looped in perpetual vibrato.

I changed out of my scrubs in the nearly empty locker room and checked my reflection at least three times. Then, upon opening the door, I nearly walked right into Dmitry, who had apparently been waiting outside like a bouncer at a very selective night club.

He stepped back, gave me a very obvious up-and-down, then let out a low, unfeigned whistle. "When did you become so fashionable?"

I looked down at myself and, before I could stop the words, the truth fell out of my mouth: "Oh. Thank you. Andreas bought these for me."

Dmitry's eyes went wide, then almost crossed as he processed the statement. "You're using the best chess player in the world as your personal shopper?"

"He is not my personal shopper," I said, but the way it came out sounded false.

Dmitry fell into step next to me as we started down the hall toward the elevators, shaking his head in a way that made his glasses slip down his

165

nose. "The kombucha drink you were raving about earlier today, didn't you say that Andreas bought that for you first?"

"Yes, but that doesn't make him my personal shopper." I tried to sound resolute, but my voice did a little trampoline bounce at the end.

Dmitry pressed the elevator button and fixed me with a side-eye. "He seems to know your tastes better than you know yourself. Didn't you say last week that your fiancé picked out the perfume you've been wearing recently? I assume you only have one fiancé."

Once we stepped inside the elevator car, I pressed the lobby button and made a low noise of defeat. "Yes. Fine. He did pick out the perfume, too."

"How long have you two been together?" The elevator doors closed, sealing us in with the hush of a confessional.

I deflected. "I've known him for a really long time, since we were kids."

Dmitry nodded. "Apparently so. For him to know exactly what cut and shape of clothes look best on you, and what color those clothes should be to flatter your complexion and bring out your eyes, and what food you'll like even before you try it yourself, and what perfume scent not only smells like heaven mixed with your unique pheromones but also uses your favorite flower, you two must've known each other since birth and he's been taking notes the entire time."

The elevator doors parted on the ground floor, and I said, "Cut it out. He should be waiting for me outside. Stop teasing me if you want to meet him."

Dmitry raised his hands, surrendering, but couldn't resist a last volley as we crossed the marble floor toward the security desk. "I'm just trying to point out, you are getting married to someone who loves you very much. A man does not pay this close attention to a woman unless he plans—or hopes—to spend the rest of his life making her happy."

My heart did a little twist and flutter, and I felt an unexpected blush prickle up my neck. Once upon a time, the thought of someone falling in love with me would have triggered a biological panic response. I would have ended the situationship. But Dmitry's words about Andreas didn't scare me. In fact, they made me . . . happy. Giddy, almost.

We passed the security desk, said goodbye to the guard, and walked straight for the main glass doors. Andreas stood waiting for me just outside, eyes on something in the distance. He wore a dark wool coat and a navy scarf, his hair swept back with the kind of effortless style that cost actual effort. I felt a tiny, irrational spark of joy at the sight of him.

"Are you ready? Your boyfriend is outside," I said, nudging Dmitry.

He stumbled for a second then hissed, "Only say nice things about me. Do not embarrass me in front of him. Or else."

I cackled. The sound actually startled a nearby student.

As we stepped outside, Andreas's gaze swung toward us and instantly focused on me. For a split second, his eyes did that thing where they got very bright. Then his gaze slid to Dmitry, and the corners of his mouth dipped slightly.

"Dmitry, this is Andreas Kristiansen. Andreas, this is Dmitry Bortnik, one of my fellow PhD candidates and my work husband." I grinned.

Andreas's frown deepened, but before he could say anything, I added, "That just means he's like my best friend at work, and I trust him, and he's very good to me."

Andreas's forehead cleared, and the side of his mouth pulled upward in a not-unfriendly way.

Dmitry shot me a look. "You should have called me your work brother, not your work husband."

Andreas took off his glove and extended his hand to Dmitry. "No, work husband is better. I do not get along with my brothers. It is nice to meet you. I am Samantha's soon-to-be real-life husband."

I tucked my chin into my scarf to hide my smile.

Dmitry gripped his hand. It was a very firm handshake but without aggression, the kind that telegraphed mutual respect. "I have followed your chess career for many years. You obviously already know this, but it is truly an honor to meet the best chess player in the world. I wouldn't let Sam marry anyone less impressive."

I did a double take at the chill in Dmitry's voice, like he was meeting an old friend for a beer and not the person he'd been fanboying over since —as per his own admission—he was a kid.

Dmitry continued, "I have to get going, but if you ever want to beat an amateur chess enthusiast, I am at your service."

Andreas grinned, a real, dazzling grin. "If you are free after the break, perhaps we could have you over for dinner."

Dmitry nodded, king of being unconcerned. "I will look at my calendar and get back to you."

As Dmitry started to walk away, I made a face at his retreating back, equal parts disbelief and admiration at how unshakable he was acting in the presence of his literal idol.

I waited until he was out of earshot before shaking my head.

"Was I nice to your friend?" Andreas asked.

"He is so weird. He's like your biggest fan and yet is all chill, acting like he has plans and needs to check his calendar before playing chess with you. What a weirdo."

Andreas's eyes sparkled. "Not all Russians are the same, obviously. But I had many chess coaches who were Russian, and my experience is if they said, 'Good job,' it was like getting a round of applause from anyone else. He seems similar. Understated."

I slotted my arm through his. "Enough about Dmitry. Why did you insist on picking me up this evening? Are we going on another date night?"

He tilted his head, feigning offense. "Did you forget? We're going to go pick out a Christmas tree."

I gaped. "We're doing it tonight?"

He nodded, entirely serious. "It is already past the first week of December. I made a list of tree vendors within walking distance."

I grinned, letting myself be led down the sidewalk. "Have you ever picked out a Christmas tree before?"

"No," he said. "I will have to defer to your superior experience."

"Indeed," I said, fairly certain my cheeks were going to be stuck in a smile for the rest of the night.

* * *

Four hours after Andreas had reduced my body to a grinning machine, we were locked in a silent domestic standoff in his apartment. The Christmas tree—our pride and sorrow—stood at one end of the living room, still oozing pine sap onto the plastic tarp we'd finally remembered to put down after the fourth try. At the other end, Andreas was slumped on the couch, arms crossed over his chest, a scowl engineered to repel all attempts at cheer.

"See? Doesn't it look great?" I said as brightly as I could without setting off his sulk sensors.

He glared at me, a thundercloud of discontent, and made a noise that might have been "Mmm."

I admired our work. The tree was lopsided. A quarter of it faced the wall because that's where the branches were the most anemic. Several strings of lights ran in drunken ellipses, not the crisp Fibonacci spiral I'd intended, and the stand oozed sticky sap onto a fortress of doubled garbage bags. I stood back, hands on my hips, channeling every suburban dad.

"Look at it this way," I said. "We couldn't enjoy the wonderfulness of this moment if we hadn't lived through the pain and suffering of setting it up."

The scowl deepened. Andreas might have been plotting to torch the tree and salt the earth with the charred remains.

Truthfully, the evening's pain and suffering had not been minor. We'd left my department together, hand in hand, and found a Christmas tree lot on the east side of Central Park, just as the sun dipped behind the buildings and threw the world into blue shadows. We had agreed on a tree in less than four minutes—a record that should have been immortalized on a plaque—but then our differing philosophies of logistics clashed like tectonic plates.

Andreas wanted to hire professionals. "I will call the building. They can send staff to pick it up and install it for us. There is no need for us to carry it," he'd said, already dialing the number.

But the whole point, I'd tried to explain, was to carry the tree ourselves. "Have you ever seen *When Harry Met Sally*?" I'd asked. "There's this part where they carry the Christmas tree back to Sally's apartment and it's iconic."

I'd pressed my case, citing romantic comedies and the importance of seasonal tradition. In the end, Andreas caved. He always caved when I made irrefutable arguments. Or, in this case, when I kissed him on the mouth until he lost the will to argue.

What followed was an hour of abject humiliation as we tried to drag a seven-foot balsam fir through the city without killing any pedestrians or ourselves. The net result was a trail of needles through the lobby, an irritated doorman who might've threatened to fine us for sap stains if I hadn't brought him so many cookies over the last few weeks, and several hundred calories burned in passive-aggressive bickering.

Then came the tree stand. Andreas had bought the most expensive one on the internet, which claimed to "self-center" and "lock in seconds." It didn't. It took us forty-five minutes to get the tree vertical, and it listed like a ship half flooded. Andreas's mood, which had started at "mildly testy," decayed in half-lives to "active volcanic rage." He began shouting in Italian. Eventually, we figured out how to fill the reservoir for water without unleashing a tidal wave onto the parquet.

We high-fived when it finally stood upright and didn't immediately topple. The moment lasted exactly three minutes, until we realized we hadn't put anything down to protect the floor. Which meant: remove tree, empty stand, mop, line with plastic, then repeat all prior steps. I'd laughed through most of it, which Andreas did not appreciate, but even he couldn't deny that the result—one haggard, needle-dropping, fully upright tree— was impressive.

But now, with the post-holiday-trauma haze settling, he looked at me like I'd personally invented Christmas for the express purpose of making him suffer.

I walked over and straddled his lap, resting my hands on his shoulders. He was all angles and tension, a physical object lesson in stubbornness. As soon as my butt hit his thighs, his hands automatically migrated to cup it, holding me in place like he'd been born with that evolutionary adaptation.

"Thank you for setting up the tree with me," I said, and kissed the tip of his nose.

He maintained eye contact, refusing to smile, a gesture of resistance that made my insides fizz. I lowered my mouth to his neck and whispered, "I'd like to show my gratitude, if you'll let me."

The hands at my backside slipped up under my shirt, fingers tracing bare skin at my lower back. His voice was wary but hopeful. "What do you have in mind?"

I licked his earlobe, slow and deliberate, then breathed, "Anything you want."

A full-body shiver passed through him, like a seismic wave. His hands roved upward, pausing at my ribs, then higher, fingers skimming the band of my bra. He found the clasp, flicked it open with deft precision, and said, "I would like very much to taste you."

I frowned, just a little. Not because I disliked the offer—far from it— but because I'd been trying to get him to let me reciprocate for days, and every single time I attempted to put my hands or mouth on him, he'd redirected the focus to me. His generosity was infuriating. I wanted to worship his body, to have him at my mercy, and he just kept giving and giving until my bones felt like they might dissolve.

I kissed down the side of his neck, letting my hair fall across his jaw. "Can we focus on you tonight?" I whispered. "I miss your body."

He exhaled, a hot rush of air against my temple, but didn't reply.

"Can I unbutton your shirt and touch you?" I murmured, letting my hands drift up the planes of his chest.

He hesitated—just for a beat—and then, voice rough, said, "Yes."

I slid my fingers down the row of buttons, popping them open one by one. As his shirt parted, I saw the flushed line of muscle down his sternum, the ridge and shadow of each ab. I could feel him getting hard, urgent and insistent against my inner thigh. The sight sent a thrill through me, and I had to lean back to really take him in. He was so beautiful, so perfectly put together, and yet right now, under my hands, he trembled.

I finished the last button and ran my hands over his skin, savoring the heat and the way he flexed beneath my touch. "Where else am I allowed to touch you?" I asked, half teasing, half daring him to answer.

He swallowed, throat working. "Anywhere you want."

Emboldened, I spread his shirt wide and let my palms roam, fingers mapping his chest, down his stomach, stopping at the waistband of his pants. "May I unbutton this?" I asked.

He gritted his teeth, seeming to wrestle with himself, and then nodded. "If you want."

I wanted. God, did I want. I slid my hands lower, unfastened the button, and began to unzip his pants. He watched, transfixed, cheeks blotched with heat and something else. Hesitation?

I reached inside, found the soft fabric of his boxers, the outline of his erection straining beneath. I stroked him, gentle at first, then more firmly, but before I could do anything meaningful, he caught my wrists.

"You do not have to," he said, the words squeezed out like he was in actual pain.

I tried to keep a frown from my forehead. "I want to. But if you're not ready, we can do something else."

His grip on me loosened slightly. "Like what?"

I considered, genuinely. What could we do that wouldn't be all about me, but also wouldn't push him past where he wanted to go? I bit my lip, then said, "You could watch me touch myself."

His eyes opened fully, dark and sharp, and his eyelashes fluttered as if the concept had winded him. For a long second, neither of us moved. Then I gave him a slow, sweet kiss. When I broke away, I easily twisted my wrists out of his lax hold and began to unbutton my own shirt.

"Would you like that?" I asked, just above a whisper.

He nodded, the motion small, his gaze molten.

I smiled, then moved to stand, but he caught my waist, grounding me to his lap. I kissed his jaw, then leaned in and whispered, "Let's move to the bed."

This time, he let me go.

I stood and slowly unbuttoned my shirt, letting it fall to the floor. Then I unzipped my jeans, shimmied out of them, and left them puddled by the couch. My bra was loose, barely holding on, so I let it slip off my shoulders and tossed it onto a chair. I was now in nothing but underwear and a cocky smile.

I walked to his bedroom, well aware he was following, and once inside, I flicked on the light and glanced over my shoulder to see if he was still watching. He was. Every step, every movement, his eyes tracked me with a hunger that bordered on devotional.

I sat on his bed and patted the spot next to me. "Sit wherever you want."

Instead, he stood in the doorway, arms at his sides, chest rising and falling. I lay back on the bed, parallel to the headboard, legs dangling off the edge. For a minute, I just let him look.

Then, with deliberate slowness, I cupped my breasts, rubbing and pinching my nipples, rolling them between my fingers. I could feel his eyes on me, like a current of heat, and I let myself imagine what he saw. My flushed skin, my hips pressed into the mattress, my hands working myself into a shudder.

I sucked my middle finger into my mouth, getting it wet, then slid it under the elastic of my underwear. The touch was electric, I barely needed to move before I began panting. I kept my eyes closed, wanting to memorize the feeling of his gaze, and started to work slow circles around my clit.

I heard him step further into the room, the sound of his feet soft on the floor. I cracked opened my eyes and saw him looming over me, shirt open, pants hanging half undone. His face was flushed and his mouth was open, as if he couldn't quite believe what he was seeing.

I got close, so close, the ache building and building. Kicking off my underwear, I brought my heels to the edge of the bed, and opened my legs wide. I slid a finger inside and let myself moan.

Andreas dropped to his knees next to the bed, face level with my body, his eyes burning with something primal. "May I?" he asked, voice hoarse and thick.

"Tonight isn't about me," I said, fighting to keep my hand in place. "I wanted to do something for you."

He licked his lips and said, "This is for me." Then, without waiting, he gently pulled my hand away and replaced it with his own, touching me with the perfect pressure, the perfect rhythm. "You are so wet," he murmured, almost reverent.

I almost came right then, the sight of his hand moving and his eyes fixed on my body was enough to push me to the edge. Before I could protest or even process, he bent forward and licked me, slow at first, then with intent.

My whole body jerked, a shock of pleasure racing up my spine. I tried to brace myself, but Andreas was relentless. He slid his thick finger inside me, curling it just so, while his mouth worked in wet, greedy laps. He groaned into me, the vibration like a tuning fork, and the sensation sent me spiraling.

I tried to hold back, to draw it out, but I couldn't. I came hard, knees locking around his head, fingers tangling in his hair as I bucked against his mouth. My voice echoed in the room, wordless and raw, and the orgasm just kept going, wave after wave, until I was certain I'd left my body behind and was now just a field of pure, radiant energy.

He didn't stop until I physically had to push him away, my skin so sensitive it hurt. He kissed his way up my stomach, lingered at my breasts, then settled over me and kissed me deep, tongue tasting me, hands cupping my face like I was something precious.

Andreas's hand drifted back down between my legs, and he stroked me, gentle and patient, coaxing. He looked down at me, his eyes hopeful and greedy all at once, whispering, "Do you think we can do that again?"

I laughed. Not a full-bodied laugh, but the soft, incredulous kind, and spoke my mind. "Don't you want me to go down on you?"

His whole body stilled. The question hung in the air, visible and vibrating. For a second, he looked shy, speechless. Utterly bashful.

I sat up, propping my arms behind me, and arched my back just a little, because if he was going to stare at me, I might as well give him a show.

He slid backward, away from the bed, and then knelt on the carpet at the edge of the mattress. He looked up at me, licking his lips. The movement was small, but it felt almost dangerous, like a warning that things were about to get very, very interesting.

"Andreas," I said, drawing his name out, "don't you want me to make you come?"

He closed his eyes and shook his head once. Not a no, but an attempt to clear it, to get back to the topic at hand. When he opened them again, the look on his face made my insides twist. It was desperation.

I let the silence bloom. I wanted him to say it, or at least admit it to himself.

Then, softer, I added, "I don't have to use my mouth. I can use my hand, like before."

He inhaled through his nose, then exhaled slow, nostrils flaring just a bit. I waited, studying the tension in his jaw, the lines of muscle along his neck.

Finally, while still kneeling, still refusing to move, he nodded. Once. Just enough to confirm that he'd heard, and he wanted. A thrill ran up my spine.

I watched him a second longer, then cocked my head and said, "Do you want me to use my hands or my mouth?"

He looked up at me, eyes wide and vulnerable. He took a deep, shuddering breath, then he said, "Your mouth," and it sounded like the words were forced out of him, a confession.

I suppressed a smile and stood up, still naked, and reached for his wrists, gently encouraging him to stand. He did, but looked uncertain, so I took charge and gave him a slow come-hither gesture toward the bed, pushing his pants all the way down his legs and turning him.

I pushed his shoulders gently and Andreas sat on the bed. Kneeling between his knees, I lowered my gaze. He still wore his black boxer briefs, but the fabric was already tented. For a second, I just looked at him, loving the way his entire body was wound up, his muscles tense, his fists gripping the mattress.

I met his eyes and didn't break contact as I reached under the waistband and tugged the boxer briefs down his hips. He lifted himself off the bed automatically, like he'd been trained in this. The second the fabric slipped over the head of his cock, it sprang up, full and flushed and utterly, beautifully exposed.

He was big. Not comically or cartoonishly, but enough that my first thought was, *That is not all going to fit in my mouth.* The shaft was perfectly straight, but with a slight curve at the end, the head thick, a slick bead of precum already gathered at the tip. The skin was smooth, and I realized with another jolt of pride that I was probably the first person to ever see it like this, up close and in the wild.

My mouth watered. I mean, literally. I swallowed, then smiled up at him, and wrapped my hand around the base. He sucked in a breath, lips parting, and his eyes rolled back for just a second before he brought them back to mine, still desperate looking.

I stroked him a few times, slow, just to get the feel of him. He was heavy, hot, the pulse of blood in the veins like a tiny earthquake under my palm.

He tried to speak, voice wrecked, and choked out, "I am not a good person."

I almost laughed, the words so out of left field I thought maybe I'd misheard. But he looked dead serious, like he genuinely believed his body was a weapon of mass destruction. Instead of arguing, I just leaned forward and, without breaking eye contact, pressed my lips to the tip of his cock.

He groaned. But then in the next moment, he shook his head and reached for me.

"No. I can't. We—we can't," he said.

Before I could say anything, Andreas grabbed me by the waist, hauled me up onto the bed, and crushed me against his chest. He kissed my neck, my jaw, my shoulder, everywhere he could reach, speaking in that frantic, beautiful language, and this time I was sure it was Norwegian and not Italian.

He kissed my breasts, my collarbone, my lips. He held my hands down so I couldn't touch him. And when I tried to speak again, ask him why he'd stopped me, he kissed me deeply and wouldn't answer.

[ 18 ]

# THE NEONATE AND THE NEW PARENTS

***Samantha***

The Friday before Christmas, Kaitlyn's apartment was a zone of clutter and chaos. Packing cubes and zipped pouches covered every square inch of the sectional and ottoman. Every open surface bore witness to at least one pile. Baby onesies in a pastel avalanche, an unsettling number of travel-size Clorox wipes, industrial-strength diaper paste, and a dizzying array of chargers, cables, and adaptors.

I'd spent the day running interference on a fifteen-pound screaming potato so Kaitlyn could do recon at the shops and come home armed for her flight to California.

Now, in the late afternoon, the apartment was a battle between two competing energies. Kaitlyn, coolly methodical, folding and zipping and stashing with the efficiency of a veteran general; and Joey, who'd managed, against all odds, to wedge his entire body under the living room coffee table and was making a series of wet, determined noises that suggested the imminent birth of a tooth. But then he cried. It was his tired cry, not his wet-diaper cry. So I made him a bottle of stashed breast milk and rocked him to sleep.

When I came out of the nursery a half hour later, I felt *tired*, but determined. My job, as I saw it, was to be a sounding board and also to keep

177

Joey from swallowing anything not on the pediatrician's approved foods list. I was failing at the second one (at last count, he'd gnawed the corners off two foam packing blocks), but I was crushing it at the first.

Because all during Kaitlyn's packing session, there had to be an emotional component. It was required by law, like how TSA makes you take off your shoes even if you're wearing Crocs and have a TSA PreCheck tattooed on your forehead. Kaitlyn's emotional component was, "Tell me everything about your sex life, and don't leave anything out."

Earlier, I'd tried deflecting. ("Don't you want to talk about Martin?") But Kaitlyn had batted that aside. ("You already know everything.")

Now she was on her fourth packing cube, expertly shuffling pajama sets and toddler socks, when she said, "So, as you were saying before you put down Joey, you're going to Rome on Monday. What's the plan—just watch him play chess and drink espresso?"

I shrugged. "There's a spa at the hotel. He's got matches, interviews, and press the whole time. I'll mostly be making sure he eats and sleeps and maybe helping him avoid the international chess paparazzi." I paired the word *paparazzi* with jazz hands. "It's going to be a lot of room service and weirdly elaborate breakfast buffets."

Kaitlyn eyed me over the rim of a Ziploc full of charging cords. "What's on your mind? Something is bothering you."

I hesitated. I hadn't planned to say any of this out loud, not yet, but it was Kaitlyn. So, why not.

"It's weird," I said, picking at a stray Cheerio glued to my thigh. "We sleep together every night, and always end up cuddling. And then, in the morning, he's—like—extremely ready to do something as soon as I wake up."

Kaitlyn snorted. "Martin is the same way. It's like, as soon as I crack an eyelid, his hands are all over me."

I shook my head, not sure how I wanted to put this next part. "But with Andreas, it's strange. He only ever wants to give me orgasms."

She stopped stuffing pajamas and looked at me, full attention now. "What do you mean?"

"He's obsessed with my body," I said, feeling both ridiculous and, if I was being honest, smug. "He stares at me all the time. Like, it's not even subtle. It's like he's memorizing every square inch for a quiz. But he never lets me return the favor. It's like he's . . ." I trailed off, realizing I didn't know how to finish.

"He's shy?" Kaitlyn guessed, still folding but now mostly on autopilot.

"I don't know if that's it. He's a little shy, I think." I stared at the ceiling, running through all the data points. "But it's more than that. Like, I know he really enjoyed it when I gave him a hand job, but I get the sense he's denying himself for some reason. He's put up this internal boundary that he doesn't let himself cross."

Kaitlyn finished a cube and zipped it with a flourish, then set it on top of the suitcase with a thunk. "That's understandable. If you remember, I was very shy when I first started becoming intimate with Martin. I hated being naked in front of him, and not because I disliked my body. It's just, it felt weird, and not good-weird. It made me feel vulnerable, like it was a risk. Do you think that's what's going on with Andreas?"

I considered this. I'd shared everything with Kaitlyn, because all people needed someone they could talk to about absolutely anything, and Kaitlyn had always been that person for me. Likewise, I had always been that person for her. So, I knew she'd listen with full seriousness.

"Maybe," I said.

Kaitlyn abandoned the pajamas and perched on the edge of the coffee table. She watched me for a second.

"Have you asked him about it?" This was the most obvious solution.

I made a noise like a deflating tire. "I don't want to push. I figure he'll tell me when he's ready, right?"

Kaitlyn smirked. "I guess you just have to accept him giving you multiple orgasms every morning and every night until he's ready to tell you why he's holding himself back from reciprocation."

"He's taken so many cold showers, he actually got a cold last week," I said, and we both laughed, but I felt a little bad for him, too.

Kaitlyn pressed her lips together and said, "Poor baby. He's got it bad for you. Why won't he just let himself feel good?"

I shrugged. "I don't know. The only thing I can do is be patient."

She seemed to study me for a moment, eyes narrowed as if looking through a microscope. Then she said, "Have his brothers harassed you again?"

I shook my head. "No, thankfully. I haven't seen either of them for weeks. Are you suggesting that the threat from his brothers could be giving him psychological cock-block?"

"Hmm. I don't know. And what about his father. Any news?"

"No. In fact, Andreas hasn't heard anything for days, which is strange, so he sent someone to investigate. He should hear back today or tomorrow."

"Then, do you think maybe Andreas is being cautious because of the 'friends-with-benefits' and 'no-strings' thing you two have going on?"

I blinked at her. "What do you mean?"

"Maybe he's falling in love with you and he doesn't want to be devastated when you leave. So, he's holding himself back, reserving parts of himself."

My heart picked up pace, and I felt my cheeks flush. "Do you think so?"

Kaitlyn nodded. "If it were me, I would do the same thing."

I fumbled for a counter-argument. "What? Hold yourself back?"

"Yes," she said. "Because why would I give myself—my body—fully to someone who doesn't also want all of me? That's how I think, but maybe that's not how Andreas thinks."

She went back to her packing cubes, folding and stacking, but I could tell she was watching my reaction out of the corner of her eye. I stared forward, feeling a weird combination of guilt and longing.

After a minute, I blurted, "I think I'm in love with him."

Kaitlyn froze. The pajamas in her hands sagged to the table, forgotten. She turned to look at me, her expression raw and shocked. "Are you serious?"

I nodded, because anything else would have been a lie.

She said, "Oh my God," and sat down hard next to me.

"I know!" I picked up a throw pillow and pressed my face to it, muffling a scream.

Kaitlyn set her hand on my knee, squeezing until I looked at her. "Are you going to tell him?"

I nodded, still half buried in the pillow. "Yes. I feel like I'll burst if I don't tell him. And it's not fair, right? It's not fair of me to keep calling this no-strings when I want strings. We're heading to Rome for his chess tournament on Monday. I think I'll tell him in Rome."

Kaitlyn smiled, real and big, then pulled me into a hug. "You're not feeling squeamish anymore about him legally adopting you?"

I shook my head. "No. Not at all, actually. I haven't thought about that in weeks. Besides, it's all for revenge. It doesn't mean anything, it's just paperwork, and I certainly don't consider Andreas a father figure *at all*."

"Have you talked to your therapist about this? This is huge for you."

"Yes. And she agrees. I should be honest with him. And, she didn't say as much, but I get the sense she approves of him."

Kaitlyn laughed, and the sound was warm and safe, like a heated blanket right out of the dryer. "For the record, I approve too. I think he's great, and I love how he pampers you. You deserve pampering."

I smiled and felt a little overwhelmed by my happy feelings, which were rare and precious.

Waving my hands in the air, I said, "Let's change the subject. I'm already too obsessed with him as it is. Let's talk about something else."

"Okay . . . How's work? You haven't talked about work in ages."

I gave her the quick version of the drama that happened with Dr. Hauser and James before and after Thanksgiving, hitting the highlights— the funding reinstatement, the departmental gossip, Dmitry's campaign to befriend Andreas.

When I finished, Kaitlyn shook her head. "I can't believe all of this was happening and you didn't tell me!" She smacked me with one of Joey's onesies. "You really are obsessed with Andreas. You didn't even tell me about something so important. Oh! Speaking of important. Wait right here."

She jumped up and disappeared down the hallway, then came back less than a minute later, carrying a pile of folders and papers. On top of the stack was a thumb drive.

"I know you told me not to, but I had Martin's people do some investigating about your dad and this is everything they found, in hard copy and digital."

I stared, stunned. I'd been so swept up in my romance with Andreas that I'd forgotten to do more digging into my dad's fraud case, a fact that now made me feel like a traitor.

"Oh my gosh," I said, clutching the folders. "Thank you. Thank you so much."

Kaitlyn shrugged, modest but pleased. "I figured you've been busy and

I know how important this is to you. It's everything from the initial fraud complaint to the bankruptcy filing—I think you had that already, right?—to his death certificate. I also had them pull Genetix's initial corporate filing paperwork, just in case. I hope you find something helpful."

"Seriously. Thank you. This is amazing." I set the pile to one side and gave Kaitlyn another hug, tighter this time.

She said, "I just want you to be happy."

After the hug, I picked up the pile again and said, "Let me go put this next to my phone. I'll be right back."

I carried the folders and thumb drive to the kitchen counter where my cell was sitting. I realized, with a pang, that the phone was dead. I plugged it in and called back to Kaitlyn, "My phone is dead, I'm using your cable to charge it."

She called out, "Sounds good. Take your time."

I hovered, waiting for it to reboot. When the power finally came on, I had several missed texts, including a few from Diya, one from Tara, and one from Andreas.

I checked the one from Andreas first.

**Andreas:** Please message me when you get this. Oskar died four days ago and I've just been notified today. I'm on my way to the airport and will fly out immediately for the funeral, which takes place tomorrow in Oslo. Tara will pick you up this evening. She has your travel and hotel information. You need to be in Paris for the will reading Sunday morning.

I sat down at the kitchen table and reread the message several times before it truly sank in.

Oskar was dead. I couldn't believe it. I didn't know what to think. I'd thought we had more time. And now . . .

Shaking myself, I texted him back.

**Sam:** I am so sorry I didn't get your message until just now. My phone was dead. I will do as you've said and see you at the will reading on Sunday in Paris. Please take good care of yourself. I miss you.

I considered texting, *I love you*, but decided against it. Not yet. Not on the day he found out his father died.

I set the phone down, and for a long, long time, I just stared at the kitchen wall, trying to process the fact that everything had changed. My world had been turned upside down by a missed text message while my phone was dead.

Silently. And with no warning.

* * *

I'd texted Tara from Kaitlyn's apartment and she'd appeared outside within twelve minutes. Now, thirty minutes after I read Andreas's message, I was in the back seat of Tara's Mercedes, staring out the window at the city, feeling oddly wired. I kept checking my phone, freshly revived and plugged into the charging port in the center console. No new messages from Andreas.

As the Mercedes sliced through the damp cold, the reality of what I was about to do caught up with me like a slap. I should have been thinking about the logistics of packing and getting to the airport, asking about travel arrangements once we landed in Paris. But all I could think about was Andreas, how he must have found out, what he was feeling right now, whether he'd had anyone to talk to on the way to the airport.

I wanted to be the one holding his hand, or at the very least the one texting him back within a reasonable timeframe, not after my phone spent six hours dead on the kitchen counter. I felt, for the millionth time, the bone-deep guilt of missing his messages, of not being there to offer a single goddamn word of comfort.

For the tenth time since Tara had picked me up, I opened the messages app and scrolled to the top, hoping for a late-breaking missive from Andreas. Nothing. But just below his thread, I noticed the messages from Diya that I hadn't yet checked.

**Diya:** Your grandfather came looking for you at the apartment today. I hope you don't mind, I told him your new address. He said he would call you and arrange a time to meet. It didn't occur to me until after he left that maybe you didn't want him to know where you live? If so, I am so sorry!

**Diya:** Please message me back.

I reread Diya's words three times, trying to parse them. The last time I'd seen my mom's father, he was packing everything that had been legally determined to be his into a moving van after my grandparents' divorce. He'd tried to hug me. I'd pushed him away.

He'd raised me from age fourteen to sixteen, and then filed for divorce the month my grandma was diagnosed with cancer. I'd never forgiven him for it. I wasn't sure I ever would.

"Hey." Tara's voice floated back from the front seat. "You want a protein bar or anything? Have you eaten? This traffic is dogshit."

I looked up at the rearview mirror. I could see the outline of her head, the edge of her ponytail, her eyes flickering to meet mine for a split second. "No, thanks. I'm good," I said, which was a lie, but she didn't press.

The car lapsed back into its private storm of engine noise and bad thoughts.

I pulled out the thermos of tea Kaitlyn had given me before leaving her apartment and tried to take a sip, but my hands were trembling too much to unscrew the lid. I jammed it back between my knees and turned my attention to the world outside. Bridges, overpasses, the blur of holiday lights in shop windows. All I could think about was Andreas's face, and how I would find him at the Paris hotel, and whether I could say anything that would make any of this less terrible. I knew he had complicated thoughts about his father, but the man was still his father.

When I next looked up, we were gliding to a stop outside Andreas's building, the familiar stone-and-glass box on the Lower East Side. I blinked, surprised at how quickly we'd arrived, then realized that my sense of time had been completely scrambled by the chemical cocktail of stress and shock. Tara double-parked and turned around in the front seat to face me.

"Can you wait here for a minute before going in?" she said. "There's someone at the door talking to Costa. Not one of our people."

I craned my neck and looked out the tinted window. Standing on the front steps, next to the doorman, was an old man in a navy peacoat and gray slacks, a heavy wool scarf knotted at his throat. He was hunched against the cold, hands shoved deep in his pockets, his head inclined toward the doorman as if listening to a secret. The angle was bad, but even at a distance I recognized the shape of his jaw, the stubborn set of his shoulders. My grandfather.

"That man is my grandfather," I said, my voice flat.

Tara raised her eyebrows, then looked out the window again. "Want me to take you around the back? Or wait until he leaves?"

I shook my head, surprising myself with the intensity of my own answer. "No, it's fine. I should see him." The words tasted bitter and unfamiliar, but I knew they were right.

Tara paused, studying me for a moment. "You sure? We can circle the block until he's gone."

"No," I said again, this time more certain. "I want to talk to him."

"Okay," Tara said, and put the car in park. "But Peter will meet you in the lobby to take you up to the apartment while I park. I'll be right behind you. If you want privacy, I'll keep the team away, but they'll be watching."

I nodded, grateful. "Makes sense. Um, can you bring up these files when you come up?" I gestured to the folders that Kaitlyn had given me, which now sat on the seat next to me. I'd placed the thumb drive in my bag.

"Sure thing," she said.

I opened the door and stepped out into the air, which felt like it had become colder over the last half hour. My legs were still wobbly from adrenaline, but I forced them into motion and walked up the steps to where my grandfather stood. He was arguing with Costa in the amiable, practiced way of old men who have spent years perfecting the art of polite combat.

He saw me first. His whole body snapped to attention, and for a second he looked exactly as I remembered him—sturdy, confident, more granite than flesh. But then I saw the age in his face, the slack at his jaw, the thinned patch at his hairline. His mouth worked for a moment, unsure what shape to make, and then a small, hopeful smile tugged at one corner.

"Hi," I said, stuffing my hands into my own coat pockets, suddenly fourteen years old again.

He nodded at Costa, who tactfully stepped inside to give us privacy. "Hey, kid," my grandfather said. His voice was softer than I remembered, a little worn at the edges. "How you doing?"

I shrugged. "I'm okay. How are you?" The words felt rehearsed, but it was the only thing I could think to say.

"I was in town and thought I'd look you up," he said, eyes skittering away from mine and then back again.

I felt my throat tighten, but I pushed past it. "I'm sorry I haven't been in touch. It's been—" I gestured to the city, the sky, my entire existence.

His eyes glistened, but he didn't look away. "Oh, it's okay. I know you've been busy."

I nodded, then blurted, "I have a plane to catch tonight, so I only have a few minutes."

His face fell just a hair, but he rallied. "That's okay. I just wanted to see you, make sure you're alright."

There was a silence, the kind that's both too short and too long, and I realized I wasn't angry at him anymore. Or maybe I was, but it was drowned out by the greater urge not to waste another second.

"I'm coming back in a week," I said. "Will you still be in town? Would you want to meet up then? Or, I don't know, maybe talk on the phone before that?"

He smiled, and this time it stuck. "Yes. Anytime. I can fly out here, too, if you want. Whenever you want."

He fumbled in his pocket for a phone. "Can I get your number? I, uh, only seem to have the old one."

I recited it, watching as he typed, then listened as he called the number. My phone, which was still in my hand, buzzed with the new contact.

I held it up and flashed the screen. "That's me."

He laughed, a little sheepishly, and then said, "I'll let you get going. But I'd like to see you. When you get back."

"Yeah," I said, and this time I meant it. "I'll call you."

He nodded, his smile going shaky at the corners. "Thank you, Sammy. I really miss you."

The words hit harder than I expected. I felt my eyes sting, and before I could second-guess it, I closed the distance and hugged him, hard. His arms came up around me, strong and warm, the same way they used to when I was a kid. He smelled like his usual aftershave and cold air, and for a second I wanted to take him with me upstairs and tell him everything.

But instead, I just said, "I missed you, too," and let go.

As I walked toward the lobby, I felt lighter, not because I'd let go of anything, but because I'd decided to carry it differently. I didn't know what would happen with my grandfather, or whether we'd ever be close again, but for the first time in years, I was done pushing people away. I wanted to believe that we all could change, including me. I wanted to believe that they wouldn't let me down, that they wouldn't leave. That it was safe to love someone.

As I greeted my guard and followed him to the elevator, I said a silent thank-you to Andreas. Without him, I wasn't sure I would've ever opened myself up again.

I felt . . . optimistic.

# [ 19 ]

## DYSFUNCTION

***Samantha***

Approximately thirty hours after I hugged my grandfather, I was sitting in a Paris hotel room, regretting every time I'd ever fantasized about waking up on another continent.

It was just past 9:00 AM on Sunday, which, if you did the math, made it about 3:00 AM New York time, or the eternal Now of jet lag. The hotel suite looked like the inside of a Fabergé egg, all gold moldings and white marble and so much velvet you could have upholstered an army of Marie Antoinettes.

I'd taken a midnight direct from JFK and my traveling companion had been Tara. We'd landed at Charles de Gaulle just after 2:00 PM on Saturday afternoon, and from that moment I had given up any hope of understanding what the fuck was happening, electing instead to simply follow Tara's lead. She produced a car from thin air, and then spirited us to a hotel so swanky I was half convinced they were going to kick me out if I ventured into the lobby.

The suite itself was another world. Two bedrooms, each with a king bed and a bathroom bigger than my undergrad dorm room. A private sitting room with a view of the Eiffel Tower so close it looked fake, like one of those Instagram filters that superimposes the Taj Mahal behind your backyard barbecue.

In any other circumstances, I would've been thrilled.

I spent the first five minutes after arrival in a sort of fugue state, staring at the pair of black dresses that had been left on the bed in my room. Both in my size, both with designer tags. One was a Givenchy, the other a Chanel. And I was supposed to pick one for the will reading, which made me feel like a paper doll dressed by a particularly chic god.

The next ten hours were a blur of attempts to sleep (fail), attempts to eat (triple fail), and increasingly desperate attempts to locate Andreas, who had not so much as texted since leaving for his father's funeral.

Earlier this morning, around 6:00 AM, Tara had claimed that his flight should have landed, and that he was probably "handling things," but as the minutes wore on and the silence grew, I became concerned something terrible had happened. What if Henrik had done something? Or Tobias had arranged for an unfortunate accident?

By 8:00 AM, I'd given up on checking my phone and moved to the sitting room, where I sat cross-legged on a cream brocade settee, clad in the less threatening of the two dresses, my hair styled and makeup applied.

My gaze strayed to the bundle wrapped in paper under the oval coffee table. For some reason, I'd brought Andreas's Christmas gift with me to Paris, the set of signed Bobby Fischer books. Now I felt strange about it. But Christmas was just days away. Even if we didn't celebrate while in Paris, I'd thought maybe I could give them to him, something to cheer him up.

Rolling my eyes at myself and how inadequate of a girlfriend I might theoretically make some day, I refocused my attention on my computer. I should have been reading over my father's files, aka Kaitlyn's gift to me. Instead, I'd been sitting with my laptop open, scrolling through the PDFs in a cycle of diminishing comprehension, never reading more than half a page before scrolling to the next.

Then, there was a knock on the door.

It was not a soft, French-hotel knock, but the kind you'd use if you were serving a warrant or delivering news of a tornado. I startled upright, staring at the door.

From inside the other bedroom, Tara called, "I'll get it. Stay put." She appeared in the corridor two seconds later, already in a black suit and boots, her light brown hair slicked back.

She opened the door.

I leaned to the side, peering around her, and saw Andreas standing in the hallway. My heart did an actual, audible restart. I set the laptop aside and bolted to the door, nearly tripping on the corner of an antique rug.

Tara started to say something, but I didn't let her finish. I shouldered her out of the way, which was sort of like shoving an iceberg, then threw my arms around Andreas's neck.

For a split second, his body went rigid. Eventually, he wrapped his arms around my waist and pulled me tight, so tight I thought maybe I'd never breathe again, and honestly, I was fine with it.

I kissed his neck because it was the only part of him I could reach without letting him go. "I am so sorry," I said, and the words came out in a rush, unplanned. "Let me know what I can do. I am sorry." I rubbed his back, which was taut and hard as a carved statue, and he shook his head, as if to say, *There is nothing.*

I heard Tara say, "I'll be in the next room," just before a door closed quietly behind us.

She was gone before I even registered the words, a true professional.

I pulled away and took Andreas's hand. He let me. I led him toward the sitting area, then shut the door behind us for privacy. I looked at his face for the first time and saw that the skin under his eyes was gray and bruised, like he'd spent the last thirty hours awake. There were faint white lines at the corners of his mouth, the kind that only appear when you've been frowning for days.

"When did you get in?" I asked, my voice soft so it wouldn't break.

He didn't answer at first, just stared at our hands like he was counting the bones. Then, all at once, he dropped my fingers and took two steps back, shoving his own hands in his coat pockets. "We need to go," he said, voice scraped raw. "Are you ready?"

Something about the way he said it—so flat, so unlike him—made me go stiff. But then I reminded myself that his father had just died. I told myself to be patient. Be normal. *Don't make this about you.*

"Yes. Let me put on my shoes and get my coat," I said, and went to fetch them. I could see him, reflected in the antique mirror above the fireplace, standing there like a dark pillar, unmoving.

I pulled on the shoes, leaving the straps at the ankles dangling, and I found the matching wool coat, shrugged it on, and turned to face him.

"Is there anything I should know?" I said, trying to keep my voice steady. "About the will reading? Anything I should be prepared for? Or is there anything I can do to support you and make this easier?"

He stared at the carpet, then at the chandelier, and then, finally, at the wall behind my head.

He spoke without emotion. "Tobias has a child. A daughter, by a woman he was involved with a few years ago. He tracked them down. He believes this daughter is the oldest and first grandchild."

I blinked, processing. "Wow."

Andreas continued, "He will be very surprised and unhappy when I show him your adoption papers. Henrik, likewise, will be unhappy, since Tobias has always taken care of Henrik, in a way. I will encourage the woman and the child to leave the room before Tobias or Henrik lose their temper, but I need you to not intervene."

I nodded, feeling sick for the woman and the girl who would have to be present for what was about to happen. "Understood," I said. "I won't intervene. But if you need me to do something, you just have to look at me."

He didn't reply, but his jaw unclenched, and I took it as a win.

Then, for the first time since he'd entered the room, Andreas looked directly at me. His eyes were cold and bright, but his expression was grave. "It is imperative that you stay close to Tara and the team. No matter what is said, or what my brothers do, or what I say, stay with Tara and the team."

I nodded, matching his seriousness, and bent to fasten the ankle straps of my shoes. "I will."

Some of the tension drained from his face, but not all. There was still something else, a thick, invisible layer of ice between us, and I didn't know how to melt it. *Be patient.*

I finished with the last strap of my shoe and straightened. Only then did I realize that every single item I was wearing—dress, coat, shoes, even the tights—had been bought for me by Andreas. And every piece fit perfectly. He'd chosen everything so that I would look the part, and now, walking toward him, I felt a bit like an accessory, one he'd designed for today's purpose.

"Tara. We are leaving," Andreas called, turning away from me.

Tara exited her room seconds later, but she hung back, her face a mask of professionalism.

Andreas opened the suite door for me, not meeting my eyes. I walked past him into the hallway, feeling the heavy thud of each heartbeat, and heard him let the door close behind us after Tara exited.

He walked in front, not beside me, setting the pace. I thought about reaching for his hand, then decided against it. Tara and four other guards who'd been waiting outside fell into step around me, a human wall.

We walked, the seven of us, through the silent, perfect corridors of the hotel. I wondered, not for the first time since reading his text message on Friday, what it would be like if I just ran away with Andreas to a place where none of this could reach us. But that wasn't reality.

Reality was a will, and a company, and two sinister brothers who would likely be blindsided, and therefore unpredictable.

Tara nudged me, a tiny, invisible reassurance, and I squared my shoulders. It was time to play my part.

As we reached the elevator, I looked once at Andreas, hoping to catch his gaze. But he was focused forward, jaw set, eyes fixed on the future.

* * *

In the back of another Mercedes, this time a limo, I tried not to sweat through my dress. Not because it was hot—it wasn't, it was very cold— but because I was so nervous. Tara sat next to me along with the four security guards from the hotel. The Parisian sky was the exact shade of the mother-of-pearl buttons on my coat.

I'd assumed I'd be in the same car as Andreas, that we'd go to the will reading together, but apparently not. Logistics had been handled with the same precision as a hostage exchange. Two identical cars, two sets of bodyguards, two separate routes through city traffic to the lawyer's office in the 16th arrondissement.

Through the window, the city unspooled in wet, gray ribbons—cyclists hunching past, children in wool coats dragging parents toward boulan- geries, impossibly thin women chain-smoking under the eaves of apart- ment buildings. I didn't know if it was the jet lag or the situation, but the city looked haunted. Every block was like a different timeline, each building a monument to some secret history. It made New York look like a freshman attempt at culture.

The lawyer's building was an old limestone hulk that looked like it should have been repurposed as a museum or the headquarters of the Illuminati. The Mercedes rolled to a halt in a semicircle cobbled drive, and immediately the doors opened, Tara barking orders and the guards forming a phalanx around me as I stepped out. There was something deeply embarrassing about being flanked by five security professionals when you yourself were the farthest thing from an international asset, but Tara seemed to relish the moment.

Inside, the lobby was cold and sterile, the kind of place where the receptionist's lipstick was the only color in sight. I caught a glimpse of myself in the glass. Pale, overdressed, a little hollowed out around the eyes. Tara was a step behind me, and in her black suit and earpiece, she looked like a bulletproof shadow.

Then I saw him. Andreas. He was ahead of us, near the elevators, standing ramrod straight in his dark suit. He had no security detail now, just himself, hands folded in front of him, jaw set.

He looked back, saw us, and did not smile. Instead, he pressed the elevator call button, then turned away, as if to telegraph that we'd be taking different elevators. And we did. Andreas got into the first elevator alone, doors closing on him. Tara guided me toward the next set of elevators, then leaned in and whispered, "We're taking a more secure route. Mr. Kristiansen doesn't want to take any chances with your safety."

The way she said it—"your safety"—made it sound like I was the target of assassins. I suppressed the urge to laugh because Henrik Kristiansen was no assassin.

We rode in silence. At the twelfth floor, the elevator doors opened to a long, echoing corridor lined with gold-leaf mirrors and the sort of furniture that looks like it's only meant for looking at, never for sitting. As a group of six, we walked the last fifty feet to the double doors at the end.

Tara stopped in front of the doors and checked her watch. I could hear voices inside, faint and heated. Then, the doors swung open and someone who I assumed was a lawyer beckoned us in.

The conference room was so opulent it was offensive. The table was a single, carved slab of something dark and old, long enough to seat thirty. The chandeliers above dripped with crystal, refracting the winter light into a haloed glare that made my head throb. The windows were so tall and thick that you could barely hear the city outside. For a second, I wondered if that was the point, to make the whole will reading feel like it happened outside of time or worldly worries.

Henrik was already in the room, seated at the far end of the table. He wore a suit, but the tie was off and the top button undone. He looked like he'd spent the night drinking bleach. His eyes were red-rimmed, and as soon as he saw me, he started to grin—an ugly, hungry grin that made me want to throw up.

Tobias stood at the head of the table, hands braced on the wood, talking in low tones to a man I assumed was the lead lawyer. He was short and trim, with silver hair and a face like an old coin. He wore the most beautiful suit I'd ever seen, and spoke French in the rapid, clipped way I used to think was beautiful. Tobias gestured wildly, then shot a glance at Henrik, and then at me. His eyes didn't register me as a threat, and I felt a perverse sense of satisfaction at being so thoroughly underestimated.

Andreas entered the room last, as though he'd timed his arrival to coincide with ours. For the first time since I'd known him, he looked small —not physically, but in the way he moved, like he was trying to take up as little physical space as possible. He glanced at me once, then at Tara, then nodded to the lawyer.

The lawyer stepped forward and greeted Andreas in French. Andreas, likewise, responded in flawless French. The exchange was smooth and struck me as friendly. *Did these two know each other well?*

Meanwhile, I hadn't even known Andreas could speak French.

Tara led me to a spot at the long table as far from Tobias and Henrik as possible. She pulled out a chair for me, and as I sat, I could feel Henrik's eyes boring into me.

The lawyer conferred with a second attorney. There was a flurry of document shuffling and whispered strategy, then the one I'd assumed was the lead lawyer seemed to call the room to order.

Henrik leaned over to Andreas and said something in Norwegian, low and rapid-fire.

Andreas barely turned his head, then replied in English, crisp and flat, "No. Sam is not pregnant."

Tobias rolled his eyes. "Then why all the security?"

The lawyer said something in French, then switched, mid-sentence, to

English so flawless it barely carried an accent. "I apologize, Ms. Jarlston. I will use English from this point forward." He bowed his head toward me.

I gave him a small smile of gratitude.

Tobias sneered, "Why pander to the childless American? The heir is Norwegian." He gestured with a dismissive wave toward the far end of the table, where a woman sat with a small child on her lap. The woman looked shell-shocked, her face locked in a stone mask of compliance. The child—maybe two—wore a miniature sailor suit and clutched a sippy cup in both hands.

I stared. The woman wouldn't look at me, and for a moment I wondered if she was here of her own free will, or if she'd been coerced.

Tobias spoke to Andreas, his tone smug. "And now father's shares belong to my child. Likewise, father's personal holdings and estate, which include all your mother's compositions, belong to me."

I stiffened. The last part was news to me. I settled my attention on Andreas, who was looking at the table, fingers laced together like he didn't have a care in the world.

The lawyer glanced from Andreas to Tobias to Henrik, clearing his throat as he did so. "Let us sit and discuss the matter thoroughly, yes?"

Tobias took his seat with an exaggerated sigh. "I guess what they say about sleeping around not paying off is all a lie, hmm? I can't wait to license your mother's songs for car commercials." He barked a laugh, then turned to the lawyer and said, "Isn't that right? Since I fathered the oldest grandchild, according to father's addendum, the personal estate passes to me, and that includes every piece of physical property that belonged to my dearest youngest brother's mother and every piece of intellectual property as well."

I shifted my attention back to Andreas again, and this time, he was smiling—but not in a way that suggested happiness. It was more like he was enjoying a private joke at everyone else's expense.

I tried to mask my confusion as my brain tried to make sense of what was happening. Meanwhile, Henrik—who must've noticed Andreas's smirk—shifted in his seat and glared at me. "Wait. What's going on?"

Andreas sat down slowly, folded his hands on the tabletop, and turned to the lawyer. "Shall we proceed?"

Henrik pointed at the lawyer and yelled, "What the fuck is going on?"

The little girl at the far end of the table started to cry, loud and abrupt.

The mother whispered something in her ear, rocking her, but the noise only increased.

Andreas, calm as ever, said, "You might want to ask your child and her mother to leave."

Tobias stood up, hands braced on the table, and leaned in toward Andreas. "You've lost," he said, but he didn't sound so certain or smug anymore. For a second, I thought he was going to vault across the table and strangle Andreas.

Andreas sat there, eyes on Tobias, expression serene. "Allow me to introduce you to your niece, who I adopted last month." He lifted a hand to me. "She is now the controlling shareholder of Genetix, and is of legal age. Thus, she will be inheriting and have control of those shares as of today."

It was like time stopped. Henrik and Tobias just stared, mouths open, eyes bouncing from me to Andreas and back again. Even the lawyers seemed to freeze, reminding me of rabbits when they suspect a nearby predator.

Andreas continued, "And since I am the legal father of the oldest grandchild, all of Oskar's personal belongings—including my mother's compositions and property in Italy—pass to me."

A beat of silence. Pure, soundless suspension, a vacuum of air and atoms and time.

And then all hell broke loose.

Tobias lunged, overturning his chair, and screamed something in Norwegian that even I could tell was a collection of the most inventive curse words in the language. Henrik, instead of going for Andreas, actually went for the lawyer, grabbing him by the lapels and shaking him. The woman at the table shrieked, clutching her daughter to her chest. She stood and stumbled away from the kerfuffle.

Someone was calling for security. My guards didn't move. They simply stood in formation around me amid all the chaos outside the bubble of their protection. And inside the bubble, where I sat miring in my own chaos while stupidly staring at Andreas, I watched this man I thought I loved grinning triumphantly in the face of his eldest brother.

I realized, with no small amount of despair, that I had also been played by Andreas Kristiansen.

When I'd asked him all those weeks ago why he wanted to help me take over Genetix, he'd told the truth. He didn't want Genetix, he never had. He didn't care about the company.

But he'd also lied.

Andreas wanted his mother's legacy, her property, the rights to her music. *That's* why he'd sought me out. That's why he'd adopted me.

Perhaps that was also why he'd bought me gifts and meticulously won me over with nostalgia and sweetness and thoughtfulness and shy smiles. He'd seduced my mind, my body, and my heart. And I'd let him.

What had I been to him? A pawn? This whole time, had I been nothing but a disposable piece in his game? He'd lied to me. And he'd gotten exactly what he wanted from me. I thought I was so smart, but I was nothing.

No. I was less than nothing.

I was a complete fool.

[ 20 ]

# UNSTABLE ENVIRONMENTS

***Andreas***

I'd been standing some distance outside Samantha's suite for five minutes. To my left, a tall blue vase loomed above the white marble pedestal like a flowerless cenotaph. To my right, a row of four security guards spaced at measured intervals along the hallway, each pretending not to see me, each one shifting in place with the periodicity of metronomes. I loitered exactly fifteen feet from her door. I'd measured it in paces when I first traversed the distance this morning.

These men worked for me. I'd hired them. Or, at least, I'd given the order for them to be here. The gracelessness of my idling in their presence didn't faze me. What I had not counted on was the pain in my stomach. The actual, physical sensation of needing to vomit and being unable to do so. The last time I'd felt this kind of visceral discomfort had been at my mother's funeral.

The hour was just past ten, Paris time. Lights in the hotel corridor were dimmed except for the spots immediately above each door. The walls were lined in blue silk the color of sea glass, and it made my black suit and shoes look funereal. I supposed, for this occasion, it was appropriate.

That moment at the will reading, when I'd revealed the truth to the room, played on repeat inside my head. Specifically, I recalled the way Samantha looked at me. Not with anger or betrayal. Not even with hurt. Her gaze exuded emptiness. As though I were a stranger, someone she didn't know and didn't wish to.

It had always been possible that Samantha might not forgive me. I'd approached her months ago with this knowledge, but it hadn't seemed to matter . . . *then*.

We'd been strangers, more or less. That we would—that I could, and almost from the very first moment I laid eyes on her, grow to care for her again so deeply after fifteen years apart seemed ludicrous. Standing outside her department building on that early fall morning, she'd unknowingly wrapped me around her finger; and she'd twisted me into knots in that café with effortless ease. But, it wasn't until the night she'd showed up at my apartment—bitter and sweet, dressed in black and stilettos—that I suspected I might be dealing with a queen instead of a pawn.

Closing my eyes, I exhaled, fighting the urge to crawl on my knees in front of her and beg for forgiveness, for absolution. Samantha would not want that from me tonight. She would despise it, and me, for being weak and inconsistent and continuing to lie, and she'd be right. She'd see through the performance.

Forgiveness wasn't what I wanted from Samantha.

However . . . *Later, perhaps*. In the fullness of time, Samantha Jarlston might someday permit me to kneel at her feet, and in that event, I would be more than happy to oblige. And if she wanted me to be sincerely sorry, if it would make any difference, I would—sincerely—be sorry. Yet, only if repentance won me her heart in the end.

But first, consequences. Pain and suffering. Which I assumed would culminate in either objects thrown at my head or a slap across the face by her own hand. Perhaps screaming. Possibly tears.

*I hope it's not tears.* I had no countermove for tears. No plan, other than to surrender. And I didn't want to surrender. I wanted *her*.

Squaring my shoulders, I checked my watch again (10:07 PM), and approached the door, ignoring the attention of her guards. I lifted my hand to knock and hesitated. What if she was already asleep? She slept fitfully under the best circumstances. I didn't wish to wake her. But I was also not a coward. Cowardice was a learned behavior, a vestige of too many years in the company of men who mistook ruthlessness for virtue.

Whereas, I was ruthless. But did not consider myself virtuous. Obviously.

I knocked, three precise raps, then braced myself.

The door opened after four seconds and Tara appeared, her face unreadable. She wore the same suit as earlier, but had lost the tie, and her arms were folded across her chest.

She looked at me and said, "She's in her room." No pleasantries.

"Is she awake?" My voice came out gravelly. I was not surprised. I'd been forced to shout over Henrik when the Police Nationale had arrived to take him into custody for aggravated assault against our father's favorite lawyer.

Tara shrugged. "She is not asleep. I'm going to take a walk. Text me when you're done."

She stepped aside to allow me entry and, as I passed her, I caught the faintest trace of—what? Pity? Disgust? I had the suspicion Tara wished to maim me, and also that she would have been entirely justified in doing so.

Tara closed the door to the hallway, leaving me in the darkness and silence of the suite's entryway. I took two deep breaths and walked into the suite proper.

The suite had two bedrooms, and the main bedroom was at the end of a short corridor lined with mirrors and low, blue-lit sconces. I walked slowly, careful to keep my steps light. Sam's door was ajar, and from the crack of it, I could see the square of bright light from her laptop screen, and her form hunched in bed, shoulders up, head down.

I stood there for a moment, staring at her, the way her long hair curled at the edges, the angle of her jaw above the collar of an old sweatshirt. She scrolled with one hand and picked at her thumbnail with the other, something she did when she felt overwhelmed. A tell, I speculated, she wasn't aware of.

Abruptly, she glanced up and spotted me in the doorway, our gazes clashing. Yet, her expression didn't alter at all.

I knocked softly, pushing the door open wider, and said, "May I come in?"

She closed the laptop with a snap. "I'll come out." Her voice rang neutral and monotone.

I retreated to the sitting room and waited for her to appear. This was not a sensation I was familiar with. In chess, you lost, and then you immediately began analyzing the defeat for lessons, weaknesses, patterns. I had never been checkmated in love before, the irony being that I'd checkmated myself. The rules were unfamiliar.

Samantha entered the sitting room and stood ten feet removed from me, hands pushed into the front pouch pocket of her sweatshirt, hair falling around her shoulders. She regarded me with what I wanted to believe was blankness, but in reality was probably contempt.

"I know it's late," I said.

She didn't move, didn't nod. Just waited.

"Before we discuss anything else," I said, "I have something important to tell you."

She blinked, her features softening just a little, eyes seeming to spark to life. "Go on."

I exhaled, surprised at my own nervousness, but forged ahead. This confession would, hopefully, be the worst part. "I am the one who froze the funding for your PI, Dr. Hauser, back in November. That was not Tobias, that was me."

She stared at me for a beat. Her face went slack. I recognized that she required a moment to process this news and I braced myself for her reaction to my manipulation. *Please, no tears. Anything but tears.*

But Samantha didn't cry. She smiled. It was a bitter, twisted thing, and it made me wish she'd cried instead.

Then, she laughed, short and sharp, and turned, walking to the window and wrapping her arms around herself. She stood with her back to me, looking out at the city.

"After what happened today," she said, her tone steady, almost academic, "I wondered if it had been you. Tobias told me, when he came to see me that second time after Thanksgiving with a bribe, that he hadn't done anything to me yet. And then, when you and I went to that wine bar, you asked me if I wanted you to get rid of Dr. Nieminen. It struck me as strange at the time, but I never would've suspected you until today."

The urge to apologize, or at least to explain myself, bombarded my better judgment. But I knew both of those pathetic displays would only make her hate me more. I stood there in silence, hands at my sides, breathing through the sting of it.

After a long pause, she said, "You did tell me once that you were not a good person. I should have believed you."

I gritted my teeth. The memory of saying those words, of believing myself to be the villain, was suddenly, acutely real. I was a villain. I'd almost let her put her mouth on me because I'd wanted it more than I'd wanted my next breath in that moment. I'd wanted her so badly, I'd almost let it happen. I didn't regret stopping her. If I hadn't stopped her, I would truly be a weak-willed coward. And I'd hate myself just as much as she hated me now.

Telling her, as she lowered to her knees, that I wasn't a good person, didn't absolve me of any sins. But absolution wasn't my goal. What good would that do me? I didn't want her to move on, I wanted her stuck, just as I was stuck. Truthfully, pathetically, I wanted her even if she hated me. Even if she never forgave me. And I would settle for any part of Samantha, at any time.

*That* was now my goal. A sliver of her attention. A bone thrown in my direction at her discretion. Given my sins, just that would be a miraculous victory.

Her back still to the room, she cleared her throat and said, "I think I know why, but tell me anyway. Why did you have Dr. Hauser's funding frozen?"

I'd rehearsed an answer to this question. "I knew, if your position were threatened and you thought Tobias was responsible, you would accept my proposal to let me adopt you. I knew Tobias interfering in your life would anger you and lead you to seek revenge against him." My statements were one-hundred-percent honest and also provided just enough detail and type of information to paint a clear picture of the situation without me self-indulgently explaining additional context for my decisions. Context would only sound like excuses.

What I'd done was ruthless and without virtue, even if the end result meant Samantha inherited the shares of Genetix that should've been hers by birthright.

She was silent again. I could see the tension in her shoulders, the way her hands curled into fists at her sides. I waited for her to say something, anything.

She didn't.

I swallowed, and found I had to focus in order to keep my voice steady. "Do you have any additional questions for me? I will answer anything."

She shook her head, slow and methodical. "No. I think you covered everything else this afternoon at the will reading."

There was a sharp, literal pain in my chest. Her dismissiveness and lack of curiosity hurt me. I wanted to say her name but knew it would sound like an entreaty, which she would likely view as deceitful.

Anything I said beyond the relaying of factual, verifiable information would be discounted, derided, filed under manipulation. Thus, appealing to her now on any personal level, or with any emotion, was not a viable strategy. I knew this.

I forced myself to swallow the hurt silently and reached into my coat pocket. I pulled out a bank card and flicked it between my fingers. "This account contains approximately the same amount of money that was in your parents' bank accounts before the fraud allegations, before the bankruptcy. The pin is your birth year and month."

She turned slightly. I could decipher the reflection of her profile in the window's glass, but she didn't look at me. "You can leave it on the table. And it goes without saying, I think, that I will not be paying you back for any expenses incurred while we lived together."

I nodded, blinking against a sudden stinging in my eyes, and masked my tone in equanimity. "I would not accept it, even if you did try to . . . reimburse me." I placed the card on the table and added, "The security team is with you for another six months, fully paid. And I have arranged for an apartment for you in New York, the lease is paid through the end of next year."

She nodded, arms still around her middle. "Looks like you covered everything. I assume my things are already out of your apartment?"

"Not yet."

Samantha seemed to pause, like this information surprised her. Then she turned and looked at me, eyes finally meeting mine, and asked, "Why not?"

"I did not wish to touch or move your things without your consent."

She barked a laugh, then shook her head. "That's funny. That's a good one."

I felt my jaw clench and grind with the effort it took to remain silent, to not explain myself or my reasoning. I'd led us here. No one but me. And if she wished to laugh in my face, she deserved the distinction of being the only person I would ever allow to do so.

When her laughter tapered, we stood in silence for a long time, simply staring at each other. I wondered what she saw, or if she suspected how carefully I'd planned this interaction.

If I weren't a villain, this would likely be where we said goodbye. I would apologize for using her and lying to her. I would let her go. This brief interaction would be the finite end of our acquaintance.

That had been the original plan because she was never supposed to care about me, or want me, or even like me. Obviously, the original plan had changed that first night she'd sleepwalked into my bedroom. I began bargaining with myself and formulating new schemes, ones where she eventually forgave me and we remained in each other's lives in some capacity. I'd studied her preferences, asked her friends for information about her, studied her partialities and dislikes, selected items as gifts I felt certain she would adore, hoping to make myself indispensable.

But that night I'd returned from London, Samantha had annihilated all my assumptions about us, about what might be possible in the future. I'd never considered the possibility that she might want *me*. And so, I'd stopped focusing on how to earn her forgiveness and friendship and began plotting how to keep *her*.

This meeting—this conversation—was part of my new plan. A necessary, albeit painful, step for us to move forward. Each move orchestrated, each statement prepared. I hadn't expected it to hurt this much, but letting Samantha go was impossible now.

If my father had just lived for another three months, I might've strategized a solution, mapped out how to tell her the truth without losing her in the short term. I might've convinced her to love me, to keep me. But the timing was off.

"I leave for the tournament in Rome soon," I said, and covered my urge to grimace at the banality of my words by glancing down at my shoes.

"I'm sure you'll win. You always do." Her emotionless statements were like ice water down my spine.

I had one more thing to say, and then I would leave. I simply needed to speak.

Yet, I couldn't force my mouth to move. I didn't wish to leave her, not even for a few days or hours. And the urge to beg, to plead, again pressed forward against my better judgement, sending my heart to my throat. My vision blurred. My breathing grew labored. I felt myself waver.

*Please. Please love me back. Please forgive me.*

Suddenly, Samantha tore her gaze from mine and turned away. "If there's nothing else . . ." Giving me no chance to respond, Samantha walked to her bedroom and closed the door behind her with a gentleness that cut more than the violence of a slam ever could.

I stood there in the blue-lit silence, staring through blurred vision at the closed door beyond the corridor, the blood rushing between my ears a dizzying commotion, drowning out all other sounds. Then, without warning, I crumpled to the floor.

I covered my face with my hands and struggled to breathe. I thought I might cry. I didn't. Just waves of numbness, followed by excruciating pain, over and over.

Eventually, I stood. Feeling lightheaded, I sat on the sofa and clutched my forehead, breathing in deeply through my nose and out through my mouth. Tomorrow, I would begin again. I would stay the course I'd set, employ an improved strategy.

I would win her over in some capacity. Eventually. Because the alternative felt unfathomable.

**Scan me to receive new book updates and news from Penny!**

**Scan me if you'd like a signed copy of this or any Penny Reid book!**

# ABOUT THE AUTHOR

Penny Reid is the *New York Times*, *Wall Street Journal*, and *USA Today* bestselling author of the Winston Brothers and Knitting in the City series. She used to spend her days writing federal grant proposals as a biomedical researcher, but now she writes kissing books. Penny is an obsessive knitter and manages the #OwnVoices-focused mentorship incubator / publishing imprint, Smartypants Romance. She lives in Seattle Washington with her husband, three kids, and dog named Hazel.

**Come find me**
**Mailing List:** http://pennyreid.ninja/newsletter/
**Email:** pennreid@gmail.com …hey, you! Email me ;-)

amazon.com/Penny-Reid/e/B00BI7A7SY

bookbub.com/authors/penny-reid

goodreads.com/ReidRomance

facebook.com/pennyreidwriter

instagram.com/reidromance

patreon.com/smartypantsromance

tiktok.com/@authorpennyreid

x.com/reidromance

# OTHER BOOKS BY PENNY REID

**<u>Knitting in the City Series</u>**

(Interconnected Standalones, Adult Contemporary Romantic Comedy)

*<u>Neanderthal Seeks Human: A Smart Romance (#1)</u>*

*<u>Neanderthal Marries Human: A Smarter Romance (#1.5)</u>*

*<u>Friends without Benefits: An Unrequited Romance (#2)</u>*

*<u>Love Hacked: A Reluctant Romance (#3)</u>*

*<u>Beauty and the Mustache: A Philosophical Romance (#4)</u>*

*<u>Ninja at First Sight (#4.75)</u>*

*<u>Happily Ever Ninja: A Married Romance (#5)</u>*

*<u>Dating-ish: A Humanoid Romance (#6)</u>*

*<u>Marriage of Inconvenience: (#7)</u>*

*<u>Neanderthal Seeks Extra Yarns (#8)</u>*

*<u>Knitting in the City Coloring Book (#9)</u>*

**<u>Winston Brothers Series</u>**

(Interconnected Standalones, Adult Contemporary Romantic Comedy, spinoff of
Beauty and the Mustache)

*<u>Beauty and the Mustache (#0.5)</u>*

*<u>Truth or Beard (#1)</u>*

*<u>Grin and Beard It (#2)</u>*

*<u>Beard Science (#3)</u>*

*<u>Beard in Mind (#4)</u>*

*<u>Beard In Hiding (#4.5)</u>*

*<u>Dr. Strange Beard (#5)</u>*

*<u>Beard with Me (#6)</u>*

*<u>Beard Necessities (#7)</u>*

*<u>Winston Brothers Paper Doll Book (#8)</u>*

<u>**Hypothesis Series**</u>

(New Adult Romantic Comedy Trilogies)

Elements of Chemistry

*ATTRACTION (#1)*

*HEAT (#2)*

*CAPTURE (#3)*

*Laws of Physics*

*MOTION (#4)*

*SPACE (#5)*

*TIME (#6)*

*Fundamentals of Biology*

*INHERITANCE (#7)*

*REPRODUCTION (#8)*

*EVOLUTION (#9)*

<u>**Irish Players (Rugby) Series – by L.H. Cosway and Penny Reid**</u>

(Interconnected Standalones, Adult Contemporary Sports Romance)

*The Hooker and the Hermit (#1)*

*The Pixie and the Player (#2)*

*The Cad and the Co-ed (#3)*

*The Varlet and the Voyeur (#4)*

<u>**Dear Professor Series**</u>

(New Adult Romantic Comedy)

*Kissing Tolstoy (#1)*

*Kissing Galileo (#2)*

<u>**Ideal Man Series**</u>

(Interconnected Standalones, Adult Contemporary Romance Series of Jane Austen Reimaginings)

*Pride and Dad Jokes (#1, TBD)*

*Man Buns and Sensibility (#2, TBD)*

*Sense and Manscaping (#3, TBD)*

*Persuasion and Man Hands (#4, TBD)*

*Mantuary Abbey (#5, TBD)*

*Mancave Park (#6, TBD)*

*Emmanuel (#7, TBD)*

## **Handcrafted Mysteries Series**

(A Romantic Cozy Mystery Series, spinoff of *The Winston Brothers Series*)

*Engagement and Espionage (#1)*

*Marriage and Murder (#2)*

*Home and Heist (TBD)*

*Baby and Ballistics (TBD)*

*Pie Crimes and Misdemeanors (TBD)*

## **Good Folks Series**

(Interconnected Standalones, Adult Contemporary Romantic Comedy, spinoff of *The Winston Brothers Series*)

*Totally Folked (#1)*

*Folk Around and Find Out (#2)*

*All Folked Up (#3)*

## **Three Kings Series**

(Interconnected Standalones, Holiday-themed Adult Contemporary Romantic Comedies)

*Homecoming King (#1)*

*Drama King (#2)*

*Prom King (#3)*

## **Standalones**

*Ten Trends to Seduce Your Best Friend*

*Bananapants*